A Perfect Performance

Cassandra turned to the bedroom door, feeling herself to be ready to go downstairs to the sitting room. However, coming face-to-face with the necessity of stepping outside the sanctuary of the bedroom to where her every word and every facial expression would be under observation, her tiny balloon of self-confidence instantly deflated.

All of a sudden, Cassandra recalled the gleam in her sister's hazel eyes and Belle's enthusiasm. She had discovered Belle to be no different in person than she had been in her letters. Her sister was warm, frank, confident, and assured.

Cassandra squared her shoulders. "Very well, then. I shall be Belle. I shall be independent and self-reliant and brave." As she reached for the brass doorknob, she said under her breath, "Oh, God, help me!"

Coming next month

LADY JANE'S NEMESIS
by Patricia Oliver

Roger Hastings' long-awaited proposal to Lady Jane Sinclair comes at a price: the devious plans of his mistress to destroy their love....

0-451-20069-1/$4.99

A PRUDENT MATCH
by Laura Matthews

A hasty wedding between a debt-ridden baron and an innocent beauty turns from a marriage of convenience into a marriage of surprising passion....

0-451-20070-5/$4.99

A PERILOUS ENGAGEMENT
by Emily Hendrickson

After the untimely demise of his reckless cousin, Jordan Robards inherits a barony, his brother's bereft fiancée, and the terrible suspicion that his cousin's death was not an accident at all....

0-451-20071-3/$4.99

Cassandra's Deception

Gayle Buck

A SIGNET BOOK

SIGNET
Published by New American Library, a division of
Penguin Putnam Inc., 375 Hudson Street,
New York, New York 10014, U.S.A.
Penguin Books Ltd, 27 Wrights Lane,
London W8 5TZ, England
Penguin Books Australia Ltd, Ringwood,
Victoria, Australia
Penguin Books Canada Ltd, 10 Alcorn Avenue,
Toronto, Ontario, Canada M4V 3B2
Penguin Books (N.Z.) Ltd, 182–190 Wairau Road,
Auckland 10, New Zealand

Penguin Books Ltd, Registered Offices:
Harmondsworth, Middlesex, England

First published by Signet, an imprint of New American Library,
a division of Penguin Putnam Inc.

First Printing, June 2000
10 9 8 7 6 5 4 3 2 1

Chapter One

Cassandra Weatherstone was a proper Bath miss. Considered beautiful, accomplished and well-bred, she was on the verge of her come-out, which her aunt had promised her would be in the spring. She had never really thought beyond the programme laid out for her, which was to make a successful debut in London and to marry well.

All of which was why she was so extremely nervous about what she was doing. She had never done anything remotely scandalous in her life. Now here she was galloping away from the manor where she and her aunt and uncle were staying as guests, after deceiving her uncle into thinking she was simply going for a sedate ride. She had managed to give the accompanying groom the slip by sending him back for her deliberately forgotten whip. She had gone to such trouble so that she could make a rendezvous.

Cassandra consoled herself that at least it was not a clandestine meeting with a disapproved suitor. Nevertheless, she knew that if her aunt and uncle had known about the person she intended to meet, they would have categorically forbidden her to keep the appointment.

Cassandra urged her horse on faster, spurred by the fear that the groom would somehow stumble upon her direction and catch up with her. Cassandra wanted no witnesses about when she got to the deserted crofter's cottage.

It was a crisp autumn morning, the kind that omened an early winter. The leaves had turned and were falling, swirled to the ground by gusts of chilly wind. The rolling countryside was shadowed by trees and clouds. Cassandra scarcely took note of the beauty around her, except to look anxiously for landmarks.

She had never been in this county before. She was relying totally on the carefully written directions in the last letter, which had set the time and place of the rendezvous. Cassandra hoped that the directions were correct, or otherwise she ran the risk of becoming helplessly lost.

But as she urged her horse up a last rise, she saw below her a ruined cottage, just as it had been described to her. The wind was blowing briskly now and wailed low through the shallow valley as she approached. The place appeared to have been deserted for quite some time, its broken door swaying slightly to and fro on its hinges, the blackened timbers obviously rotted by wet and termites. "Oh, my, it doesn't look at all safe. Not at all the sort of place that I would ordinarily wish to visit," she murmured to herself, drawing the mare up outside the door.

The door was pushed open. A slender figure in a dark green riding habit and netted hat stepped over the threshold. The netting was pulled firmly down over the young woman's face and tied under her chin so that her features were completely obscured. "There you are! I've been watching for you through the shutters. I was beginning to think that you would never come. I thought you had changed your mind."

"Not I," responded Cassandra. Her heart was pounding, but she made an effort to appear as calm as the other had sounded. "Will you hold my horse, please?"

"Of course." The young woman came out of the shadowed doorway and took hold of the mare's bit. "We can put her in the stable with my own Rolly. No one will see her there."

Cassandra dismounted with some awkwardness, her long skirt wanting to snag as she unhooked her leg from the ladies' saddle and slid free. She landed evenly on the tufted grass. Catching up her skirt hem and draping it over her arm, she remarked, "I hope I can remount again."

The other girl shrugged. "There's an old log out in back of the cottage. It shouldn't be too difficult. Come along." Leading the way with the mare, she took Cassandra round the side of the crofter's cottage. There was indeed an old stable, in somewhat better condition than the cottage itself. Hay had recently been scattered inside, and the sweet scent combined with the dank smell of damp earth. In one rough stall was a well-knit gelding that whickered at the sight of the other young woman. She murmured something to the gelding and patted his nose before she led the mare into the adjoining stall. "Help me to set the bar."

Cassandra did so, then dusted her gloved hands. She looked around her curiously. The stable was small, typical of what a crofter would have built for his sturdy draft animals. She wondered what had happened to the crofter and his family. It was a fleeting thought at best, for the other woman was already turning to face her.

"You wore a veil, too," said the woman with satisfaction. "I think it makes everything a bit more melodramatic, don't you think?"

"Indeed," said Cassandra dryly, her sense of humor tickled by the other's cheerful observation. "Shall we reveal ourselves to each other now?"

"Oh, yes! I can scarce wait another instant!" said the other woman, laughing. She began to untie the netting.

Cassandra untied her own veil and lifted it to lay its folds over the top of her riding hat. She looked then at her companion and sucked in her breath in amazement.

The other woman was also staring, with widened brown-flecked hazel eyes. "It is like looking into a mirror that one did not know existed."

"Yes, isn't that what being a twin means?" asked Cassandra, trying to gather her shaken senses. "But it is truly amazing. I had no idea that—"

"Nor I!" interrupted the other young woman. She gave a small laugh. "How odd. How very odd. I knew that you and I were twins, but until this very moment I did not realize how very alike we sound and appear."

"Belle." Cassandra hugged her sister, overcome by several emotions too ambivalent to identify. Belle Weatherstone's embrace was equally as strong around her. "It has been such a long time."

"Yes, since Mama and Papa were killed in that awful carriage accident." Belle's voice was muffled against Cassandra's hat. She drew back, holding Cassandra at arm's length. Her eyes searched her sister's face. In a voice of discovery she said, "I think that I have missed you."

Cassandra gave a shaky laugh. Her sister's words struck a chord of recognition in her. Her aunt and uncle had been good to her, treating and raising her as though she was their own daughter. Indeed, they had been childless when they had taken her in and had lavished on her the affection that should have been given to their own. Cassandra had never felt herself to be short of love. Despite her good fortune, however, she had always felt a certain restlessness, a feeling of incompleteness. She had once expressed her feelings to the vicar, a wise, learned man who had astonished her with his observation that no doubt she was missing her twin sister.

Cassandra had never been encouraged to think about her sister, who had always lived with their paternal grandfather, nor to correspond except during holidays or other special occasions. After her conversation with the vicar, she had begun to write Belle more often. They had come to know each other quite well through their letters. They had even learned some of the most trivial things. Cassandra was allergic to chocolate, and Belle, at the age of nine, had exchanged promises to wed with their grandfather's godson.

"I know that I have missed you, terribly," said Cassandra. "I am so glad that we were able to do this."

"I only wish that it had come about under other circumstances," said Belle, nodding, and a slight frown on her face. "Grandfather is still not at all well. The physician seems to think that he will not last out the winter. Old nanny! I have told him a thousand times that Grandfather is tougher than a leather whip, but he will only shake his head and sigh. I could cheerfully strangle him."

"Then . . . he is bad?" asked Cassandra, a sinking feeling in her stomach.

Belle looked at her swiftly. Her expression cleared.

She squeezed Cassandra's arm. "Pray do not be so anxious, Cassandra. You do not know Grandfather. He has always rallied before. When I wrote to you, I was very fearful that this illness would indeed be the end of him. But Grandfather is very stubborn. He told me himself that he does not intend to die just yet. He says that he has matters to set right before he will allow death to claim him, and I believe him."

Cassandra smiled, thinking privately that her sister was exhibiting just the kind of optimism that she had come to associate with Belle. "Nevertheless, it does not alter my desire to become acquainted with our grandfather."

"Of course it does not! It would be strange indeed if you should turn about now," said Belle. She shook her head. "I still do not understand how Grandfather and my uncle could have built such enmity between them that they cannot bear to be in each other's company. It has certainly been unfair to us, since they separated us when Mama and Papa died."

"My aunt says that no one felt able to take us both into the same house, especially since no one could tell us apart. So Grandfather took you, and my aunt and uncle took me." Cassandra's smile wavered a little. "I do not regret my life with my uncle and aunt. They have been very good to me. I do regret all of the years that we have been apart."

"My understanding is that there is still very little love lost between Grandfather and his son and daughter-in-law," said Belle shortly. She sighed. "We have both lost a part of ourselves as a consequence. I should have liked visiting you and my uncle and aunt in Bath. I have never been to the shops or to the Pump Room or a Lending Library or done anything outside the environs of the Hall. I am naught but a country bumpkin, I fear." There was mingled longing and regret in her voice.

Cassandra was beginning to realize just how different her life had been from her sister's. While she and her sister looked alike in face, figure and coloring, there were slight differences to be found between them. Belle's skin was brushed to a rosy tan by country life, and though her riding habit was well made, it could not compare with Cassandra's own, which had been made by a skilled modiste. Cassandra was used to the slow pace of the small city, while Belle knew little beyond her own small corner of the world.

"Can you get me into the Hall to see Grandfather?" asked Cassandra.

The possibility that she might see her grandfather was the reason she had come to this lonely spot. When she had received the letter from Belle detailing their grandfather's illness, she had suddenly had the strongest desire to get to know the old gentleman in person. She had only dim recollections of him, but she had developed an affection for her grandfather through Belle's letters. It had been obvious that Belle loved the old gentleman who had had the raising of her, and Cassandra had cherished the hope that some day, some way, she could meet him.

She had known that her uncle and aunt would never consent to her visiting the country manor, despite her grandfather's illness. There was too much bitterness between the two parties. However, her uncle and aunt had decided to join a house party at an old friend's home that was within riding distance of her grandfather's manor. After their visit, they intended to continue up to London to set things in train for Cassandra's come-out.

Cassandra had conceived the notion that if she could slip away from the house party for a few hours, perhaps Belle could smuggle her into the Hall to meet their grandfather. Belle had responded enthusiastically to the idea, and so this rendezvous had been planned. It had all gone off perfectly thus far. Now she only needed Belle's reassurance that the rest of their plan could be put into effect.

"Of course I can. There is nothing simpler," said Belle. "In fact—" Her eyes began to gleam. "I have the most marvelous notion, Cassandra. You will adore it, I swear! Until we met, we neither of us knew how alike we are. But now we have, and I think it would be the easiest thing imaginable for us to switch identities for a little while. Don't you think so? Then you could spend

a few days with Grandfather, while I could get to know
my uncle and aunt. Isn't it a splendid notion?"

"You mean . . . trade places?" asked Cassandra,
appalled.

Belle made a face. "You make it sound so shocking."

"It *is* shocking!"

"But is it really? Only consider, Cassandra! We have
only to change clothes, and the deed is done. What could
be simpler or more advantageous to us both?" said Belle
urgently. "You will be with Grandfather, and I shall be
at the house party. We each get a bit of what we want.
And there is far less risk this way. What do you think
Grandfather would say if I introduced you and he had
to send word to my uncle that you were to be fetched
away?"

Cassandra could well imagine that circumstance. Her
uncle and aunt would be furious. She considered everything Belle had said. Belle was right, up to a point. It
would be so easy to exchange clothes. That Belle was a
little rosier in the face was a bit daunting. She would
have to expose her complexion to the sun for a short
time, thought Cassandra, but that was a small sacrifice
and certainly a minor abuse of her skin that could be
rectified.

"But what about Grandfather and the staff? I don't
know anything about the Hall," said Cassandra aloud.

"Oh, I can tell you all that you need to know. You
won't have the least difficulty. No one will expect you
to be anyone else but me, of course, and I can describe
to you where my bedroom is and the other rooms,"
said Belle.

"That's all very well, Belle. But surely Grandfather, at
least, will notice something different about me," retorted
Cassandra. She was feeling excitement and trepidation.
Did she dare? Did she really dare to do this outrageous
thing? Her breath shortened at the thought.

"Grandfather sleeps most of the time. I suspect it is
the nasty vile potion that the physician made up for him.
Believe me, he will notice nothing amiss, and if he does,
he will put it off to his own weakened faculties," said

Belle confidently. "Why shouldn't he? He won't be expecting you to be you!"

"There's my uncle and aunt, and the house party! What of Sir Thomas, who invited us? He might suspect you—me!—if you betrayed too much knowledge of his family or the surrounding neighborhood," said Cassandra.

"Surely I know my uncle and aunt well enough from your letters to pass as you! As for Sir Thomas—well, he has known me since I was small. He is the local physician, you see. But I cannot see how that will be a problem. He knows our family history as well as anyone, I suppose, and he will not embarrass my uncle and aunt by referring to the trouble between them and Grandfather. Quite frankly, I do not anticipate any difficulty," said Belle. "Sir Thomas will not be expecting anyone but Cassandra Weatherstone at his house party. Has he said anything to you about me?"

"No, he has not," said Cassandra slowly.

"You see!" Belle exclaimed as she threw out her hands.

"I hope that I am not making a mistake," said Cassandra, shaking her head.

"Oh, Cassandra! Thank you!" Belle hugged her. "You shan't regret it, I promise you. Nor shall I!"

Chapter Two

Cassandra entered the rear door of the Hall with her heart pounding. She struggled to maintain a calm expression, but she could not help how her eyes darted anxiously here and there. Perspiring from nervousness, she grasped her sister's riding whip with clenched fingers.

She had made a misstep in the stables when she rode in. The elderly groom, whom Belle had told her was called Young John, had taken the gelding. He had stood looking at her while she had shaken out her skirt, and when she had looked up at him inquiringly, he had said, "Bain't you going to feed him the carrot, Miss Belle?"

Cassandra had felt her face flame. Belle had told her about the treat that she always carried for the gelding, but she had forgotten. Cassandra thrust her gloved hand into her pocket and pulled out the carrot. "Of course I am! Here, Rolly, that's a good boy."

With a backward stare, the old groom had led the gelding away toward the stables while Cassandra turned toward the manor door. She had been profoundly shaken that she had made such a simple and noticeable error at the first opportunity.

Now as she traversed the dimly lit hallway toward the front of the manor, she had difficulty drawing a decent breath. She shrank from the thought of making another mistake and hoped that she would meet no one on the way up to Belle's bedroom. At that moment she wanted nothing more ardently than a private corner in which to orient herself and gather her shattered nerve.

"Miss Belle."

Her heart jumping, Cassandra turned quickly. Her eyes searched swiftly for the owner of the deep, wavering voice. Belle had described all of the household staff, but Cassandra was not at all certain that she could put names to any of them. Some of her anxiety must have shown in her expression, for the white-haired man coughed apologetically behind his hand.

"It was not my intent to startle you, miss. I only wished to inform you that the post has come."

Cassandra realized at once, both from what the man had said and his attire, that he was the butler, Steeves. She did a swift survey—stooped, white-haired, long nose. Yes, it was Steeves. Belle's description had been perfect.

"Th-thank you, Steeves. I shall be glad to open it as soon as I have put off my habit," stammered Cassandra. She wondered whether the faithful old retainer would notice anything different about her. Thank goodness that the hallway lighting was so gloomy, thought Cassandra, so that her pale complexion could not be as noticeable.

"Very good, Miss Belle. I shall take it to the sitting room." The butler hesitated, then said, "There is a letter from Sir Marcus's man of business. Perhaps you will wish to open it as well."

"But my grandfather—"

The butler shook his head regretfully. "I fear not, miss. I have been informed by Weems that Sir Marcus is very restless and not himself this morning. Weems holds out very little encouragement that Sir Marcus will come out of his delirious state for some hours. As you will recall, that is the nature of the illness."

Cassandra stood quite still, hit by several emotions at once. First and foremost was fear—fear that she was in a fair way to being unmasked and fear that her grandfather's precarious health had taken a decided turn for the worst. "I wish that you had not given me such ill tidings, Steeves," she said, her fingers clenching more tightly about the shaft of the riding whip.

"Of course not, Miss Belle." The butler's voice was compassionate. "However, we must all remember that Sir Marcus has always rallied before."

"Yes." Cassandra stood a moment longer, thinking over the dilemmas that had been thrust upon her. It was obviously not a good time to go up to visit with her grandfather, as she had hoped to do as soon as she had changed. There was also this matter of the letter that the butler had mentioned. She had no notion what she should do, but obviously the butler expected her to do something.

"This letter—do you know anything about its contents, Steeves?" she asked cautiously. She was hoping that she would not be forced into the position of making herself mistress of her grandfather's private correspondence. It was one thing for her sister to open their grandfather's mail, but she felt it would be the height of indelicacy for her to do so. She had no right, after all. Surely, there was nothing so important that it could not wait until Sir Marcus had regained his senses.

"Not in so many words, miss. I am aware, however, that Sir Marcus had written a rather urgent communication to his man of business just before his last bout. I assume that this letter is in response. Sir Marcus will undoubtedly wish to know at once what his man of business has to say. However, if he does not recover as Weems anticipates, and it is an urgent matter, it may be something that you will need to address," said Steeves.

"I see." Cassandra sighed. Little as she wished the position or the responsibility, it was hers because it would have been Belle's. She had to do what Belle would do, at least for the time being. Cassandra felt that the masquerade was a bit rockier than either she or her sister had anticipated. At least she had recalled that Weems was the name of her grandfather's valet. She hoped that she would be able to recognize him from her sister's description as easily. She fleetingly wondered how Belle was doing in her shoes. "Very well, Steeves. Bring the letter to me."

"Very good, Miss Belle."

Cassandra fled up the narrow backstairs to the second landing, where she hesitated long enough to carefully count doors. When she was confident of the right one, she turned the brass knob and stepped inside the room. A maid was cleaning the grate of ashes, and upon Cassandra's entrance rose to dip a curtsy.

"I was just finishing, miss."

"Oh . . . that's quite all right," stammered Cassandra, a little taken aback. She hadn't expected anyone to be in the bedroom, and she had bolted into it like a rabbit taking refuge in its hole. Now she felt unbelievably awkward. She didn't know where to look or what to do. The maid had returned to her task and was cleaning up. Should she say something else? Cassandra jerked the whip through her gloved fingers, feeling the curls of panic again. What was the girl's name?

She saw that the girl was glancing at her, and a moment later had again looked over her shoulder at her. Cassandra swallowed, trying to think of something, anything—

"Don't worry so, miss. The master is a tough old bird. He'll fight his way back. That's what we all say belowstairs," said the maid.

Cassandra was startled. "I beg your pardon?"

The maid flushed and cast down her eyes. "Forgive me for speaking out of turn, miss. You just look so worried, is all."

"Oh! That . . . that is quite all right. I . . . I appreciate your concern." Cassandra was hugely relieved. The maid had taken her ill-concealed trepidation to be worry over her grandfather. She was safe, after all. Then Cassandra felt guilty, because of course she should be thinking more about her grandfather than herself. All of a sudden she felt monstrously self-centered, and tears started to her eyes.

The maid dipped a curtsy, picked up her covered bucket and exited the bedroom. Cassandra made certain that the heavy oak-paneled door was locked, and then she sat on the canopied bed and had a good, quiet cry. She felt immensely better afterward. She got up and went to the washstand. Pouring cool water from the pitcher into the washbowl, she splashed her heated face. She had never thought herself as being of a nervous disposition before, but now Cassandra solemnly considered it. She had never simply broken down like that, over such trivial happenings, too. However, in a few moments she had recognized that she had never borne such stress before. She had lived such a sheltered life. All life-shaping decisions had been taken out of her hands. The most momentous decision that she had ever had to make on her own had been the choosing of the perfect shade of ribbons for her new bonnet.

Until this day, Cassandra amended. She had made the decision to rendezvous with her sister, resorting to subterfuges that were reprehensible. She had agreed to the momentous step of exchanging places with her twin. And she had actually carried it through, without wavering and with far more bravado than she had ever believed she possessed. Really, she was quite impressed with herself.

Feeling calmer, Cassandra finally took stock of her surroundings. She had been too preoccupied by the maid's presence and her own turbulent thoughts to notice anything about her twin sister's bedroom.

It was a small room of pleasing proportions and very well-furnished. The matching carved set of bed, wardrobe and vanity were from a previous decade that had since fallen out of fashion, but there was nothing drab or worn in any of the upholstery. The drapes at the windows were velvet and of the finest quality, as was the carpet.

The tall, lead-paned windows overlooked an expanse of lawn that would be pleasant to look out on in the spring, but was now browned and strewn with leaves from the trees bordering it.

Cassandra turned back from the windows. A generously built fire crackled quietly on the hearth, warming the room to a comfortable temperature. It didn't appear that the chimney smoked, which was a good thing. She thought that during her short visit at the manor that she would feel at ease in her sister's bedroom.

Cassandra took off the riding habit and found a dark blue merino day dress in the wardrobe. She was a little clumsy with the mother-of-pearl buttons, being unused to doing without a maid. She was fortunate to be able to reach all of the buttons, she thought; but then she concluded it was not all that surprising, after all. Belle had told Cassandra that she generally dressed herself since she did not have a lady's maid. Naturally, her

clothes would not be made with the more fashionable
rows of tiny buttons down the back that required help
from a lady's maid. Cassandra wondered with a half
smile what her sister felt about having a lady's maid and
being dressed. She found a gold-fringed Kashmere shawl
and placed it over her shoulders as the final touch to
her new outfit.

Cassandra looked at herself critically in the burnished
mahogany cheval glass. She looked like herself, and yet
did not. She puzzled over the odd notion that something
was different about her. Then she realized that Belle's
day dress was not as sophisticated as what she was used
to wearing. There were not the deep ruchings of lace at
the bodice and hem. The cut of the gown was not as
good, and it was slightly out of fashion, the skirt being
longer than what she was used to. Only the Kashmere
shawl could make claim to being fashionable.

Once again, Cassandra was brought face-to-face with
the realization that her sister's life was even more retir-
ing than her own. Not for Belle a come-out that spring.
Cassandra felt a surge of compassion for her sister. Belle
would have spurned self-pity, of course. Cassandra felt
confident enough of that. However, it really was little
wonder that Belle had expressed a longing for a taste
of society.

Cassandra turned to the bedroom door, feeling herself
to be ready to go downstairs to the sitting room. However, coming face-to-face with the necessity of stepping
outside the sanctuary of the bedroom to where her every
word and every facial expression would be under observation, her tiny balloon of self-confidence instantly deflated. She could be impressed with herself all she
wished behind this sturdy door, but it was quite another
thing to imagine the hurdles she might have to face on
the other side of it. The initial excitement she had felt
at the beginning of this masquerade had unequivocally
faded.

All of a sudden, Cassandra recalled the gleam in her
sister's hazel eyes and Belle's enthusiasm. She had discovered Belle to be no different in person than she had
been in her letters. Her sister was warm, frank, confident

and assured. Cassandra felt certain Belle would have pooh-poohed the feelings of inadequacy and trepidation that crashed over her. Belle would surely have laughed and swept all difficulties before her.

Cassandra squared her shoulders. "Very well, then. I shall be Belle. I shall be independent and self-reliant and brave." As she again reached for the brass doorknob, she said under her breath, "Oh, God, help me!"

Chapter Three

Dominant in Cassandra's mind as she made her way down the long hall was the terrible thought of the looming post. She knew it was ridiculous to feel such timorousness, but she could not help herself. Most terrifying of all was the letter from her grandfather's man of business. Its contents would mean nothing to her, of course. She simply hated so much the necessity of opening that letter that she could scarcely bear it. It was so utterly foreign to her to rifle through someone else's possessions.

But wasn't she rifling through someone's life? The thought was startling in its intensity. Her hand on the smooth banister, Cassandra faltered on the worn stairs. The masquerade was different, she told herself, resuming her descent. She and Belle had willingly chosen to trade identities for a few days. It was scarcely her fault that she was thrust into the position of making decisions that should rightfully only be made by her sister. She *was* her sister for all intents and purposes, and she might as well get over these misplaced scruples of hers as soon as possible. If Belle wished to call her on the carpet later for her brash behavior, then she could, and with Cassandra's goodwill. In the meantime, she had to play the part that she had taken to the very best of her ability, even if that meant opening and reading the post and, yes, the all-important letter from Sir Marcus's man of business.

On that bleak thought, Cassandra entered through an oak-paneled door to what she hoped was the sitting room. It was, she saw with relief. Her sister's insistence that she repeat over and over the geography of the house was standing her in good stead. She quickly surveyed the well-appointed room, taking instant note of the fire burning on the stone hearth and the deep carpets. Her grandfather did not stint on creature comforts, she thought fleetingly, which gave her a good indication that Sir Marcus was not of a pecuniary nature. She looked for the silver salver holding the small stack of envelopes and discovered it sitting on the gleaming occasional table on the wall opposite. She started toward the table.

"Good morning, my dear. I trust that you enjoyed your ride."

Cassandra started, assuming until that moment that she was alone in the room. She now saw that a slightly-built lady was seated on the settee, half concealed by a painted wooden screen that reflected back the heat from the fire. The elderly lady's soft white hair was swept up under a delectable lace cap, and there were discreet touches of lace at the high throat and at the cuffs of her gown. The lady was tatting an intricate piece of lace, her thin, agile fingers handling the delicate thread and needles with skill.

Cassandra at once recognized the lady. She strove to respond in the manner she thought her sister might. "Yes, thank you, Biddy, I did. The wind was a trifle brisk, but I do not regard that."

Miss Bidwell, who had been retained as Belle's governess, and was now comfortably situated as Belle's companion, gave a small chuckle. "No, I wager that you do not. I have known you practically all of your life, Belle, and I have never observed that you gave the snap of your fingers for any of those things that other young ladies might find daunting."

Cassandra was pleased that she had struck just the right note. At last she had done something right. The knot in her stomach eased, and she breathed freer. Yet, the next instant she was thrown off balance again.

"My dear Belle, you appear pale today. Are you feeling quite the thing?" asked Miss Bidwell. Behind her spectacles, her keen blue gaze was fixed on Cassandra's face.

Cassandra swallowed and managed to summon up a smile. "Am I? I can't imagine why. I don't feel in the least unwell."

"No, perhaps not. But it is always difficult to maintain one's optimism in the face of such anxiety as you have had thrust upon you these past few months," said Miss Bidwell with a sympathetic note in her voice.

"Steeves told me when I came in that my grandfather was in a delirious state," said Cassandra quietly. She thought the less she said the better it would be. She would not make any excuses for the paleness of her complexion; let the lady make what she might of it. As she had hoped, Miss Bidwell instantly made the connection that Cassandra had intended she would.

"I thought that might be it." Miss Bidwell nodded. "Like many other high-strung young ladies, you allow your emotions to rule you too much, Belle. You mustn't dread the worst. Sir Marcus is a very determined gentleman."

"Yes, I know." A smile played about Cassandra's mouth as she recalled her sister's assertion, and she repeated Belle's words as her own. "He said that he had matters to set right before he allowed death to claim him. I must believe that."

"That sounds much more like you, dear," said Miss Bidwell.

It crossed Cassandra's mind that if her grandfather had not been ill, this masquerade would quite probably have been impossible. She was simply not an actress. As it was, however, her nervousness and her mistakes were all being put down to anxiety over her grandfather's physical state. She was fortunate in that much, at least.

Cassandra only wished that Sir Marcus was well enough for her to see him. That was the whole point of this outrageous endeavor, after all. It was extremely unfortunate that her grandfather had taken a turn for the worst, in more ways than one. She and Belle had agreed to exchange places for just a few days. At the end of that time, they planned to meet again at the deserted crofter's cottage and resume their own identities. Cassandra fervently hoped that her grandfather would recover in time for her to get to know him a little before she had to leave the Hall.

"I do wish you would stop fidgeting all over the room, my dear," said Miss Bidwell, glancing up at her young companion.

Cassandra felt herself color. "I am sorry, Biddy. I didn't realize that was what I was doing." She set down the porcelain figurine that she had been unconsciously turning in her hands.

Miss Bidwell cocked her head to one side, the slightest frown on her face. "There is something different about you today. I can't quite put my finger on it."

Cassandra's heart jumped. She tried to keep her expression bland. "Is there? I can't imagine what." Nervously, she reached up to smooth back a rebellious lock.

"That is what it is! Your hair. You have done your hair differently."

Miss Bidwell looked appraisingly at her, while Cassandra waited with dread for the verdict. It was ghastly that she and Belle had been so careless as not to change something so simple. Of course their hair had been dressed differently. Cassandra had come from the ministrations of a lady's maid, who had arranged her hair in a simple but elegant style at the back of her neck. Belle's hair, Cassandra recalled, had been pulled back and loosely tied with a ribbon.

"It suits you very well, Belle. You appear more grown up than is your wont," said Miss Bidwell, almost with surprise.

"I am eighteen, after all," said Cassandra. She was almost fainting with relief. She at once made the decision to brush out her hair as soon as possible and redo it in her sister's style.

"So you are. Belle, I know that you have a great deal on your mind. Why don't you read the post? It might divert you. Perhaps there is a letter from your sister, Cassandra," said Miss Bidwell, her gaze once more dropping to her handiwork.

Cassandra gave a slight start, quickly staring at the lady's face to see if Miss Bidwell was voicing coy suspicions about her. However, there was nothing in Miss

Bidwell's placid expression to lead Cassandra to believe
that the lady was hinting at anything. "Yes, Steeves told
me that he would bring it in here."

Miss Bidwell looked up from her tatting, the light
glinting on her spectacles. There was an element of surprise in her eyes. "Steeves always brings the post into
the sitting room."

"He made particular mention of a letter from my
grandfather's man of business," said Cassandra, desperately attempting to retrieve her mistake. She went over
to the occasional table to pick up the mail, enabling her
to turn her back so that Miss Bidwell could not see her
expression. Cassandra knew that her renewed anxiety
must show in her facial expression and her eyes.

"Oh, I see." Miss Bidwell contemplated the information given her. "I suppose it has something to do with
that letter that Sir Marcus was so insistent be sent. You
shall have to open it, of course."

Cassandra turned, having found the correspondence in
question and holding it doubtfully in her hand. "Do you
think that I should? It is Grandfather's business, after
all."

"I do admire your scruples, my dear. However, in this
instance I think we may dispense with them just a little,
don't you think? With Sir Marcus incapacitated as he is,
and knowing that he was very anxious for this business
of his to be attended to with the utmost speed, I think
it is imperative that you make yourself mistress of the
contents of that letter." Miss Bidwell seemed to hesitate,
before she added quietly, "Belle, you may be required
to make some decision on Sir Marcus's behalf."

"That is precisely the reason that I am so reluctant to
open it," said Cassandra, almost to herself, and frowning
down at the envelope she held.

"Bravo, my dear! I see that some of my admon-
ishments toward caution have not gone for naught, after
all. You are learning discretion, Belle," said Miss
Bidwell.

"Oh, bother," said Cassandra under her breath, irritated. Once again she had acted out of character for
her sister. Without further ado, she took up the letter

opener and slit the green wax seal securing the envelope.
She slipped out the sheets and began to read the letter.

When she was done, she looked up. Her brows were
knit in a frown. "I do not understand all the fuss. There
is nothing here of any great import that I can see."

"Er . . . would it be out of bounds of me to ask about
the subject of the letter?" asked Miss Bidwell with nicely
restrained curiosity.

Cassandra shook her head. "No, of course not." She
was immensely relieved that she had not been forced
into being made privy to some matter of paramount importance. "There is nothing here requiring anyone's decision, including Grandfather's. Apparently, Grandfather
had suddenly taken it into his head that he had to discover the present whereabouts of his godson, Mr. Philip
Raven, and he had written Mr. Petrie-Downs to request
that an inquiry be set afoot. Mr. Petrie-Downs writes that
he has been successful in locating Mr. Raven, and that he
is on his way to the Hall now."

"Philip Raven! Why, it has been years since I saw
him. As I recall, he was a dark-haired, handsome boy a
few years older than you. He stayed here at the Hall for
a year or two. He was a much easier student to tutor
than you, my dear! Do you remember him?" said Miss
Bidwell.

"N-not really," stammered Cassandra. She suddenly
remembered something from one of her sister's letters.
"Though I do seem to recall that when I was nine years
old, my grandfather's godson and I pledged ourselves to
be wed."

"That would be Philip," said Miss Bidwell, nodding.
She looked curiously at Cassandra. "I don't believe that
you ever told me that before, Belle."

"Have I not? Why, I suppose it wasn't important.
Such childish stuff, really," said Cassandra airily.

"Undoubtedly, Sir Marcus wished to find his godson
because he was feeling very mortal just at that time. I
imagine that it had something to do with his will," said
Miss Bidwell reflectively.

"His will?" repeated Cassandra, feeling rather stupid.

"Of course, my dear, what else? Philip Raven is your

grandfather's godson, after all. I would be surprised, indeed, if Sir Marcus did not intend to provide something for him," said Miss Bidwell. "I wonder how Sir Marcus lost contact with him at all?"

"I think that I can answer that," said Cassandra, glad to be able to offer something that would not place her in an uncomfortable position. "Mr. Petrie-Downs says in his letter that Mr. Raven had sold out of the army, but had remained on the Continent because of business interests." She looked up at Miss Bidwell. "I wonder what sort of business interests?"

"An interesting question, indeed. Mr. Raven is apparently not anxious to return to his native shores. One wonders why, really," said Miss Bidwell. "Of course, I understand now why Sir Marcus had lost contact. That war was such a hurly-burly affair. No one quite knew what to believe. Was Wellington retreating, or was he gaining ground? Well, Boney has abdicated at last, and that's the end of it, thank God. Belle, it will undoubtedly ease Sir Marcus's mind to know that his godson has been located and is alive. You will naturally let him know when you go up to visit him."

"Yes, of course I shall." Cassandra refolded the sheets and slipped them back into the envelope. She was glad to have come off so well in her first encounter with one of the household who could be considered to know Belle intimately. "I suppose Weems will let me know when I can go up."

Miss Bidwell looked up quickly and stared fixedly at her for a moment. "Yes, I suppose that he shall," she agreed.

Cassandra tapped the envelope nervously into her palm. She knew that she had made another misstep, but intuitively she hit upon the right note. "I shan't wait on Weems. I shall go up in a bit and see for myself how Grandfather is."

Miss Bidwell smiled without comment. Her agile fingers worked the tatting needles, growing the bit of lacework.

Cassandra picked up the rest of the post and sat down in a wing chair near the fireplace. The crackling of the burning wood was a quiet accompaniment as she sorted through the envelopes. There were communications that she recognized to be bills against various household accounts. Those she set aside for the housekeeper or steward to attend. The remainder were personal correspondences addressed to Sir Marcus, but there was one addressed in her own hand to Miss Belle Weatherstone. It was rather a shock to see the letter. She knew its contents, after all. And yet she was supposed to open it and read it as though she was completely ignorant of what she, Cassandra, had had to say to her sister, Belle. What a very odd situation she was in, to be sure.

"There is a letter from Cassandra," she announced casually, taking up the letter opener.

"Oh, how nice. Her letters are always entertaining," remarked Miss Bidwell. "I am always reminded of my own times in dear Bath."

Cassandra threw a glance at Miss Bidwell, surprised. She had never given a thought to Miss Bidwell's personal history. She racked her memory. Had Belle ever mentioned that Miss Bidwell had family in Bath or perhaps had some previous place of employment there? Cassandra could not recall anything of the sort, and hoped that she was not expected to comment on Miss Bidwell's past confidences. She bent her head, pretending that she had not been listening, and opened her letter to her sister. She spread apart the sheets, scanning the lines quickly for anything that could possibly be incriminating. Of course Belle could not have confided their secret to Miss Bidwell, and so obviously she had not read everything from Cassandra's letters to Miss Bidwell. Cassandra thought she would be safe if she gave Miss Bidwell only bits and pieces. It would probably be very out of character for her to read the letter in its entirety. "The subscription rate for the balls has gone up," she offered.

Miss Bidwell exclaimed disapprovingly. "What nonsense! As though one was made of silver! What else does your sister say?"

Encouraged, Cassandra went on to tell Miss Bidwell what she had written about the latest romance from the

Lending Library and whom she had met in the Pump Room and the ravishing bonnet that she had bought. When she was finished and proceeded to fold the letter, Miss Bidwell sighed.

"Do you mind very much not living in Bath, Biddy?" asked Cassandra, feeling very bold to be posing a personal question.

Miss Bidwell shot her a glance. "Certainly not! I am perfectly content at the Hall."

"But you would like to go to the Pump Room and to the Lending Library again," ventured Cassandra, hoping to discover a bit of Miss Bidwell's history, something that Belle probably would already have known.

Miss Bidwell did not deny her statement, only giving a dismissive sniff. "And you, my dear, would undoubtedly spend all of your time trying on bonnets!"

"Oh, no. I would try on gloves and gowns and stockings, too," said Cassandra with a smile.

Miss Bidwell chuckled. "I have little doubt of it, Belle. Aren't we a pair, to be mooning over something that we cannot have? Well, your sister's letters are always welcome and entertaining, but I discover that they also rouse a bit of envy in my breast."

"In mine, too, Biddy," said Cassandra, feeling that her sister would have certainly expressed such a thought.

"Never mind, Belle. I told you that I have talked to Sir Marcus about letting me take you to Bath or some other fashionable watering spot for the summer. He has not yet consented, but I do not give up hope yet. I shall speak to him again, once he has recovered sufficiently," said Miss Bidwell. "In the meantime, we must be cheerful and patient."

"Oh, and let patience have its perfect work?" asked Cassandra, smiling.

Miss Bidwell raised her brows, a surprised expression in her blue eyes. "Belle, I don't believe I have ever heard you express sarcasm before. It does not suit you, my dear."

Cassandra felt her face grow warm. She was dismayed that her little play on words had been taken in such error. Obviously, Belle was not clever with phrases or quotations. She would have to remember that. Cassandra stood up. "I . . . I think that I shall go talk to Weems," she said, and on that pretext she fled the sitting room.

Chapter Four

Cassandra held her skirt up in one hand so that she did not trip on it as she hurried back upstairs. She felt like running, but naturally one did not succumb to such temptations no matter how shaken one's nerve had become. She started for Belle's bedroom, wanting nothing more than to hide away until she felt it was safe to emerge. And when that would be, she thought morosely, was anyone's guess. It wouldn't surprise her if she decided to remain cowardly in the bedroom until it was time to meet Belle again at the crofter's cottage. It was certainly safer than seeing anyone or talking to anyone in the house. Every time she opened her mouth she betrayed herself. She could not believe that there was not someone who was going to point a shaking finger at her and accuse her of duplicity.

Cassandra toyed with the idea of pretending to be ill. That would allow her to hide in the bedroom. But such a plan of action had its distinct disadvantages. First of all, it would undoubtedly draw unwelcome attention because she could not imagine her vivacious sister ever becoming sick. And of course, if she were pretending to be ill, ever visiting with her grandfather was completely out of the question. She would not be allowed to leave her sickroom and "infect" Sir Marcus with whatever complaint she was pretending to have.

"Bother," said Cassandra to herself, annoyed and frustrated and afraid. She felt trapped. It was all supposed to have been so simple. Belle was going to let her quietly into their grandfather's room so that she could spend an hour or two with him. Then she would have returned to her uncle and aunt. Cassandra could not imagine how simple a plan could have ballooned up into such a horrid monstrosity as this masquerade.

She had almost reached Belle's bedroom when a short, supercilious little man came quietly out of an oaken door into the hallway. Upon seeing her, he nodded in a stiff manner. "Miss Belle, I was just coming to find you. Sir Marcus would like to see you."

Cassandra stopped. Her heart felt as if it were plummeting to her toes. "Does . . . does he?"

The valet nodded. A smile flickered across his clever face. "The turnaround was quite sudden this time, Miss Belle. I am glad to say that Sir Marcus has regained his full faculties, though he is naturally very weak from the fever."

"Perhaps I should wait until later to go in, then," said Cassandra diffidently. "He might wish to sleep."

The valet's brows twitched upward, and he stared very hard at her. "Normally, I might agree with you, miss. However, Sir Marcus will fret himself to flinders if he does not have his way, as you well know."

"Yes," agreed Cassandra, as seemed expected of her. She felt very nervous. "Then I must see him at once, of course."

The valet opened the door and ushered her through the dressing room to the bedroom beyond. Cassandra entered her grandfather's bedroom with both curiosity and trepidation. She blinked at the lavish brocade draperies hanging at the windows and the velvet curtains that had been corded back from around the massive four-post bed. All of the furniture was imposing in size and handsomely carved. Several deep Oriental rugs covered every corner of the floor so that no step could be heard crossing them. Bunches of candles in candelabras lit the room almost to full day, despite the drawn drapes. On one wall a bookshelf had been built from ceiling to floor. Strange figures of brass and beautiful vases of obvious value cluttered every shelf. Cassandra had not known what to expect, but certainly not this extravagant splendor. She recalled that her grandfather had been said to have traveled extensively as a young man in foreign parts and had returned with many curious pieces.

"Belle? Is that you?" The deep voice was whispery and fretful. "Come closer, child. I cannot see you."

Cassandra drew a breath. She had reached the true test. If anyone could tell the difference between Belle and herself, surely it would be their grandfather. Sir Marcus had raised Belle almost as his own daughter. Almost cringing within, she approached the four-post bed. She grasped one of the posts, her fingers curling on the heavy gold cord that held back the rich wine-colored velvet. "Yes, Grandfather. Here I am. You . . . you wished to see me?"

"Weems told you so, so I must have," said Sir Marcus, almost growling. He tried to pull himself up higher on his pillows. The valet appeared instantly to lever the elderly gentleman into a more comfortable position.

While the two men were occupied, Cassandra studied her grandfather with open curiosity. She had vaguely recalled a tall, wide-shouldered gentleman. Her memory had served her well. Sir Marcus was but a shell of his former self, but his bones were long and large, and Cassandra could well understand why all of the furniture had been built on such heavy lines. It had been built to match the man. Her uncle was also tall, but she did not think that he could ever have been as large a gentleman as her grandfather had once been.

"What are you staring at, puss? Don't I pass muster?" asked Sir Marcus, his bushy brows forming an unbroken line across his long nose. His eyes were winter blue, with no lack of awareness in their depths.

Cassandra thought she had better be more careful. "I suppose you look better than you did," she said casually.

Sir Marcus gave a bark of laughter that was cut short by a coughing spasm. The valet picked up a goblet set on the night table and put it to his master's lips. Once Sir Marcus had drunk a little, he waved the goblet away. "Enough, Weems! You tend me like an old nursemaid. Let me be, I say."

"Very good, my lord." The valet set down the goblet and adjusted the pillows once more. He bowed and turned away from the bed. Before he passed Cassandra, he gave her a significant look and the slightest shake of the head.

Cassandra interpreted the valet's glance as meaning that Sir Marcus should not be kept long. She moved toward the chair beside the bed and sat down. She smiled at her grandfather, who had turned his gray head to regard her. Very boldly, she said, "And I, sir? Do I pass muster?"

"You always do, my dear. That blue gown becomes you very well," said Sir Marcus, his deep voice but a thread.

"A compliment indeed, my lord," said Cassandra with another smile.

"My lord? Why are we so formal, Belle? Are you perhaps angry with me?" asked Sir Marcus.

"Oh, no! Of course I am not," said Cassandra, appalled. Once again, she had done something out of character for Belle.

Sir Marcus waved his hand. "No, no, do not deny it. I frightened you this time, I know. That is why you are angry with me, is it not?"

"Perhaps," said Cassandra noncommittally.

Sir Marcus sighed. "I am sorry, Belle. I am an old man, and I have not long to live, I suspect."

"Pray do not say so!" exclaimed Cassandra, her heartstrings touched. She took Sir Marcus's hand between her own in her distress. His skin was wrinkled and cool, and his signet ring felt too heavy on his finger.

"You are a good girl. Always have been. I am glad you came to me," said Sir Marcus. His eyes drifted past her. He stirred restlessly under the coverlet. "I wish I had some word from Petrie-Downs."

"You had a letter from Mr. Petrie-Downs this morning," said Cassandra, glad to be able to offer something helpful.

Sir Marcus's gaze focused and sharpened again on her face. "A letter? From Petrie-Downs? You opened it, of course. What did he say?"

"Your godson, Philip Raven, has been located. He sold out of the army and remained on the Continent for business reasons," said Cassandra.

"Business reasons! What possible business might he have, I should like to know?" exclaimed Sir Marcus.

"Mr. Petrie-Downs did not convey that information, Grandfather," said Cassandra. "He also wrote that Mr. Raven was en route to the Hall."

Sir Marcus's jaws worked as he stared beyond Cassandra out into the bedroom. His eyes suddenly returned to her. "You might as well know. I told Petrie-Downs to send word to Philip that I am on my deathbed."

He threw up his hand at Cassandra's involuntary protest. "Aye, you don't like to hear it, my dear. However, facts are facts and must be faced. I am an old man and not likely to see the spring. You and I both heard that long-faced physician predict it. It's not what one wishes to hear, but the truth has a way of getting down into a man's spirit. I told you that I had matters to settle, and so I have. I am in hopes of seeing everything tied up nice and pretty before I die. So I had Petrie-Downs send for Philip Raven to come to us here at the Hall."

Cassandra hoped that Mr. Raven would not arrive until after she and Belle had exchanged places again. "I wonder when Mr. Raven will arrive?"

"I don't know. I wish I did. And I'll not put up with any of your nonsense, Belle, so don't think it," said Sir Marcus, frowning at her.

"Of course not. I haven't a clue as to what to think," said Cassandra truthfully.

Sir Marcus snorted. He shook a long finger at her. "Aye, play off your tricks against me if you will, but I know better than to believe that look of blank innocence. You'll be civil to Philip. He is my godson, and I wish to talk to him privately. That's enough for you to know right now."

"Yes, Grandfather," said Cassandra with a smile. She noticed the valet had come back into the bedroom and was standing near the door. She took that to mean that her time with her grandfather should come to an end. Indeed, Sir Marcus did appear to be rather wearied. His energy seemed to have been sapped with the delivery of his scold. He had sagged back against the pillows, and his eyes had closed.

Cassandra stood up. She leaned over to brush a soft kiss against her grandfather's cheek and then started to tiptoe away.

"Belle."

She turned, surprised. She had thought that Sir Marcus had fallen asleep on the instant, but she saw that his eyelids had lifted a trace and that he was looking at her with a stern expression.

"I mean it, Belle. I'll have you be civil to Philip."

"So I shall be," said Cassandra, nodding. It was highly unlikely that Mr. Philip Raven would arrive before she and her sister regained their rightful places, so she felt completely at ease in making the promise that was demanded of her. She wondered why Sir Marcus was so adamant. Surely, Belle would not be rude to their grandfather's guest, especially one that was so nearly related.

"Aye, a young tigress with sheathed claws," murmured Sir Marcus, his mouth stretching in a wan smile. "Poor Philip. He does not know what he is walking into, does he?"

The valet advanced. "It is time for your draft, my lord."

"Is that you, Weems? Of course it is. How long have you been standing there eavesdropping? Never mind! Nothing is a secret for long in this house. I shall want to see you again after supper, Belle," said Sir Marcus.

Cassandra agreed and left the bedroom. Sir Marcus's words echoed in her mind. She wondered how long it would be before her own secret was exposed. She had made missteps all morning. Would it be so bad to be found out, though? After all, Sir Marcus was her grandfather. Surely, he would be delighted to reacquaint himself with her after all of these years. Cassandra longed to be able to tell him who she really was, to be known for herself and not as Belle's substitute.

Cassandra shook her head. Reluctant as she was to acknowledge the truth, she knew that Sir Marcus would not take kindly to the announcement that he and all of his household had been duped. And if the little that Belle had said was true, Sir Marcus would like even less sending word to his son and daughter-in-law, as he would be forced to do in order to return her to their care. Cassandra thought she knew, too, what her uncle's feelings would be to discover that he and his spouse had been deceived and then forced into communication with his father. No, it was far better to play this thing out the original way she and Belle had planned it, with no one the wiser and no one stirred to outrage.

Cassandra again wondered how her sister was getting along in her new role. If she was making mistakes, surely Belle, too, was having her own difficulties. Cassandra smiled, however, because she believed that her twin was perfectly capable of carrying anything off with aplomb. Belle exuded enthusiasm, and that went a long way in proving confidence.

Chapter Five

When Cassandra returned downstairs, thinking that she would rejoin Miss Bidwell in the sitting room, she received the shock of her life. She was informed by Steeves that Mr. Philip Raven was awaiting her in the drawing room.

"Oh, dear!" Cassandra felt panic and wondered what she should do. She hadn't even gotten used to the idea of possibly meeting her sister's childhood friend, and now he had arrived. How she wished that it was Belle who was the one standing in her shoes instead of herself.

The butler was watching her with an impassive face. He was patiently awaiting instructions, she realized. Cassandra pulled herself together. "Have you informed Weems that Mr. Raven has arrived and wishes to see my grandfather?"

"Yes, miss. Weems sent word down that Sir Marcus is resting and cannot be disturbed. I suggested to Mr. Raven that you would see him when you had returned downstairs," said Steeves in a neutral voice.

"Perhaps Miss Bidwell—"

"Unfortunately, Miss Bidwell went up to rest only twenty minutes ago," said Steeves. "In view of that and your own absence, I have taken the liberty to order that the best rooms be made ready for Mr. Raven. I have also informed Mr. Raven that you would join him as soon as you returned. I knew that would be what you would wish me to do."

"Thank you, Steeves," said Cassandra quietly, although thinking that she could cheerfully have throttled the butler for his efficiency. Now she had no choice but to meet this gentleman whose arrival had been precipitated by her grandfather's fear of dying.

Well, perhaps it was better this way, thought Cassandra. She would join Mr. Raven and point out, in a subtle way, of course, that the timing of his arrival was a bit inconvenient. If she was fortunate, he would think to remove himself to the local inn rather than incommode the household. After all, Sir Marcus was very ill still and could not be expected to entertain even a guest whom he had himself summoned. She would certainly encourage such a decision. No matter how much her sister had assured her otherwise, she was very unsure that she could handle another twist to this masquerade.

"I will see Mr. Raven now," said Cassandra, starting down the hallway toward the drawing room.

"Very good, miss. I have already seen that Mr. Raven has been offered refreshment, of course," said the butler.

Cassandra half turned. Restraining herself again, she said quietly, "Thank you, Steeves. You think of everything."

The butler bowed and went on his way.

Cassandra opened the door to the drawing room, taking a deep breath as she did so. As she entered, a tall, broad-shouldered gentleman attired in a caped greatcoat turned toward her. Cassandra was struck at once by the piercing keenness of Mr. Raven's gaze. Her heart gave an unaccountable skip, and she momentarily forgot her major concern.

Mr. Raven was a well-built gentleman, wide of shoulder and well-proportioned. His hair was dark above a lean and very tanned face. Glimpses of his clothing under his greatcoat gave an impression of quiet respectability. His boots, though somewhat soiled, were obviously of good quality.

Cassandra met the gentleman's gaze again. His gray eyes were deep-set under arching brows, and they held an arrested expression that she found unfathomable. "Mr. Raven."

"At your service, Miss Weatherstone."

Cassandra offered her hand to him. "Welcome to the

Hall, Mr. Raven. I am sorry not to have been available when you arrived.''

Mr. Raven shook hands with her. His grasp was firm. When he smiled, his entire coutenance seemed to lighten, the lines at the corners of his eyes crinkling as he looked down at her. "Forgive me for arriving at such an unusual hour, Miss Weatherstone. I should have guessed how it would be, but it has been long since I was familiar with the tranquil patterns of an English country house."

Cassandra felt at a loss. She had wanted to throw him off balance, and instead he had neatly turned the tables. What could she do but graciously deny that he had caused any inconveniene? It would be churlish to do otherwise. "Pray do not apologize, Mr. Raven. I understand that Steeves brought refreshment? I hope that you have not been kept waiting long."

Cassandra listened to herself and marveled. She was almost babbling. Of course, he had not been waiting long. He was still wearing his greatcoat and gloves, and his beaver hat was placed on the settee. Now that was odd, thought Cassandra, glancing again at the beaver. Why hadn't Steeves offered to take the gentleman's hat and gloves?

Mr. Raven's gaze followed hers. "You are wondering why I still possess my hat and gloves. That is easily explained. I was not certain that I would be staying. However, Steeves has assured me that Sir Marcus is on the mend and that he would be unhappy if I did not remain. I had meant to ride into the village if my godfather was dying, not wishing to intrude on your household at such a time."

"That . . . that was kind of you, Mr. Raven," said Cassandra, once more made to feel churlish, but she was irritated, too. It was really too bad. She had actually almost been spared the necessity of playing the part of her sister with this old acquaintance of Belle's. Cassandra was all too aware that she had the butler to thank for the present circumstance. If left to his own inclinations, Mr. Raven would not now be ensconced in the best rooms.

"I wished to speak with you before accepting the hospitality offered to me," said Mr. Raven.

"Of course." Cassandra smiled, then turned and sank down on a silk-striped chair, inviting him with a wave of her hand to be seated also. "Steeves has told me that he has already bespoken rooms to be made ready for you. Undoubtedly, that is just how Sir Marcus would wish it."

"Thank you. You have relieved my uncertainty." Mr. Raven sat down and crossed one leg over the other. His booted foot swung gently. "Miss Weatherstone, have I offended you in some way?"

Cassandra was disconcerted. "Why, how could you have, Mr. Raven?"

"We were once such good friends that you called me Philip, and you were Belle to me. I must admit that the years have dimmed my memory considerably, but I do remember that much," said Mr. Raven with a fleeting smile.

Cassandra felt color rise in her face. "It has indeed been a long time," she hedged, wondering what other confidences would be disclosed.

Mr. Raven apparently took her hesitancy to mean that the former intimacy between himself and Belle was at an end. "Miss Weatherstone it is, then," he said with a nod. Before Cassandra could think of a suitable response, he asked, "How is my godfather, truly?"

At least on this much Cassandra felt sure of her ground. She relaxed her guard slightly. "He has been very ill. He has just recovered from a strong bout of fever and was left very weak."

Mr. Raven's brows rose a fraction in inquiry. "Then the illness has run its course?"

"I am hopeful that it has. He has regained his faculties, so that I was able to visit with him for a few moments," said Cassandra.

"I am glad to hear it, especially on your account," said Mr. Raven. "As I recall, you were always in your grandfather's company. Unless, of course, you were badgering me to skip our lessons to go riding." He smiled again, the expression in his eyes friendly. He was not in the least standoffish in either his address or demeanor.

Cassandra felt heat in her face again as her mind worked quickly. Apparently, Philip Raven remembered quite a lot about his stay at the Hall. She wondered just how much he recalled about Belle in particular. Would he ask what others had not—about Belle's past, for instance? She would simply have to plead a faulty memory if she was asked any pertinent questions. Her excuse must be that she had only been a child and could not be expected to recall all the details of her childhood.

"Did I badger you? Then I must certainly apologize," she said civilly. "I see that you have had tea. May I offer you another cup? Or perhaps a biscuit or piece of plum cake?"

"No, thank you to both. I am not one to overindulge," said Mr. Raven, shaking his head. "My youthful passion for sweets has long since been dulled by my army service."

"I fear that I know nothing about your life since you left the Hall," said Cassandra, feeling certain of her ground. After all, Sir Marcus had had to have his man of business track down Mr. Raven's whereabouts. "Were you in the army long?"

"I saw all the major campaigns in Spain," said Mr. Raven. For a moment, his expression was grim. Then he shook his head and smiled again. "I am thankful that that part of my life is over. It is odd to me now how idealistic I was, my one burning ambition being to become a soldier."

Cassandra hoped to learn more without making it obvious. "I suppose we have both changed," she said, setting aside the teapot after pouring a cup for herself. She added cream and lifted the cup to her lips, looking across inquiringly at Mr. Raven.

He was watching her. "Yes; for instance, you used to never take your tea white. I see that you have developed a taste otherwise."

Cassandra nearly choked on her tea. She set down the condemning cup hastily. "Er . . . yes. What a funny thing to have noticed! It was such a long time ago, after all."

"And how would you say that I have changed?" asked Mr. Raven, lounging at his ease. The slightest smile touched his lips as he regarded her.

Cassandra felt the sense of panic that was now all too familiar. She strove to hide her insecurity behind a cool, contained smile. "Why, you are taller."

Mr. Raven laughed, to her immense surprise and relief. "Very good, Miss Weatherstone! You have made a neat joke of it, indeed! I had hoped one day to live down that onerous nickname. Do you recall what you used to call me?"

"Oh, but I have no memory of it," said Cassandra, quite truthfully.

He laughed again. "Thank you! When you breezed in, quite in your old style, I had the strangest feeling of déjà vu. You can have no notion how I dreaded hearing myself addressed as Stubby again!"

"I would never be so uncivil," said Cassandra, smiling.

"Strange, is it not? We are so formal, just as though we had this moment met. Yet we are able to converse with an ease that comes from common memories," said Mr. Raven in a thoughtful voice.

"It is very strange, indeed," said Cassandra, feeling heartfelt agreement. She decided that it was time to put an end to this unnerving interview. She did not know how much longer she could speak to the gentleman without somehow exposing her ignorance of those "common memories."

She hoped that his visit did not prove to be a long one. It was a pity that the butler had been so efficient in offering hospitality. She really felt inadequate and at quite a loss with Mr. Raven. He seemed determined to recall the past with her; it was unfortunate that it was such a wasted effort. "Steeves told me that you were informed that my grandfather was not well enough to receive visitors as yet."

Mr. Raven at once frowned. "Yes, I was naturally unhappy to hear that Sir Marcus was indeed so ill. Mr. Petrie-Downs had indicated that Sir Marcus was very nearly on his deathbed. That was why I was uncertain whether I should stay until I had spoken to you."

"What are your plans, Mr. Raven?" asked Cassandra forthrightly.

"I have none to speak of, Miss Weatherstone. I came

as quickly as I was able, bringing only what I and my batman could conveniently carry on horseback," said Mr. Raven.

"You came by horseback?" asked Cassandra in surprise. She had assumed that Mr. Raven had arrived in a carriage. Her glance dropped back to his boots in sudden comprehension. But of course, that was why his footwear showed signs of neglect.

He seemed to understand her astonishment. "As a former soldier, Miss Weatherstone, I am practiced in swift travel. It seemed more expedient to ride cross-country so that I would arrive as soon as possible. Mr. Petrie-Downs's letter led me to fear that I might not be in time to see Sir Marcus again," said Mr. Raven. "You may imagine my dismay when I was told that Sir Marcus was unable to see me at all."

"My grandfather *is* making a recovery, Mr. Raven. You needn't fear, I assure you. His valet is merely careful and husbands his strength, sometimes with a jealous zeal," said Cassandra, rising from her seat. She held out her hand again. "I shall see you again at supper, I daresay. I will ask Steeves to see to your comfort."

"My batman has undoubtedly done all that is necessary," said Mr. Raven. He had taken her hand and now looked down searchingly into her face. "Belle—forgive me—Miss Weatherstone, I am aware that it has been a number of years since we last saw each other. In some ways, you are just as I remembered you. Those were good days, when I lived here at the Hall and we became friends. I trust that my friendship is recalled just as fondly. I hope that we may become friends again."

Cassandra was very aware that he still held her fingers captive in his. She tried not to glance down at their clasped hands. "I, too, hope that we may become friends, Mr. Raven." She uttered the civil rejoinder a little breathlessly.

The door opened, and Miss Bidwell entered. "Belle! And this must be Philip Raven! I was utterly disconcerted to learn from Steeves when I rose from my nap that you had arrived, Mr. Raven. I most certainly bid you welcome."

Mr. Raven let go of Cassandra's hand and moved forward to bow over Miss Bidwell's fingers. "My dear Miss Bidwell, I have never forgotten you. You were a mainstay of my young life during my time here at the Hall."

Miss Bidwell appeared very pleased that he had recalled her so favorably. "Thank you, Mr. Raven. I have not forgotten you, certainly. You were always a good student. I regretted when it became time for you to leave."

"As did I, Miss Bidwell," said Mr. Raven, throwing a smiling glance in Cassandra's direction. "However, despite my youthful fears to the contrary, all turned out well. I suppose you know why I have come?"

"I surmised that Sir Marcus must have sent for you because of a question having to do with his will," said Miss Bidwell. She looked over at Cassandra. "Has Sir Marcus been informed that his godson is here?"

"Weems sent down word to Mr. Raven that my grandfather was resting and could not receive visitors as yet," said Cassandra. "I was myself informed just a quarter hour ago that Mr. Raven had arrived."

"I see," said Miss Bidwell with a hint of disapproval in her voice. She glanced askance at Cassandra, her expression frowning.

"I am still in all my dirt," said Mr. Raven smoothly. "If you ladies will excuse me, I shall go up to my room and make myself more presentable."

"Of course, Mr. Raven," said Cassandra cordially, glad that her initial meeting with Mr. Raven was at last over. She had sustained such a shock when she heard that he was at the Hall, and another upon meeting him. He was such a fine-looking fellow, and his manners left nothing at all to be desired. It was such a pity that she had not met him as herself, thought Cassandra with a pang of regret.

Mr. Raven retrieved his hat and gloves before making a formal bow to each of them. He then exited, his greatcoat swinging jauntily from his broad shoulders.

When Miss Bidwell had closed the door quietly behind Mr. Raven, she turned to Cassandra. "Really, Belle, how could you! What Philip Raven must have thought when you received him alone! It was poorly thought on your part."

"I know it was, Biddy," agreed Cassandra with a nod. In truth, she was feeling a little ashamed of herself. It was so unlike her to behave with such impropriety. Her only excuse must be that the constant tension she had felt since coming to the Hall had rendered her temporarily deranged.

"And you haven't a trace of remorse, either," exclaimed Miss Bidwell. "I am angry with you, Belle. You have shown a lack of judgment that I never expected of you. What's more, you have probably given Mr. Raven a very odd notion of the sort of hospitality that may be had here at the Hall."

A sliver of irritation ran through Cassandra at Miss Bidwell's scolding censure. Really, her sister was treated exactly like a schoolgirl in this house, she thought. However, she dared not allow her real feelings to surface. Instead, she said calmly, "I admit that I hoped that Mr. Raven would choose to remove himself to the village, but Steeves made it quite impossible. He had already assigned rooms to Mr. Raven and his servant."

"Whyever would you want Mr. Raven out of the house?" asked Miss Bidwell in amazement.

"I was thinking of my grandfather, of course," said Cassandra. She was already regretting her frankness. When she noted Miss Bidwell's expression of disbelief, her innate honesty made her try to make the lady understand at least a little. "And my time with him. I know that sounds horridly selfish, but— Oh, Biddy, I do not know this man. I really do not wish to know him, not right now. I have too much else on my mind."

At once Miss Bidwell's expression softened. "I do understand, Belle. I do not fault you for it, though I could wish— However, I shall say nothing more. Why do you not run along now? I know how difficult it is for you to sit about, and it has been a trying day. No doubt you would do better for a period of solitary reflection. If Mr. Raven returns downstairs before luncheon, I shall set myself to entertain him."

Cassandra smiled at Miss Bidwell through a mist. "Thank you, Biddy."

Chapter Six

After Biddy departed, Cassandra wondered what she was to do with herself, given what was left of the morning. Obviously, she could not spend more time with her grandfather until that evening, which meant that she had to occupy herself otherwise. But what would Belle do in similar circumstances? Certainly Belle would not sit in her bedroom all day, thought Cassandra, and so neither could she. Cassandra would still have liked to take refuge in the bedroom, emerging only for luncheon and supper. However, that really was not an option, Cassandra felt certain, overriding her trepidation.

Refuge. What a lovely word. It conjured up a place that was peaceful, out-of-the-way, safe. A tiny smile flitted across her face. She could think of nowhere better suited to her purposes than the library. She could sit down at the writing desk and write a letter to herself in reply to the one she had written to Belle. That would be an interesting exercise, indeed. She almost laughed out loud at how nonsensical it all was. She felt as though she were surrounded by mirrors and had to turn this way and that to discover which of her images was the real one.

Cassandra found the library after a little difficulty. Her sister's description of the house had not been as detailed in every respect, or perhaps she had simply not paid close enough attention when Belle was instructing her. However, as she had assumed, there was a writing desk that held ample supplies of paper and pens and inkwells.

Before sitting down at the desk, which was situated between two long narrow windows through which the late autumn sun shone, Cassandra quietly walked about the room. She had closed the door behind her when she had entered, and she felt perfectly at ease in exploring a little. The bookshelves had been built into the walls and extended almost to the high ceiling. A railed ladder on metal casters was attached to a railing that extended the length of the shelves so that a browser could slide it along to whatever location that was desired and climb up to the uppermost shelves quite comfortably. Cassandra was impressed. She had never seen such a thing. It was obvious that Sir Marcus and his ancestors had taken pride in collecting such a substantial library and had used it.

Cassandra experimentally rolled the ladder back and forth. Then she grasped the rail with one hand and pulled up her skirt out of the way so that she could climb up. She picked up a random volume here and there from the shelves closest to her. There were several of the classics in the original Latin or Greek, an informative text on animal husbandry and a treatise on the law.

Cassandra made a face. Such reading did not appeal to her, and she suspected that her sister would not have found it interesting, either. Just as she was climbing down, Cassandra paused and pulled out one other volume. It was a hand-tooled leather-bound volume, the title quaintly scrolled in Old English. Cassandra took the time to make it out, and realized with a spurt of excitement that she held a family history written by none other than her grandfather, Sir Marcus Weatherstone.

She climbed down off of the ladder and blew dust from the thick volume. The leather was a trifle brittle along the spine when she opened the book, but Cassandra paid not the slightest attention. She had found a treasure. Before she left the Hall, she would be able to take something very precious with her. She would be able to take some knowledge of who she was and where she had come from. Her uncle had rarely spoken about his family, so Cassandra had never had the opportunity to feel a sense of roots. She had always felt awkward at the girls' seminary when others had talked about their relations and their own place in the scheme of things. Cassandra had had very little to say. That probably went a long way in explaining her desire to come to know her grandfather, who was, after all, her only other link in the world.

At one end of the library loomed a massive fireplace. A fire had been built in it and warmed the chill air. A settee and wing chairs had been arranged near the hearth. Cassandra was glad for the heat as she curled up on the settee and began to turn the pages of the book written by her grandfather.

It was hours later when she heard the bell sounding for luncheon. She looked up, blinking at the clock on the mantel, and disbelievingly took in the time. She would have to hurry if she was to change her dress.

Cassandra left the book upstairs on the bedside table in her bedroom, but her thoughts were still filled with the images conjured up by her grandfather's history. As she entered the morning room, she greeted Miss Bidwell almost absently. She sat down at the table, completely free of the anxiety that had dogged her from the beginning of the masquerade.

Miss Bidwell greeted her in return, then said, "You appear preoccupied, my dear. Is everything quite all right?"

"Oh, yes. I was just thinking of something that Grandfather wrote in his family history. I am up to the Crusades now," said Cassandra. She indicated her preferences to the serving man that waited on her and turned her attention to the barley soup.

"Family history? I was not aware that Sir Marcus had written such a thing," said Miss Bidwell, obviously surprised.

"Nor I," said Cassandra. "I found it quite by accident this morning in the library. It is absolutely fascinating. Did you know that the name Weatherstone according to legend is said to have originated because the family had a reputation for weathering trouble like so many stones? One must wonder how much truth there is to such old tales."

"You were in the library?"

Cassandra became aware that Miss Bidwell was staring at her with a stunned expression. Cassandra regretted her inattention. She simply had to be more cautious. "I was going to write a letter to Ca . . . Cassandra," she said in hasty explanation. "And then I started amusing myself with the ladder, you see. One thing led to another and I . . . I found this book . . ." Her voice trailed off, and she covered her inadequacy by picking up her teacup and putting it to her lips.

Miss Bidwell smiled and nodded. "I do see, Belle. It is very natural to desire to reaffirm one's sense of identity when one's world threatens to change."

"Yes," agreed Cassandra, scarcely understanding what Miss Bidwell was saying, but quite willing to go along if it meant that suspicion would be averted.

Miss Bidwell reached her hand across to pat Cassandra's arm gently. "My very dear girl, you mustn't worry so. I am certain, even if our worst fears are realized, that Sir Marcus has made ample provisions for you."

Cassandra stared at Miss Bidwell's earnest face. "But I never gave a thought to—" She shook her head. The very thought of her grandfather dying was completely obnoxious to her. As for provision, she was very sure that that would have been Belle's least concern. "I shan't think anything of the sort, and I do not wish you to either, Biddy. Grandfather made a surprising turnaround. Weems said so. He will be fine once he has gotten his strength back, I am sure of it."

Miss Bidwell nodded. "Of course he will be, Belle. Of course he will be."

There was only the sound of spoon against china for a few moments. Cassandra's reflections had been firmly turned into less diverting channels. She could not forget what her grandfather had said about expecting death. But surely he was not completely resigned to it if he had invited his godson to come to see him, even if he had said it was for a deathbed visit. Following her train of logic and in an effort to reassure Miss Bidwell that the future was not as gloomy as that lady apparently believed, Cassandra said, "This morning Grandfather told me that he had requested Mr. Petrie-Downs to send for his godson. I doubt that Grandfather would have done so if he had not believed that he was strong enough to outlast Mr. Petrie-Downs's search for his godson."

Suddenly, Cassandra realized that Mr. Raven had not joined them at table. She looked around, a small frown knitting her brows. "Where *is* Mr. Raven, Biddy?"

"Steeves informed me that when Sir Marcus woke from his sleep and learned that Mr. Raven had arrived, he insisted that his godson take luncheon with him in his rooms," said Miss Bidwell.

"Indeed! Well, there you are, Biddy. I don't expect Grandfather to pass on just yet," said Cassandra.

"No, I quite agree with you, my dear," said Miss Bidwell with a thoughtful nod.

Cassandra smiled, feeling somewhat relieved that her companion had concurred. "Perhaps we should all be grateful for Mr. Raven's arrival, after all."

Miss Bidwell looked fixedly at her for a moment. "Er . . . how do you really feel about Sir Marcus's invitation to Philip Raven, Belle?"

"Why, how *should* I feel about it? I think it a good sign that my grandfather wishes company." Cassandra realized that was not quite what her companion had meant. "Biddy, surely I am cognizant enough of what is due to a guest that I shall be able to make him feel comfortable."

"Of course you shall. There is no question of that, naturally," said Miss Bidwell hastily.

Cassandra looked at her companion, who was busying herself with a small piece of chicken. "Biddy, is there something that I should know?"

"About what, my dear?" asked Miss Bidwell, glancing up momentarily before returning her gaze to cutting her chicken.

"About Philip Raven," said Cassandra. She rather thought, after what her grandfather had said about his godson's visit and now Miss Bidwell's odd reaction, that there must be something that she was missing. Perhaps Belle already knew what it was; but then again, Belle might not, in which case it was her sister's duty to find out what was in the wind so that she could warn Belle.

"I am sure I don't know what you mean," said Miss Bidwell with a studied indifference.

Cassandra's suspicions were confirmed. Something was in the wind, something connected with Philip Raven. She decided to press Miss Bidwell a little. "It is very odd, you know. Grandfather seemed concerned that I might not be civil toward Mr. Raven. Now why should he think that, Biddy?" asked Cassandra.

"I cannot presume to read Sir Marcus's mind, dear," said Miss Bidwell briskly. She signaled to the serving man for another serving of the poultry. "The chicken is very well prepared, don't you think? So tender and flavorful. I wonder what herbs were used? I must remember to ask Mrs. Fleming when I see her. Would you like another piece also, Belle?"

Cassandra had no difficulty in recognizing the attempt to change the subject. She said dryly, "No, thank you. I have had quite enough, I think. Of everything."

Miss Bidwell looked up, a look of startlement in her blue eyes.

Cassandra laid aside her napkin and rose. "If you will excuse me, Biddy, I believe that I shall return to my reading."

"Belle—"

Cassandra paused at the door, looking back at the elderly lady. Miss Bidwell had a perturbed expression on her face. "Yes, Biddy?"

Miss Bidwell seemed to hesitate, as though it was difficult to form the words that she needed. She cast a glance toward the serving-man, who was moving about at the serving board. Miss Bidwell sighed. "Never mind, my dear. I shall speak with you later."

"Of course, Biddy," said Cassandra coolly. She left the morning room, still determined to find out what Miss Bidwell knew and was concealing from her.

She rather thought that her strategic retreat had taken Miss Bidwell by surprise. Apparently, the lady had been prepared for an interrogation from her charge, not a gently delivered setdown. The unexpected tactic had seemed to shake Miss Bidwell's resistance. In view of that, Cassandra had every expectation of being able to

persuade Miss Bidwell to confide in her; and if that was
not characteristic of her sister's personality, then so be
it. She would be gone within a few days, and Belle would
be reestablished in her rightful place.

As Cassandra made her way back upstairs to retrieve
the history, she wondered what there could possibly be
about Mr. Philip Raven that was so unusual or undesir-
able that Belle should object to his coming. Sir Marcus
and Miss Bidwell had both assumed that his arrival
would be frowned on by her sister. It was very curious,
indeed.

Her sister must have liked Philip Raven well enough
as a child, or otherwise Belle would not have made that
childish pledge to wed him when she was old enough.

Something must have changed that. Perhaps it had to
do with Philip Raven's leaving the Hall after living with
his godfather for so long. Cassandra then wondered why
Philip Raven had lived at the Hall at all. Had he been
orphaned? Was it an experience in common that had
created the original tie between Belle and Philip Raven?
These were unanswerable questions, of course, until she
had an opportunity to speak to Belle.

In the meantime, Cassandra fully intended to finish
the history that her grandfather had written. She had
spoken the truth to Miss Bidwell. She did find it fascinating. It was intriguing to Cassandra to read about her
ancestors. She had never known anything very much
about her precedents. It probably should not matter to
her, and perhaps it would not have if she had been
raised along with her sister. However, Cassandra felt
something like a pecuniary relative come to visit at the
Hall. She was accepted, but she really did not feel at
home.

After retrieving the book, Cassandra decided to take
the volume to the sitting room. The light would be better
there, and if someone should wish to find her, such as
Miss Bidwell, she would be readily available. Cassandra
rather hoped that Miss Bidwell would seek her out. She
was very curious about Mr. Philip Raven and what his
visit might mean to her sister.

Cassandra occasionally glanced up at the ormolu clock

on the mantel, but an hour passed without Miss Bidwell making an appearance. Cassandra gradually forgot to look up at the clock as she became more and more involved in the history. She curled up on the settee in front of the fire, her feet tucked under her skirt on the cushion. Sir Marcus was a master storyteller. He had taken even the driest of facts and managed to weave them into a whole that would keep a reader's interest. She was reading about Sir Marcus himself and his adventures when she heard a bell peal in the distance.

Chapter Seven

Cassandra glanced up, startled. Almost immediately the door to the sitting room opened, and the butler entered. "What is it, Steeves?" she asked.

"Sir Thomas is here, miss."

Cassandra straightened abruptly, bringing her feet to the carpet. Her heart was suddenly thudding. *Sir Thomas—her host at the house party!* Would he recognize her? There must have been a startled expression on her face, for the butler gave a slight nod, as though answering a question.

"He wishes to see Sir Marcus," said Steeves.

"I see." Cassandra carefully marked her place in the history, giving herself a moment to gather her thoughts. She looked up. "Has Weems been informed?"

"I sent word up only a moment ago," said Steeves.

"What of Mr. Raven? Is he still with my grandfather?" asked Cassandra curiously.

"No, miss. Mr. Raven went riding this hour past."

"Very well, Steeves. Then I think that we may allow Sir Thomas to see Sir Marcus," said Cassandra with a smile.

The butler gave a slight cough. "I told Sir Thomas that you would wish to escort him upstairs yourself."

"Of course I shall," said Cassandra, sounding more assured than she felt. The butler's meaningful statement had hinted strongly her sister's probable course of action. Though she was grateful for the prompt on how to act out her part, she was also insecure about how well she could carry it out. For instance, what would Belle do if Sir Thomas decided that he could very well see himself upstairs?

As Cassandra stood up, a voice sounded behind the butler, and Steeves turned to reply. The next instant, the butler gave way before a short, portly gentleman. The visitor had put off his coat and gloves and was attired in a dark driving coat. His frowning expression deepened when he saw Cassandra.

She stepped forward, offering her hand. She had instantly recognized him. "Sir Thomas, I am happy to see you."

"Very pretty of you, Belle," said Sir Thomas with a lessening of his frown. He bowed over her hand. When he straightened, he directed a searching glance at her face. "You know why I have come, of course."

For an instant, Cassandra thought wildly that he meant to tell her that he knew everything and that he had immediately recognized that it had been Belle, and not Cassandra, who had sat down with him and his guests at luncheon. Clutching her hands together unobtrusively in the folds of her skirt, Cassandra strove for mastery over herself.

"Of course. You wish to see Grandfather," said Cassandra with a semblance of cool self-possession.

"I received the message from Weems but half an hour ago. Steeves confirms to me that Sir Marcus made a turnaround earlier today. If true, that is the swiftest recovery that he has ever made," said Sir Thomas.

Cassandra felt almost weak from relief. She was not going to be unmasked and shamed after all. She struggled to maintain her facade of calm. "I spoke to Grandfather myself this morning," said Cassandra. "He seemed quite cognizant. We are all quite encouraged."

"I shall judge his condition for myself," said Sir Thomas. "I know it will not make the least impression upon you if I were to request that you remain belowstairs while I see to my patient."

"Not the least," agreed Cassandra, glad for the clue as to how her sister would have handled the physician's visit. "Shall we go upstairs, Sir Thomas? You will want to speak with Weems, also."

Sir Thomas agreed, somewhat sardonically. He bowed her out of the sitting room, retrieving a black bag from

the butler's care, and escorted her upstairs to Sir Marcus's apartments. Cassandra knocked on the massive oak
door. It was opened immediately by Sir Marcus's valet.

"Weems, here is Sir Thomas come to attend my
grandfather," said Cassandra.

"Sir Thomas, pray come in. This is a welcome visit,"
said Weems, opening the door wider so that the physician and Cassandra could enter.

"I understand that Sir Marcus has made a remarkable
turnaround, Weems," said Sir Thomas, carrying his black
bag toward the bed.

"Yes, sir, he has," said Weems without expression.

As Cassandra passed the valet, he caught her eye and
gave her a look of significance. She wondered what the
valet was trying to convey.

Sir Thomas put down his bag on the bed. "Well, Sir
Marcus? How do I find you this fine day?"

The invalid snorted, even as he held up one hand to
be grasped in a handshake. "My old friend, to what do
I owe this pleasure? I quite thought I had run you off
for the last time."

"I wish that you would," retorted Sir Thomas, check-
ing his patient's pulse. "Have you been taking the potion
that I prescribed for you?"

"Weems makes certain that I am poisoned with it
every day at the same hour," said Sir Marcus sourly.

"Good. I am glad to hear it," said Sir Thomas, quite
unperturbed. "It is doing you good, as anyone can see."

"Is that you, Belle? Come around where I can see
you. This blasted candlelight is too dim for me. I cannot
see you properly," commanded Sir Marcus.

"Yes, Grandfather," said Cassandra, obediently drawing nearer.

"Does the light seem too dim? Weems, perhaps you
should open the drapes," said Sir Thomas, turning his
head toward the valet with his brows raised. As the valet
made as if to go to the windows, he held up his hand to
motion him back. "Is that better, Sir Marcus?"

"Yes, yes! I can see much better now," said Sir Marcus in a testy voice.

Cassandra looked at the physician and the valet in

consternation. The valet had not drawn open the drapes at all. There had not been the least change in the light whatsoever. In any event, the several branches of candles had made the room quite brilliant. "Weems—"

The valet shook his head at her, while Sir Thomas again threw up his hand, this time to silence anything Cassandra might say. "Well, you seem to be coming along splendidly, Sir Marcus. I am very pleased to find you in such fine stirrups. We will have you up and about quite soon, I daresay," said Sir Thomas.

"Of course I shall be up and about," said Sir Marcus. He put a hand up to his eyes and pressed his fingers briefly to them. "I am tired of a sudden. It is your fault, sir. I am not yet up to your poking and prodding."

"Then you must rest. Weems, I leave you in charge. We will continue with the potion that I have prescribed for Sir Marcus. And now, my friend, I must leave you. I am hosting a house party, as you may have heard, and my duties do not allow me to stay away for long," said Sir Thomas, closing his black bag.

"Away with you, then. Pray give my regards to Amanda," said Sir Marcus. He stirred restlessly. His voice slurred a little. "Would that I could join your entertainments. It is deuced dull being confined to this bed."

Sir Thomas said good-bye again and motioned for Cassandra and Weems to follow him out of the bedroom.

As the valet closed the connecting door between the bedroom and dressing room, Sir Thomas looked at both of them with a serious expression. "It is as I feared. When Steeves told me that Sir Marcus was doing so unexpectedly well, I suspected as much. We have the calm before the storm."

"What do you mean?" asked Cassandra sharply.

Sir Thomas laid his hand on her arm for a short, comforting second. "My dear Belle, you must recognize the signs by now. I am sure that Weems understands."

The valet nodded, his expression troubled. "Aye, it always happens just this way. The master comes to himself for a few hours, and then he succumbs to another,

worse bout of the fever. When he complains about the
light, it is a certain sign of it happening. It is as though
his eyes forget how to see."

"But you said that he had made a surprising turnaround, Weems," said Cassandra quickly. "How can you
say he is going to be worse now?"

"Belle, you must prepare yourself," said Sir Thomas
quietly. "And I greatly fear that this might be the worst
struggle that Sir Marcus has yet faced, simply because
the time between bouts is shortened. He has not had the
usual time to gather his strength."

"Are you trying to say that he might not live?" asked
Cassandra. What she read in the physician's expression
answered her question. "No! I shall not believe it! You
are wrong, Sir Thomas!" She turned quickly away, then
whirled back about. "You will forgive me if I do not
show you out. You know the way, of course."

Sir Thomas bowed. He opened the dressing room
door for her. Cassandra turned away from the physician
again and quickly made her escape down the hall; however she was not yet far enough away that she could not
hear the physician's sad observation to the valet.

"Ah, Weems, it will be very hard on her when the
time comes. Very hard, indeed."

Cassandra fled without giving thought to where she
was going. She was already well past Belle's bedroom
when she began thinking again. She wanted to be alone
for a while to gather herself. Miss Bidwell would probably be in the sitting room at that time of day, so she did
not want to go there. She kept walking until she found
herself in a part of the manor that she did not recognize.

Cassandra opened a door and looked down the long
length of a gallery. It was deserted, and she slipped inside, closing the door behind her. The gallery served a
dual purpose. It connected the west wing of the manor
to the east wing. On the one hand was a row of tall,
stately lead-paned windows that looked out on the ex-
tensive lawns and gardens at the back of the manor. On
the other hand the oak-paneled wall was covered with
tapestries and countless portraits, both great and small,
serving as a portrait gallery. The portraits captured Cas-

sandra's attention and suspended her distressed thoughts.

She went slowly down the gallery, her footsteps soft on the several carpets that covered the polished wooden floor. She discerned at once that the portraits were ancestral, and that was what made them of interest to her. Gentlemen in velvets and lace, in slashed doublets and hose, in somber coats and white cravats. Ladies in ringlets and frills, in high white wigs and panniers, in decorous gowns and ribbons. All stared back at Cassandra with very nearly the same painted expression, their eyes knowing and their expressions distant.

She had been reading in Sir Marcus's family history about many of those same personages who looked down on her from out of the wooden frames. It seemed so very odd that their lives actually formed a part of her.

There were two portraits that she looked at for a very long time. One was of her uncle and her father when they had been young boys. They had posed in a careless fashion, leaning against marble columns, their youthful figures radiating life. The other portrait was of her parents, with two infants in long white gowns held protectively between them. Their expressions were serene and confident.

"How much I wish that I had known you better," she said quietly, lightly touching the painted canvas.

Her thoughts were somber. She had learned much about herself and her background, true. She had met her grandfather and had learned to care about him in a very short time. The advantages of the masquerade were plain. But she had not expected to experience such trepidation and pain because of it.

Cassandra leaned her head against the massive gilt frame that had captured her family in a stilled, perfect moment of time. "Oh, Grandfather."

After a moment, she straightened and left the gallery. She did not look back. There was nothing there but memories, and most of those were not hers.

That evening at dinner there was scarcely a word spoken amongst the company. Mr. Raven had joined Cas-

sandra and Miss Bidwell, and it would have been natural
that the addition of a handsome gentleman to their number would have enlivened the conversation. However,
they had all been informed by Weems only a few short
hours after Sir Thomas's departure that Sir Marcus had
once more lapsed into fevered delirium. The depressing
news had served to squelch the desire to exchange more
than the polite civilities. The candlelight flickering
against the gloom only enhanced the melancholy atmosphere.

Cassandra and Miss Bidwell ate quietly the tender
meats and vegetables set before them and sipped spar-
ingly at their wine. Mr. Raven's appetite did not seem
to be as adversely affected as that of his dinner companions. He made a fair dinner and afterward sent his com-
pliments to the cook. Catching Cassandra's gaze upon
him, he smiled at her. There was a sympathetic expression in his own eyes. "You should try to eat a little
more, Miss Weatherstone. Uncomfortable times are always faced better when one is well fed."

"I have little appetite this evening, I fear," said Cassandra simply.

Cassandra knew that she and Miss Bidwell must both
be thinking the same thoughts about the ill gentleman
upstairs, for every once in a while Miss Bidwell would
make a comment that reflected her concern. Cassandra
caught herself and Miss Bidwell glancing often toward
the dining room door, as though willing someone to
bring some word, whether of good or evil report. It
would simply be a relief to be told something, anything
at all.

As was the customary habit after dinner, the ladies
retreated to the drawing room and left Mr. Raven to his
after-dinner wine. However, he did not remain long, and
after no more than a quarter hour, he joined them for
coffee. The butler rolled the coffee urn into the drawing
room promptly at the hour.

When Miss Bidwell inquired of Steeves if any word
had been sent down by the valet regarding Sir Marcus's
status, the butler merely shook his head in a regretful
fashion.

"At least Weems has not sent out the alarm," remarked Miss Bidwell, giving a cup of coffee to Cassandra.

"Yes," agreed Cassandra.

"Then we may assume that Sir Marcus is making a good fight of it," said Mr. Raven, also accepting a cup from Miss Bidwell. He looked somberly from one to the other of the ladies. "You must understand, that is always a hopeful sign, for it is when a man gives up the fight that death usually comes. I have seen it any number of times during the war."

"Thank you, Mr. Raven," said Cassandra quietly. "I appreciate your attempt to reassure us."

Miss Bidwell nodded. "Yes, indeed. Thank you, sir."

The conversation lagged again, and the falling of a log in the fireplace sounded abnormally loud. Miss Bidwell bestirred herself to do something for the entertainment of their guest. "Mr. Raven, I believe that you will find the most recent newspapers there on the occasional table."

"Thank you, Miss Bidwell," said Mr. Raven. He went over to pick up the newspapers and returned to his chair. "I hope that you will forgive me if I glance at all the news. I have been gone so long from England that I fear I am grown quite ignorant of what is happening in our country."

"Of course," said Miss Bidwell, inclining her head.

Cassandra murmured her concurrence. She was actually relieved to be freed of the necessity of making conversation with Mr. Raven. She had been feeling some anxiety that he would wish to bring up old memories, which of course she couldn't have responded to with any degree of lucidity, and that would have displayed her ignorance to Miss Bidwell, as well. She thought it a very good thing that Mr. Raven had taken up Miss Bidwell's suggestion so readily. As for herself, she thought that she could endure the evening better if she were not put on the spot.

Cassandra had taken only a few token sips of the coffee before setting aside the cup. She noticed that Miss Bidwell had not finished her coffee, either, but had also

set it aside in order to take up her tatting. Cassandra
envied her companion the release that such creative ac-
tivity provided and longed to be doing something with
her hands, as well. But she had nothing to do and had
to content herself with looking over the fashion plates
in back issues of the *Ladies' Magazine.*

She realized that Mr. Raven occasionally glanced in
her direction, and she pretended not to notice, burying
her nose a little deeper in the magazines as though she
were riveted by what she was perusing.

It was scarcely nine of the clock when Miss Bidwell
wound up her tatting in a decisive manner. "Well! I suspect that Belle and I would both be better for an early
night's rest. What do you think, my dear?"

"Yes, yes, I quite agree," said Cassandra with some
relief. It was nerve-racking to merely wait and listen to
the clock tick. It seemed she had been turning the pages
of the *Ladies' Magazine* forever, and yet she could not
recall one illustration out of the whole.

Miss Bidwell seemed to perceive her state of mind.
"Never mind, Belle. You must know by now that Weems
will inform us if anything does happen, one way or the
other," she said gently.

"Of course I do," said Cassandra with more assurance
than she felt. She dropped the magazine and rose to her
feet. "I shall say good night, then, Biddy."

"Good night, my dear," said Miss Bidwell. "I shall
just tidy up a bit here before I go up."

Cassandra turned to Mr. Raven, who had risen when
she stood up, the newspaper still in his hand. She extended her hand to him. "Mr. Raven, I shall say good
night."

Mr. Raven took her hand and lightly pressed her fingers, as though in reassurance. He smiled down into her
eyes. "I shall look for you again in the morning, Miss
Weatherstone."

"Yes."

Cassandra left the drawing room and went up the wide
carpeted stairs, her fingers trailing along the burnished
banister. Wall sconces lighted her way. She felt more
exhausted than she had ever been in her life. It had been

a thoroughly unnerving day, and it did not appear that the morrow would be any less harrowing, especially in light of Sir Marcus's critical lapse.

She still hoped that the physician and Weems had been wrong in their gloomy pessimism. It would be horrible to have been able to see her grandfather so briefly, only to lose him altogether so swiftly to death. As for Belle, how ghastly it would be if she were to return to her place amidst such terrible circumstances.

As she prepared for bed, Cassandra prayed that things would not come to that. She would rather cut out her heart than be required to inform her sister that the old gentleman who had raised her had died in her absence.

There was a knock on the door. At once Cassandra leaped to the conclusion that a message concerning her grandfather was being brought to her, and she called out. Upon her hurried permission, the maid who had cleaned the grate earlier that day entered the bedroom.

"Oh, it is only you," said Cassandra with relief. She discovered that she had clenched her fingers in the bedclothes, steeling herself against hearing bad news from Weems or Miss Bidwell. However, no such message would be entrusted to a lowly maid, and she was well aware of it.

" 'Tis only Meg, indeed, miss," said the maid cheerfully.

Cassandra was glad to know the maid's name at last. It would make it so much easier when she needed to address her. "Yes, Meg?"

"I have brought your chocolate, just as you like it, miss."

"Chocolate!" Cassandra stared in consternation at the cup that the maid had set down on the bedside table. "I do not want it. Take it away!"

"But, miss, you always take a cup of hot chocolate before you retire," said the maid, her expression surprised. "I've heard tell that you've done so since you were a child."

"Have I?" Cassandra was shaken, but she quickly rallied. "Well, I don't want it anymore. I have decided that it is too sweet before bed."

The maid's expression cleared. "Oh, is that it! Well, I can't say as I blame you, miss." She whisked the cup away and exited the bedroom.

Cassandra leaned back against the pillows. It had never occurred to her that her sister might have developed a habit of drinking something before bedtime. She herself never did. And chocolate, of all things! She had always been allergic to chocolate. She could scarcely take up her sister's habit of imbibing a cup of chocolate every night. It would make her deathly ill.

However, it was certain that she could not suddenly and completely abandon such a well-known and ingrained habit, either. She would have to do something to conform to her sister's known tastes.

Cassandra decided that she would drink milk each evening before she retired, if only to still any questions amongst the household. It was but for a short time, after all. And when Belle returned, she could tell the servants that she had changed her mind again and preferred chocolate after all.

Her dilemma solved, Cassandra reached over to blow out the candles. She slid under the warm coverlets and was asleep almost instantly.

Chapter Eight

The next three days were anxious ones for Cassandra. She started to pen a short note to Belle to apprise her sister of Sir Marcus's condition. It was in Cassandra's mind that she could have the note delivered sealed to her sister. Almost at once, however, she crumpled up the unfinished sheet as she realized what degree of curiosity would be generated if one of Sir Thomas's guests, and not Sir Thomas, was to receive a communication from the Hall.

Undoubtedly, it was already filtering through the servants' grapevine that Miss Belle had a spitting image of herself staying at Sir Thomas's. A sealed note from Miss Belle to that other young lady could well lead to unwelcome speculation that they had somehow met. It would be a very short leap to question whether they might have exchanged places, for that would certainly make sense of whatever mistakes Belle must be making in her role and explain Cassandra's own gaffes to those at the Hall.

Having ruled out a sealed correspondence, Cassandra went riding daily and always made her way back to the old crofter's cottage on the chance that she might run across her sister. However, she saw nothing of Belle. She felt a confusing mixture of relief and guilt. Instead of her sister, she was the one who was up at the Hall keeping vigilance over her grandfather.

Belle was not due to meet her yet, as she very well knew. Though she wanted more than anything else to remain at the Hall until she at least knew how her grandfather was going to be, she yet hoped that Belle would somehow suspect that something was wrong. Foremost in her mind was the thought that her sister must be made aware of the crisis in Sir Marcus's health. If he was to die while Belle was away, Cassandra did not know what she was going to say to her sister. It was Belle's place to be with their grandfather at such a time. They simply had to trade places again, even though it pained Cassandra to think about leaving her grandfather.

At the crofter's cottage Cassandra left a note for Belle concerning their grandfather, in the event that her sister did happen to ride out before the date of their rendezvous. Cassandra did not know what else she could do, short of the desperate notion of riding over to Sir Thomas's manor and demanding to see her sister.

"That would put us in the basket," she said to herself, thinking of the certain scandal that would arise as a result. Every one of Sir Thomas's guests would be privy to their deception, and the tale would almost certainly find its way to London, just in time for her come-out. Her uncle and aunt would not be pleased, to say the least.

In addition to Cassandra's uncertainty about what to do concerning her sister, she was uncomfortable also with the situation at the Hall. In a word, with Mr. Raven.

She took pains to avoid the gentleman, hoping to discourage any other references that he might make to a mutual childhood. She saw Mr. Raven as more dangerous to her than perhaps any other personage at the Hall, for he was the only one who made attempts to reminisce with her. She sought twice to take refuge in the library.

Once he entered and discovered her reading. Mr. Raven stopped short, his hand still on the doorknob, and regarded her with surprise in his eyes. "Reading, Belle? You?"

"Pray address me as Miss Weatherstone," said Cassandra primly, instantly closing the book. She stood up, still holding the volume and wishing very much that she could hide it. Her cheeks burned. She was annoyed to have been caught by Mr. Raven, for he would certainly recall that Belle had not cared for books.

Mr. Raven walked over to her and gently took the book out of her reluctant hands. "May I, Miss Weatherstone?" He glanced at the title, and his brows rose.

"*The Classical Ages,* pertaining to Rome and Greece. I am bowled out, I must admit. You were never one to give much attention to history."

"I . . . I have discovered that I like reading about Rome and Greece," stammered Cassandra. An inspiration struck her. "The Colosseum games and Grecian athletic contests and wars are rather fascinating."

"Now that sounds more like you," said Mr. Raven, a smile curving his lips. His eyes reflected amusement. "You always had plenty of nerve and had a liking for vigorous exercise."

"Really, you make me out to be some sort of Amazon," retorted Cassandra.

"When I look at you, it is scarcely a heathen woman warrior that I see," said Mr. Raven quietly. A new expression came into his eyes as his gaze traveled slowly over her.

Cassandra's heart gave a bump. She was unnerved by his regard, and she turned away. "Perhaps I should go upstairs and discover from Weems whether there has been any change."

"Pray do not run away on my account," said Mr. Raven softly.

Cassandra turned around, raising her chin a little at his challenge. She saw that he had leaned against one of the steps of the moving ladder, his hand resting on the railing, and that he was regarding her with open amusement. "I am not running away," she stated with dignity.

"Are you not, Miss Weatherstone? Haven't you been running away from me ever since I arrived?" asked Mr. Raven.

"Of course not," said Cassandra, half afraid that she was betraying her inner nervousness.

Mr. Raven held the book out toward her. "Here is your history, Miss Weatherstone," he said gently.

Cassandra snatched the book from him and hastily retreated. "I shall undoubtedly see you at supper, Mr. Raven." She made good her escape before it occurred to him to ask her something else.

Another time, it was she who interrupted Mr. Raven. She went in to the library and found him seated at the large desk. He was dipping a pen into the inkwell and a sheaf of sheets was under his hand. "Oh! I am sorry, sir."

Mr. Raven had looked up with a frowning expression, which dissipated upon seeing her. "You are not disturbing me, Miss Weatherstone. I am merely in the throes of composing the latest installment of my ongoing correspondence."

Cassandra came a bit farther into the room, her interest roused. "Has it to do with your business on the Continent?"

Mr. Raven's expression became more closed, something unreadable in his eyes. "Yes, I fear so."

Cassandra did not feel able to pry any more closely, though she was still curious to know the nature of his business. "I hope that all will transpire just as you wish, Mr. Raven.

"As do I, Miss Weatherstone," said Mr. Raven on a sigh. "Was there something that you wished of me?"

"O , no! I had just come in with the intention of—" Cass: dra bit back what she had been about to say, appalled at her own stupidity. She had very nearly told him that she had come in after another volume about Rome. That would be so unlike the Belle Weatherstone that he had known. She said hurriedly, "That is to say, I came to inquire whether you wished to ride with me!"

Mr. Raven grinned suddenly. His eyes lit up as he chuckled. "Now *that* brings back a score of memories! I could not begin to count the number of times that you tried to persuade me to leave my books in favor of some excursion or other!"

"Yes, and no doubt I asked more often than you ever consented!" retorted Cassandra.

Mr. Raven threw back his head and laughed. "Well, yes," he admitted. His expression was at once rueful and contrite. "Forgive me, but I must refuse the treat again."

"Very well, but I shall not easily forget how hardly you have used me, sir!" said Cassandra teasingly.

Mr. Raven laughed again as she left the library. Cassandra had closed the door with a small smile and a warm feeling. At least this once she had acquitted herself well.

She had not tried to use the library again to hide. Apparently, Mr. Raven was comfortable in such an atmosphere, and Cassandra had thought it wise not to put herself in his way.

Meanwhile, true to Sir Thomas's prediction, Sir Marcus's most recent bout of fever proved to be more violent than the previous episode. The constant care that the sick gentleman required was exhausting to Weems, so much so that he enlisted Miss Bidwell's help in the nursing.

The valet categorically refused to consider Cassandra's own offer to sit with her grandfather. "Begging your pardon, miss, but you would be made too upset in seeing the master's thrashing about and moaning and such," he had said apologetically.

When Cassandra tried to convince him otherwise, Miss Bidwell took her firmly to task. "Really, Belle, I thought you had more sense than to badger poor Weems at such a time," she said with asperity. "He is stretched to his limits now, and you are certainly not helping matters by adding to his burden."

"I only wish to help in some way," said Cassandra with a helpless gesture.

"I know, my dear. However, you would only be in the way, as I suspect you probably already know." Miss Bidwell patted Cassandra on the arm consolingly. With the air of someone throwing out a crumb but not really expecting it to fall on receptive ground, she said, "Now do be good enough to take over for me in dealing with the household. That would be the greatest service that you could render your grandfather at this point."

Cassandra acceded to the suggestion, relieved to be given something to do. She had felt useless. She could scarcely stand just waiting about while upstairs her grandfather, with whom she had been able to exchange no more than a few sentences in her entire life, was fighting for his very existence.

Besides, it gave her a very good excuse to avoid Mr. Raven.

That same hour Cassandra plunged into all the household affairs with not an ounce of trepidation. She knew she was well taught in housewifery. Her aunt had made certain that she understood how to run a house, and in fact had groomed her to be the chatelaine of a large estate. Cassandra might not be her daughter by blood, but that had not dimmed Margaret Weatherstone's ambitions for her niece in the least. Mrs. Weatherstone was determined to see that her niece made a good marriage and became well established in the world.

Cassandra called the housekeeper and the steward to her and talked to them about the running of the household. She saw the servants' incredulous expressions as they exchanged glances, but she ignored the obvious indications that her sister would probably never have embarked on such a course.

Out of character for Belle though she now knew it to be, Cassandra was determined to become familiar with the workings of the Hall. She felt certain that she would become just a bundle of exposed nerves if she did not occupy herself in some fashion, and at least her thoughts did not dwell on Sir Marcus when she was busy.

Cassandra dove into all of the business connected with the household. She consulted with the cook about menus. She began to handle the household accounts and bills. She requested that the housekeeper give her a tour of the Hall from attic to cellar, ostensibly to inform her of what was needed, though it also served the purpose of making Cassandra thoroughly familiar with the Hall and all of its environs. In the process, Cassandra discovered an old trunk with every color thread and size hoop imaginable, and she conceived the happy notion to cross-stitch new chair covers to replace the worn ones in the dining room. For the first time since she had begun the masquerade, she actually began to feel at home.

It was several days before the fever broke, and Sir Marcus was pronounced by Sir Thomas to be very weak but recovering. Cassandra expressed heartfelt thanks. Miss Bidwell agreed, saying that it was a testament to Sir Marcus's formidable constitution that he had once more cheated death.

"I am only sorry that I have neglected you, my dear," said Miss Bidwell.

"I am not complaining, Biddy," said Cassandra with a smile.

"No, of course not. It would be totally out of character for you to do so," said Miss Bidwell.

While Cassandra was still absorbing the lady's statement, Miss Bidwell continued, "What have you been doing with yourself, Belle? I understood Steeves to say something about touring the house and making a list of items that were needed or of things that needed to be done?" she asked with a raised brow, her expression dubious.

"Yes, I have done my best to keep the house running just as smoothly as you would, Biddy," said Cassandra.

"My dearest girl," said Miss Bidwell, embracing her with a suspicious moistness in her blue eyes behind her spectacles. "I am certain that you did the very best that you could."

"Is my grandfather well enough for me to sit with him?" asked Cassandra.

Miss Bidwell squeezed her hand. "Dear Belle. He is very weak, and he sleeps most of the time now. Weems and I discussed it, and we agree that it would be best to wait until tomorrow. Can you wait that long?"

"Just knowing that Grandfather is better is enough to carry me through," said Cassandra with a trembling smile. She felt immense disappointment. Tears stung her eyes suddenly, but she managed to say, "You cannot comprehend how very relieved I am, Biddy."

"Can I not, my dear? Now go on with your ride on Rolly. No doubt you will benefit from the fresh air," said Miss Bidwell.

Cassandra, who had already attired herself in her habit and had her gloves and whip in hand when Miss Bidwell had found her, nodded and ran down to the stables. She made short work of mounting and riding out of the stable yard.

Chapter Nine

As Cassandra headed into the wind, she had very mixed emotions. She wanted desperately to see her grandfather, but she knew that she could not wait until the morrow.

This was the day that she was to meet Belle and return to her own life. She would not be returning to the manor that afternoon, so she would not see her grandfather again.

At the crofter's cottage, as she had expected, she found Belle already waiting for her. The sisters embraced, then Belle said anxiously, "I found your note but a moment ago. Is Grandfather all right? He hasn't worsened, has he?"

Cassandra shook her head. "The fever broke just a few hours ago. Biddy assured me that he was weak but sleeping peacefully. She and Weems seem to think that our grandfather has made the turning point."

"Thank God! I was so afraid that—" Belle put her gloved knuckles to her lips, stopping what she had almost uttered; but Cassandra knew exactly what her sister would have said.

"Yes, so was I," said Cassandra quietly.

Belle broke the silence that had fallen between them. She almost appeared to shake herself free of the worry that had weighed on her. "But did I not tell you that Grandfather would recover? He is too stubborn to die," said Belle, her expression lightening with her natural optimism.

"Yes. I only wish that I could have spent more time with him. He was able to see me only for a few minutes one evening," said Cassandra on a sigh. She determinedly pushed aside her regret and put on a smile. "Well, how is the house party? Have my uncle and aunt suspected anything at all?"

Belle chuckled. "Oh, I don't believe that they have *suspected* anything precisely. However, I have confused them once or twice. It is due to my 'unusual liveliness,' you see."

"Oh, dear. I do see," said Cassandra, slightly dismayed. "We are different in some of our mannerisms."

"Since Aunt Margaret's remark, I have tried to subdue my speech and my ways," said Belle, frowning slightly. "But it is so hard to remember to be so very cool and to watch what I say before I say it."

"I know precisely what you mean. About watching what you say," said Cassandra, nodding. "I have put my foot into my mouth nearly every time I have opened it."

Her sister looked at her in surprise. "I don't understand how that can be. Why, I told you all that you needed to know about everyone."

Cassandra laughed. "So you did! But you didn't tell me everything about yourself! I have discovered that you do not make literary allusions and you do not enter the library for any reason. Nor do you read family histories. However, you do drink chocolate at bedtime, and I don't! Oh, and you are expected to be rude to Philip Raven for some reason that I have yet to discover."

Belle blinked. "My goodness, have you really fallen foul so badly? It is a wonder that Biddy or Weems or Steeves haven't tumbled onto you yet. But I suppose that you have managed."

"Yes, I have managed," said Cassandra dryly. She thought it was characteristic of Belle not to dwell on the problematical.

"But what is this about Philip Raven? Philip Raven! Why, I haven't seen him in years," said Belle.

"Grandfather asked his man of business to locate Mr. Raven some months ago. He arrived the very day that you and I traded places," said Cassandra.

"How disconcerting for you!" exclaimed Belle.

"Yes, very," said Cassandra. "Especially when Mr. Raven kept trying to jog my memory."

Belle laughed, but there was a sympathetic expression on her face. "No wonder you have had such a difficult time of it." She frowned. "But I wonder why Grandfather sent for Philip. He left the Hall so many years ago."

"Why was Mr. Raven at the Hall at all?" asked Cassandra curiously.

"Oh, there was something about the delicacy of his lungs and the salubrious effect of our air here. However, I think that was just an excuse given out. Philip was as healthy as you or I," said Belle. Her brows knit, deepening her frown. "I seem to recall talk about a new stepfather who didn't want him around and some sort of agreement between the gentleman and our grandfather. Finally, Philip went away to school, and we saw little of him after that."

"Well, he is back. I don't know why, however. When I was with Grandfather, he did not tell me, and he fell into that horrid fever the very next day," said Cassandra. "Biddy seems to think that the reason our grandfather sent for Mr. Raven has to do with his will since the gentleman is his godson."

"I suppose that must be it, then," said Belle, leaning negligently against the stall gate. Her gelding put his head over the top rail and snuffled at her hair, giving a whinny of recognition. She reached up to rub his nose, murmuring endearments.

Watching her sister, Cassandra said, "That is another thing. Rolly doesn't like me half as much as he does you. He'll take the treat from my hand, but very stiffly as though I am just a friendly stranger. Young John looks askance, let me tell you."

Belle laughed. "Of course Rolly knows! No one else does, but you do, don't you, boy?" She patted the gelding's nose, and a thoughtful expression came over her face. "You say that Young John watches you?"

"Yes, I think that he may guess, but he is not certain," said Cassandra.

Belle shrugged. "Well, if he does say something to you, just tell him that I am impersonating you at Sir Thomas's house party. He won't approve, but he won't worry, either. More important, he won't betray us to anyone."

"It doesn't matter now, Belle. You're going back to the Hall today," said Cassandra resolutely.

For a moment Belle stared at her as though stricken. Then her expression smoothed. "Bother! I had forgotten. When you told me that Grandfather was better, I started to think that—"

"That we might continue the masquerade a bit longer?" Cassandra turned the thought over in her mind. It would be the answer to all of her suppressed yearning. She would be able to see Sir Marcus on the morrow after all.

Belle nodded, looking a little guilty. "Yes, I did. You see, I am enjoying myself so much. It is the novelty of being in society."

"I suspect that the challenge of playing me has its allure, too," said Cassandra, making a shrewd guess.

Her sister laughed, sliding a glance at her from twinkling eyes. "Yes, I admit that there is a certain piquancy to that! My word, Cassandra, you have no notion how gauche I have felt. I have never been dressed by a maid before. I've never been to so many parties before or been made up to by gentlemen who are not Grandpa's age. And I have learned to like our Uncle Phineas and Aunt Margaret very well. It is like a pleasurable dream that one does not wish to end."

"And I feel the same. At least, I do about not wanting to end my stay at the Hall just now. I haven't had nearly enough time with Grandfather," said Cassandra.

"Then let's not change places today," said Belle, straightening from her negligent pose, appeal in her expression. "Oh, Cassandra, pray let's let it go another fortnight."

"I will admit that I am sorely tempted," said Cassandra honestly. "But I have done such a bad job of impersonating you."

"You did say that you had managed," said Belle.

"Well . . . yes," agreed Cassandra slowly. "But I think only because every mistake I've made has been put down to my—or rather, your—anxiety over Grandfather."

"Well, I see nothing to worry about, then. Oh, Cassandra, I know that you will do just fine. And I am going along splendidly. I have had my moments of doubt, of course, but I believe that I am quite able to pull it off," said Belle.

Cassandra laughed. "I am not at all surprised." She sighed suddenly. "I do envy your confidence in yourself, Belle. I wish I were as intrepid as you."

"All it takes is a bit of fortitude, which you have, dear Cassandra," said Belle fondly. "Only see how well you have done already."

"Yes, well. Belle, I don't know. Now there is Mr. Raven to think about. I have been avoiding him as best I may, but that cannot continue indefinitely. It is very awkward. I don't know what to do or say to him," said Cassandra.

"Well, neither would I," said Belle with a shrug. "As I said, I haven't seen him in years. It is not as though he actually knows me, nor I him."

"Perhaps not, but our grandfather and Biddy appear to believe that you might treat him unkindly even so," said Cassandra.

"I can't imagine why they—" A light seemed to come on in Belle's eyes. She began laughing. "Oh, I wonder if that is it? Cassandra, I think I may have put my finger on it."

"I wish you would tell me," said Cassandra.

"It is simply too amusing. You see, two or perhaps three years ago Grandfather started talking about how grown-up I was becoming and that he must see me settled in the world before long. He told me that he had been thinking about a proper husband for me, and that since Philip and I had gotten along so well as children, he thought Philip might be just the man," said Belle.

"Oh, dear. What did you say?" asked Cassandra, fascinated and appalled all at the same time. She knew that her uncle and aunt would allow her to make her own choice of husband. Of course, they meant to look out for her best interests; but that was not the same as prearranging a marriage. How very medieval of Grandfather, Cassandra thought.

"Naturally I told him what a nonsensical notion that was!" Belle shook her head, smiling at her memories. "I told him that I didn't want a husband. I wanted a proper come-out in London. Oh, we had a battle royal! Biddy sided first with Grandfather and then with me and finally threw up her hands, saying that there was no use in going on about it because it would be years before either of us need concern ourselves with the matter. That silenced both of us, which was just as well."

"Then . . . do you think that is the reason that Grandfather has sent for his godson? To see you affianced?" asked Cassandra.

Her sister looked startled for a second, then burst out laughing. "No, no, I'm certain that it is not! Why, even Grandfather would not entertain such a silly notion all of these years. And even if he did put forth such a suggestion to Philip, I am positive that Philip would reject it. I know that he would. We knew one another just as children. Why would he agree?"

"You did exchange a vow to wed," Cassandra reminded her.

"Yes, but that was just child's play. Philip probably wouldn't recall that we had done so, and even if he did, what is there in that? I certainly don't consider myself bound by words I spoke when I was nine years old, and it stands to reason that he won't expect me to, either!" said Belle. She shook her head. "No, Philip's visit has only to do with Grandfather's will, I am certain."

"Grandfather did say that he had sent word to Mr. Raven that he was on his deathbed," said Cassandra.

"There, you see!" said Belle. Her brows drew together again. "Though I do dislike Grandfather talking about himself like that."

"Never mind. He was undoubtedly simply feeling at a low point. He will improve in the days to come," said Cassandra, as much for her own benefit as her sister's.

Belle's expression cleared. "Yes, of course. That is only to be expected. He is getting better, isn't he?"

"Yes, that is what I am told," said Cassandra.

Belle nodded. She drew her whip through her hands for a moment, before she looked up and smiled. "Come, Cassandra, the hour grows late. I am expected back shortly, even though I know that you are not. How very hedged about I—you!—are! We must make a decision. Shall we continue the masquerade for a little longer?"

"A fortnight," said Cassandra, nodding. "I should be able to see more of Grandfather in that time."

"And I shall drink my fill of society while I might," said Belle. She shot her sister a mischievous glance. "I am flirting quite desperately with a certain young gentleman. Perhaps when we reclaim our own lives, you shall discover yourself to be engaged!"

Cassandra laughed. "I trust not. I should not like to have to jilt him."

As they both remounted and prepared to go their separate ways, Belle called out, "Do not be concerned about Philip Raven! I daresay he doesn't recall much about me at all. I was such a flighty girl, always on the go, and he was very studious. He was a dear, but a bit of a bore, I thought!"

Chapter Ten

Cassandra kept busy for the remainder of the day with housewifely duties, consulting with both the house-keeper and the cook on how best their newly arrived guest could be made comfortable. She learned quickly enough via the servants' grapevine that Mr. Raven's servantman was not at all an uppity fellow. Quite the contrary, in fact. The man waxed loquacious below-stairs about the adventures that he and his master had survived. It seemed that Mr. Raven had at one point been captured by the French and had made a daring escape back to his own lines, carrying with him a wounded comrade-in-arms. There had been a rare set-to with Spanish brigands, and the servantman had hinted at a romance with a Spanish *señora* while in winter quarters. Oh, yes, the servantman was more than willing to tell his tales of wartime, but when asked about Mr. Raven's present circumstances in the world since selling out of the army, the batman became strangely reticent.

"Which must lead one to wonder, Miss Belle," said Steeves, giving a swipe with his handkerchief at an imaginary speck of dust on the mahogany desk. He carefully picked up the salver, preparing to take away the post that was to be franked. He had come in upon hearing the bell pulled and had added his own bits of news to what Cassandra had already heard.

"Yes, indeed it does," agreed Cassandra. She leaned back in her chair, thinking about Mr. Raven. There certainly was something odd about the gentleman. He had sold out of the army and remained on the Continent, ostensibly for business reasons, until the letter from Mr. Petrie-Downs had found him. His batman talked about everything under the sun, except what his master was presently doing in the world. It was very odd, indeed. She shook her head and smiled at the butler. "Well, Steeves, I am certain that all will come clear in the end. If you will post my letters, I shall be grateful."

The butler lingered. His lined face was impassive, but his knowledgeable eyes were fixed upon her face. "Miss Belle, I thought you should know that Sir Marcus wakened not above an hour ago and demanded to see Mr. Raven at once."

"My grandfather asked for Mr. Raven and not for me?" asked Cassandra quickly, looking up at the elderly butler.

Steeves bowed slightly. "So Weems informed me, miss. The gentleman is above-stairs still."

"I see." Cassandra felt a spurt of jealousy. She had waited and waited to see her grandfather. When Sir Marcus had finally wakened and was able to see someone, this stranger, this interloper, had usurped her right. Then it hit her. She was as much, or even more, of a stranger than Mr. Raven. Cassandra wondered, with some hurt, whether Sir Marcus had ever wanted to become acquainted with his other granddaughter. She tried to put a good face on it. "Apparently my grandfather's mind has been exercised more about his will than any of us knew, Steeves. He wanted Mr. Raven found because there were things he wished to discuss with the gentleman, and I perceive that he is wasting little time in doing so."

"As you say, miss," said the butler.

"That will be all, Steeves," said Cassandra quietly.

"Very good, miss." The butler exited, slowly closing the door behind him.

Cassandra rose from her chair and walked over to one of the library windows overlooking the tumbled gardens. She looked through the leaded panes, one hand grasping the corded edge of the drape. It was not a brilliant day, being overclouded and threatening rain. The weather exactly suited her present mood, she decided—a bit dreary and gray.

She heard the door open and turned, expecting to see

Miss Bidwell or one of the servants. Instead, she met the gaze of Mr. Philip Raven. Neither of them said a word of greeting. Cassandra's heart skipped a beat and then began racing. Mr. Raven stood for a moment in the doorway, looking at her, then came in and closed the door.

"Steeves said that I might find you here," he said.

"Indeed. I was leaving just this moment, actually," said Cassandra coolly, starting toward the door. She had no desire for a *tête-à-tête* with the gentleman. Further, if Mr. Raven was no longer up with her grandfather, then she most certainly intended to go up to see him herself.

Mr. Raven did not politely move aside as Cassandra had anticipated he would. Instead, he lightly possessed himself of her elbow so that she was forced to stop beside him. "Miss Weatherstone, I came downstairs with the precise intention of talking with you. I beg your indulgence for a few words." He indicated with a gesture of his free hand the wing chairs in front of the blazing fireplace. "Pray, won't you grant me a few moments?"

Cassandra looked down pointedly at his hand on her arm until he removed it. Then she looked up, a somewhat angered expression in her eyes. "Thank you, Mr. Raven. I am not used to being accosted in such a manner."

"Of course you are not. Forgive me. It seemed to me that you intended to brush past me without even a nod," said Mr. Raven, a slight smile touching his mouth. "And it is very important that I speak to you without delay."

Cassandra raised her brows. "Truly? I did not know that there was anything of such immediacy between us, Mr. Raven."

Mr. Raven once more gestured toward the chairs situated in front of the hearth. "Please, Miss Weatherstone."

Cassandra stood undecided for all of a split second. Then she nodded. "Very well, Mr. Raven."

He escorted her to the chairs and politely handed her into one of them. As Cassandra sank down on the seat cushion, he seated himself in the other wing chair. "Thank you, Miss Weatherstone. I find this an awkward task, one which I had never anticipated. However, in

talking with Sir Marcus it became more and more obvious to me that it was very necessary to speak to you,"
said Mr. Raven. He stopped, turning his eyes away from
her to frown into the fire.

Cassandra's attention had been firmly caught by his
reference to her grandfather. She was no longer so impatient to be gone. She clasped her hands in her lap. "Yes,
Mr. Raven?"

He looked back at her, his frowning expression still in
place. "I find this very awkward, Miss Weatherstone."

"Yes, so you have already said," said Cassandra dryly.

A fleeting grin suddenly touched his lips. His expression lightened, and his gray eyes actually twinkled. Then
the gravity returned to his face. "That is so very like
you, Belle, to make a joke in an effort to smooth
things over."

Cassandra was startled by his unexpected renewal of
intimate address. She was made nervous by it. She hoped
that he did not intend to bring up again the brief time of
childhood that he and her sister had shared. Cassandra
touched her lips with her tongue in an unconscious gesture that revealed her discomfort. "Mr. Raven, you said
something about my grandfather."

Mr. Raven had been watching her, and now he nodded. "Yes. You may guess what we spoke of, Miss
Weatherstone."

"I would really rather not," countered Cassandra,
quite certain of it.

Mr. Raven brushed one hand through his thick, dark
hair. "You are going to make me say it, I see," he muttered, half under his breath.

"I am sorry, Mr. Raven. I did not precisely hear you,"
said Cassandra, wondering what was the matter with the
man. He was displaying definite signs of discomfort, and
she found that fascinating. Discomfort was supposed to
be her role to play in this scene, surely, she thought
irrelevantly.

Mr. Raven settled back against the squabs, squaring
his broad shoulders. His long fingers beat a nervous tat-
too on the chair arm. "Miss Weatherstone, I believe that
there has been enough history between us that we may

lay aside all constraints. We know one another well enough not to play games. In short, we must be honest with each other, you and I."

"Well, of course," said Cassandra. She shook her head. "I am sorry, Mr. Raven. You will have to make yourself more clear. I have no notion what you are actually trying to say."

"Miss Weatherstone . . . Belle . . . what I am trying to say in my poor fashion is that you have nothing to fear from me," said Mr. Raven.

"I should hope not!" said Cassandra, her brows rising in surprise. It scarcely registered with her that he was once more addressing her in a familiar manner. That fact paled beside the astonishing thing that he had said. "Why should I fear you, sir?"

Mr. Raven sighed, as though a weight had escaped him. "I am glad. I was afraid that everything had been so settled in your mind that— However, I perceive that we may come to an understanding, after all."

"So I should hope," said Cassandra, floundering for something intelligent to say in response to what was to her a completely obtuse statement. It seemed safe enough, however, to agree with his sentiment.

"Good. Miss Weatherstone, I would naturally not cavil for a moment to perform your grandfather's request if I thought that you stood in the least need of succor," said Mr. Raven. "However, it became obvious to me that you are well cared for and that Sir Marcus plans to leave adequate provision for you so that you shall never want. Therefore, I thought it unnecessary to accede to his wishes. I trust that this is acceptable to you?"

Mr. Raven looked at her, his expression inquiring but his eyes a bit guarded.

Cassandra sat there for several seconds, feeling quite at a loss. She had no idea what he had been talking about. What request? What task had Sir Marcus wished his godson to do that Mr. Raven was so obviously reluctant to perform? She had to say something. He was staring at her, waiting for her to respond.

Cassandra cleared her throat. "Are . . . are you certain

that you shouldn't simply do it? Grandfather is in rather a precarious state of health. Surely, it would not tax you overmuch to set his mind at ease."

Mr. Raven reacted as though he had just that moment noticed he had sat down on a horse tack. He leaped up from the chair. "Are you mad? Simply do it! Not tax me! My dear girl, have you any idea what you are saying?"

"Actually, none at all," said Cassandra candidly. A bubble of laughter came out of her. It *was* mad. The whole thing was mad. He was talking in riddles, and she was trying to answer them without being caught while she was doing it. She chuckled again.

When his face darkened, Cassandra was instantly contrite. "I am sorry, Mr. Raven. But your expression—if only you could have seen it. And this situation is so . . . so *bizarre!*" She waved her hand helplessly, for he would not understand. He could not possibly understand her position.

Mr. Raven breathed heavily through his nose. There was a wry look in his eyes. "I had forgotten. I had forgotten how you could always get the best of me. You little devil, playing me along like some poor fish on your line."

"Was I? I was not aware of it," said Cassandra, managing a weak smile. There, he was doing it again. Referring to Belle and their childhood relationship.

"Not aware of it, indeed! You must do better than that, Belle," said Mr. Raven with a small laugh. He shook his head. "I am amazed, nevertheless. It is a bizarre situation, and yet you are still able to find the fortitude to poke fun."

"Mr. Raven, I would prefer that we maintain a formal footing," said Cassandra. She almost trembled at her own daring in bringing him up short on the matter. "Pray do not address me by my given name. It . . . it is disconcerting, given the circumstances. I am positive that you will understand."

He nodded, looking suddenly thoughtful. "You are very right." He threw an appreciative glance at her. "Is that why you have held me at arm's length in our conversation? Why you have not responded to my gambits to join me down memory lane? Your insight amazes, Miss Weatherstone."

Cassandra inclined her head, hoping that would be sufficient reply. She could find nothing to say. Her fingers twisted in her lap. Mr. Raven was dangerous to be around. She never knew what to say or what she was talking about when she did speak.

Mr. Raven noticed the unconscious movement and put his own construction upon it. "I understand that knowledge of your grandfather's request to me must have been quite disturbing to one of your temperament. It would have been shocking to any well-bred young woman. I am only surprised that you received me as graciously as you did."

"My grandfather wished to see you. That was all that actually mattered," said Cassandra, bending her head. She was ashamed now. What she had felt or wanted had nothing to do with the circumstance, which was that Sir Marcus had bent considerable effort to find his godson. "I apologize if I appeared rag-mannered. I am not usually so."

"It was an ultimatum, wasn't it?" asked Mr. Raven quietly.

She looked up, startled. "What?"

"Sir Marcus told you that you were to wed with me."

Cassandra stared up at him, her lips parting in shock. She could not formulate a single coherent thought, but a tumble of emotions passed through her breast.

Mr. Raven bent to pick up one of her unresisting hands and raised it, holding it clasped gently in his own. He regarded her solemnly. "My dear Belle, you only had to express your objections to me. Surely, you knew that I would not agree *carte blanche* to such an archaic arrangement."

Cassandra nearly choked. She snatched her hand away and leaped up from the chair. Now she knew. She knew exactly what it had all been about, and the situation was more than she could possibly handle at just that moment. In fact, it was intolerable. "Excuse me! I . . . I must go."

"Belle!" Mr. Raven put out his hand as though he

would delay her, but Cassandra backed away, evading him.

"I cannot stay. Forgive me!" She practically ran from the library, leaving the door wide open in her haste to be gone.

The gentleman stared after her with a look of consternation on his handsome features.

Chapter Eleven

Cassandra fled upstairs, her chaotic thoughts running ahead of her. By the time she reached the landing, however, everything she was feeling had crystallized into anger. She found herself standing outside her grandfather's door, and with only a bare knock to announce her presence, she went in.

"Miss Belle!" exclaimed the valet, turning as she emerged from the dressing room and entered the bedroom.

"Is my grandfather awake, Weems?" asked Cassandra without preamble.

"Why, yes, miss, but—"

"I shall speak to him, Weems, if you please," said Cassandra, marching up to the bedside.

Sir Marcus had watched her approach from under heavy lids. "Now what has overset you, puss?"

Cassandra looked down at his heavily lined face. "As though you did not know! Grandfather, how could you tell him such a thing!"

Sir Marcus gave a deep chuckle. "I thought there might be a few fireworks when you found out. But it is not a great thing, after all."

"Really, Grandfather! You have tried to arrange a marriage! I think that a rather great thing," said Cassandra. "How could you do such a thing without saying a word to—"

"Now, Belle, you mustn't allow yourself to be so taken by emotion," said Sir Marcus soothingly. He lifted his hand to brush her arm in reassurance. "I am merely attempting to settle your future comfortably. Philip is a good man, as good as they come. He has expressed some reservations, which I do not think ill of him. Naturally, he felt some surprise, some reluctance when I first told him. I recommended that he reflect on it. I am confident that when he does, he will see all the advantages."

"He might, but I do not! This is utterly ridiculous, Grandfather." Cassandra had caught hold of her anger, thankful that she had not betrayed herself. She had so nearly blurted out her sister's name. She sat down on the chair beside the bed. "Come, Grandfather, let us reason together. You know that what you have done can have no favor with me."

"Aye, well I know it. You made yourself very clear two—no, three years ago. I had not forgotten that row. And so I said nothing, in hopes that when you met Philip again your objections would fall away," said Sir Marcus.

"Well, I *do* object," said Cassandra.

"Is he ill-favored? Does he repulse you?" demanded Sir Marcus.

Cassandra was taken aback. "Why, no, of course not. Mr. Raven is pleasing to the eye, and his manners are very nice. That is not it at all, Grandfather, as you would realize if you would but think about it."

"I fail to see what other objection you could possibly have. Philip Raven is my godson. I shall see that he is well provided for in my will, as you will be. He is a fine figure of a man, honest and direct in his speech. You have liked him all of your life," said Sir Marcus. He started to close his eyes. "It is decided, Belle. You are to wed Philip Raven."

"No, it is not decided," said Cassandra tightly. "I will not allow you to dictate my future so arbitrarily."

"You will not allow? You will not allow?" Sir Marcus roused himself, pushing up against his pillows. His bushy brows were drawn tight making a solid line across his long nose. His raspy voice rose. "It is not for a young girl to tell me what she will and will not allow! You will do as I say, Belle."

The valet hurried over, alarm registering on his face. "Pray calm yourself, sir. Miss—"

"Go away, Weems! At least *you* must obey me!" Sir Marcus glared first at the valet and then at Cassandra, before dropping back down on his pillows. A tic jumped in his jaw. He closed his eyes again.

The valet gave Cassandra a reproachful look as he retreated.

Cassandra drew deep breath. "Grandfather, I do not wish to anger you. You must know that you are very dear to me. Nor do I wish to disobey you."

Sir Marcus opened his eyes and stared at her. His winter blue eyes looked cold. "Then you will wed Philip Raven. That is how you may show your affection toward me."

Cassandra saw that she was not making much progress. "Grandfather, I shall most willingly wed Philip Raven—if I fall in love with him. But you cannot expect me to agree to this ridiculous plot of yours as it stands. What's more, I am positive that Mr. Raven has no more intention of tamely falling in with it than I have."

"Told you so, did he? Well, I cannot fault him for it. He struck me as a careful man, and anyone could see that you would be a handful, Belle," said Sir Marcus sharply.

Cassandra decided to ignore that provocative statement. She mustn't let herself be sidetracked from the main issue at hand. She remembered what her sister had said about Philip Raven and how Belle had said it. Belle had expressed only a mild curiosity about her old playmate's arrival. There had been nothing in Belle's attitude or words to lead one to suppose that she would wish to be married to the gentleman. Quite the contrary, in fact. Belle had said that Philip Raven was a dear but a bit of a bore. Cassandra thought that scarcely constituted grounds upon which to base her sister's entire future, and she certainly was not going to agree to something now that Belle would most assuredly later regret.

"Grandfather, I've never had a proper come-out. I've never been presented to society. I've never been made up to by a circle of admirers," said Cassandra, thinking that it was all true and how much more so for her sister.

"I'll not have a bunch of young jackanapes dangling after you, Belle," said Sir Marcus bitingly. "Philip is worth more than the whole lot. He has been to war. He knows what it is to fight for his life. He knows who he is, and that is more than any lounging London Lothario can claim, I can tell you! As for society, bah! You are missing nothing great there, either. It is why I have remained here at the Hall all of those years."

"You know that is not quite true, Grandfather. I am certain of it," said Cassandra quietly. "You know that it is important to become known in society, if not for yourself than for your descendants. I used to wonder about our family. I felt awkward because I did not know anything about my antecedents. What could I talk about when I came in contact with others? How should I act? How would I establish common ground and make friendships?"

Sir Marcus's expression altered, losing some of its testiness. It seemed that she had at last struck a chord.

"Ah, Belle. I did not realize that I had cloistered you so closely," said Sir Marcus regretfully. "I am a selfish old man. No, no, do not gainsay me. I am and I admit it."

Encouraged, Cassandra leaned toward him. "That is why it is so important for me to come out, Grandfather. I should like to experience what other girls do and go to parties and form friendships. I might find a suitor that you would think acceptable. Or I might discover that Mr. Raven was right for me, after all. Is that so wrong?"

Sir Marcus worked his jaws. "You have always been able to tie me around your little finger, from the time that you were a baby."

"Then you will agree to a come-out?" asked Cassandra, her heart lifting. She could imagine how Belle would feel when she told her sister that she would be going to London. It would be the most exciting thing imaginable to be able to do something so wonderful for her sister.

"I know no one to sponsor you," said Sir Marcus, shaking his head.

Cassandra looked at him. She suspected that he simply did not wish to trouble himself by putting his mind to the problem. However, she would not accept his sweeping statement so tamely. "Surely, you know someone—a friend or relation of some sort."

Sir Marcus shook his head again, quite firmly. "No, I know no one. If I once did, they're all dead now."

"Then Biddy could—"

"Miss Bidwell! Why, she could no more introduce you to polite society than you could do it for her," said Sir Marcus, waving aside the suggestion. "She is naught but a paid companion, Belle. She has no connections to speak of, worthwhile or otherwise. No, there is not any way that I can arrange a proper come-out for you. You must resign yourself to it, Belle."

Cassandra realized that when she had visualized her sister in London, she had seen Belle and herself together. Suddenly, she knew what could be done. She saw no hindrance, for she knew the depth of heart possessed by her own guardians. She was confident that they would accede to her plan. "Uncle Phineas and Aunt Margaret—"

Sir Marcus shot up from his pillows. He shook his finger at her, roaring, "Never mention those names to me, miss! Never, do you hear! I'll not have it!"

Cassandra was shocked by her grandfather's vehemence, but she recovered sufficiently to hold her ground. "Nevertheless, Grandfather, I shall say it. Uncle Phineas and Aunt Margaret could bring me out. Why, they are bringing out my sister this very spring. Cassandra wrote me about it. I do not perceive a problem in asking them to sponsor me as well."

Sir Marcus's face had darkened as she spoke and was now mottled with his fury. "That is enough! I'll hear no more about it! There will be no come-out, this spring or any other, do you hear?"

The valet rushed over to the bedside and started to murmur soothingly to his overwrought master.

Cassandra stood up. She looked down at her grandfather. Very quietly, very precisely, she said, "Oh, yes, I hear you very well. I thought you to be quite fond and indulgent. I see now that I was wrong. Very wrong, indeed! You are a selfish, pitiful old tyrant, and I wish that I had never come here."

"Miss! Pray do not—!"

"Do not worry, Weems. I am leaving. I am leaving as

soon as I may," said Cassandra. She turned on her heel
and walked rapidly from the presence of her irate
grandfather.

"Come back here, Belle! Belle! I'll not have you defy
me, do you hear?"

Cassandra retreated to her bedroom, and it was not
long before the tears began. She did not know how long
she cried. She only knew that her heart was breaking.
She had built up such a wonderful picture of her grandfather. She had always longed to see him and to have
him know her. She had been so certain that he would
be everything that she had envisioned him to be.

There had been hints in her sister's letters. As Cassandra dried her eyes, she remembered them now. Belle
had more than once expressed her frustration of being
shut up at the Hall without any social life to speak of.
She had written several times that she only felt free
when she was riding cross-country on her horse. Now
Cassandra understood perfectly her sister's yearning for
company and her willingness to embark upon a masquerade as her twin. A whole new world had opened up
to Belle.

Cassandra could not imagine that her sister would
ever wish to give it up and return to her former existence, once having tasted such heady freedom.

Cassandra changed into her riding habit. She had
made up her mind to leave her sister a note at the crofter's cottage. She did not wish to continue the masquerade for the agreed-upon fortnight. In any event, it would
be a welcome relief to get out of this place for an hour
or so on Rolly.

Cassandra hurried out of the manor before anyone
saw her. She took her ride, and she felt much better for
the fresh air and exercise by the time she returned to
the yard. When she slid off the gelding's back, she saw
that Young John was peering out of the stables at her.
Defiantly, she stared back while she fed Rolly a carrot.
Let the old groom think what he would, she thought. It
made no difference to her.

The elderly groom came up to take the gelding's reins.

He nodded to her. "A good day for riding, miss. Ye'll not see many more of them, though."

"What do you mean?" asked Cassandra suspiciously.

The old groom jerked his chin upward. "The weather be fixing to turn, miss. We'll see a bad storm soon, I'll warrant." With that, he turned and led the gelding away.

Cassandra cast a glance upward at the leaden gray sky. It did look rather ominous, as a matter of fact. A shaft of anxiety struck her, but she shook it off. She and Belle would be able to make their switch without complications, she was certain of it. It was really too early in the year for bad weather.

When Cassandra entered the manor, it was to be accosted almost at once by one of the servants with the news that the master had taken a turn for the worse. Cassandra felt something sick in the pit of her stomach. She hurried upstairs to discover the truth for herself.

When Weems refused to open the door to her, saying that it would not do the master any good to see her, Cassandra was devastated. She had been angry, but she had never meant to cause her grandfather harm.

"There you are, Belle!"

Miss Bidwell caught hold of her elbow and practically dragged her down the hall to Belle's bedroom. She opened the door and gestured for the younger woman to precede her. "In with you, my girl."

Cassandra obeyed, feeling that she definitely deserved whatever terrible scold Miss Bidwell should see fit to dish out to her. Cassandra set aside her whip and gloves and started to take off her hat.

"What in the world did you say to Sir Marcus earlier? Weems told me that he was ranting in the bed after you left him," said Miss Bidwell sternly. "Now we have had to send for Sir Thomas to come bleed him before he puts himself into one of his fevers."

Cassandra did not reply directly to Miss Bidwell's question. Nor did she acknowledge the information that had been given her, though she felt extremely guilty. There was something more that was exercising her mind just then. "Biddy, did you know that my grandfather had summoned Philip Raven here to request him to wed me?"

Miss Bidwell sat down rather suddenly on the settee in front of the hearth and stared at her. She put up a hand to touch the lace at her throat in an unconscious gesture of dismay. "Oh, dear! I think that I understand now. I understand all too well, in fact."

"Well, did you know?"

Miss Bidwell shook her head, the light refracting from her spectacles. "No, my dear. I did not. I thought that foolishness had been put aside the last time that you fell into such an argument with your grandfather. Sir Marcus has apparently harbored his ambition all this time, quite without comment from me or anyone else."

"But you suspected, did you not? That was why you wanted my reassurance that I would be civil toward him, isn't it?" asked Cassandra, beginning to change out of the riding habit. She looked straight at Miss Bidwell and saw the guilt shift across the elderly lady's face. "I see that you did. Biddy, why ever did you not tell me so that I would have some sort of warning?"

"I hoped I was wrong. I did not wish to set your back up against Philip Raven needlessly. I hoped that you and Philip—I am sorry, Belle. I have failed you miserably. It was just that I hoped that everything would turn out for the best," said Miss Bidwell, sighing.

"That I and Philip Raven would fall instantly in love and ask Grandfather's permission to wed," said Cassandra with a tiny smile. "Yes, I see. That would be so much easier, wouldn't it? After all, you probably knew that my grandfather would not consent to my uncle and aunt sponsoring a come-out in London for me." She went to the wardrobe and selected a light blue gown to put on.

"Did you really ask Sir Marcus for that?" asked Miss Bidwell, her eyes widening behind her spectacles. "Why, my dear, you were taking your life in your hands. No wonder he was thrown into such a passion."

"I am sorry for that," said Cassandra, biting her lip in anxiety. She buttoned up the gown. "Weems refused to let me in."

"It hardly surprises me. Weems watches over Sir Marcus like a flustered hen does a new chick," said Miss Bidwell tartly. "He is by far too protective of his master, to my mind."

"Then . . . you do not believe that I harmed Grandfather overmuch by talking to him in the way that I did?" asked Cassandra hopefully. She crossed to the vanity and picked up a hairbrush. Her hair was windblown even though she had been wearing a hat.

"Well, it certainly did not do him any good, Belle. However, Sir Marcus is responsible for his own passions, not you nor I nor anyone else," said Miss Bidwell with a sharp nod that was somehow reassuring to Cassandra. She took the hairbrush out of Cassandra's hand and began smoothing out the tangles. "You mustn't blame yourself for his lack of self-control, my dear. And he is always calmer once he has been bled. You know that. Sir Marcus will no doubt rest easily enough tonight."

"I suppose I shouldn't have mentioned my uncle and aunt," murmured Cassandra. Miss Bidwell had finished, and Cassandra tied a bit of satin ribbon about her hair.

"Your timing was perhaps not as perfect as one could wish," agreed Miss Bidwell, setting down the hairbrush. "Not that the thought hadn't crossed my mind more than once to write to Mr. and Mrs. Weatherstone myself and plead on your behalf that some effort should be made to repair the breach. It is a terrible thing for a family to be split apart. And I so wished that advantageous connection for you, dear Belle."

"Thank you, Biddy. I know that you have done your best for me," said Cassandra, smiling fondly at the elderly lady.

Miss Bidwell took out her handkerchief and genteelly blew her nose. "Yes, well! I suppose that I should leave you to finish dressing, my dear. I must change for supper, as well. Shall I see you downstairs?"

"Of course," said Cassandra.

Chapter Twelve

As Cassandra descended to the foyer, Mr. Raven emerged from the billiards room. He walked down the hall toward the staircase, his dark head tilted as he watched her descent. "Miss Weatherstone! I am happy to have run into you. May I speak with you privately? Perhaps in the drawing room?"

"Of course, Mr. Raven." Cassandra joined the gentleman, who was awaiting her, and preceded him into the drawing room. She turned as he closed the door. At once on her guard, she quickly informed him, "My companion, Miss Bidwell, will be down shortly, Mr. Raven. What is it that you wished to say to me?"

Mr. Raven approached her. He had a lithe stride, economical and graceful, an expression of concern on his face. "I have gathered that Sir Marcus has taken a sudden turn for the worse. Can you tell me how serious it is?"

Cassandra shook her head. "I fear not, Mr. Raven. Though I have been told that the physician has been sent for to bleed him. He will be better for it, I assure you."

Mr. Raven regarded her with a frown. "You do not appear particularly overwrought, Miss Weatherstone."

"I hope that I am more self-possessed than to go screeching down the halls, sir," said Cassandra with the tiniest of smiles. She cocked her head. "If it comforts you to know it, Mr. Raven, I was quite concerned."

"Was concerned," repeated Mr. Raven, emphasizing the words. "Then you believe that Sir Marcus is in no immediate danger."

"I do not anticipate it, Mr. Raven," said Cassandra with a cool assurance that she hoped concealed the still niggling unease that she felt despite Miss Bidwell's reassurance.

"Thank God for that," said Mr. Raven. He took a turn about the room, his hands clasped behind his back. He had changed into a dark blue frock coat that was perfectly tailored to his broad shoulders and lean form. When he came to the mantel, he stopped to look down into the yellow-tipped fire. "Miss Weatherstone, may I speak frankly?"

Cassandra moved to a wing chair and sat down in it. She hid a tiny sigh. "I thought that you already had, Mr. Raven."

He turned, laying one long arm atop the mantel, and looked over at her from his negligent stance. "You refer to our conversation earlier today, of course. That was a badly botched business on my part. I apologize. I assumed that Sir Marcus had already spoken to you about why he wanted to see me."

"I had no reason to think that my grandfather actually had any such plan up his sleeve," said Cassandra, thinking about her sister's casual reference to the old argument between herself and Sir Marcus. Belle had believed that Sir Marcus and Miss Bidwell had been concerned about her reaction to Philip Raven's arrival solely because of an old argument. She had not actually believed that Sir Marcus had any intent to approach his godson concerning a match, and had brushed aside the possibility with the observation that Mr. Raven would most certainly decline such an honor.

Cassandra was curious. She wondered what Mr. Raven's true thoughts had been. "Mr. Raven, I gathered from some things that you said earlier that you had declined my grandfather's request. May I ask why?"

He looked thunderstruck. "Why?"

"Yes, why."

Mr. Raven smoothed his expression. "Is it so difficult to understand? Such an archaic arrangement, between two strangers, in this day and age. I found it ludicrous."

"Are you perhaps already wed?" asked Cassandra boldly.

Mr. Raven's face altered with something akin to

shock, then became impassive again. "No, of course not!"

Cassandra leaned back at her ease, resting her elbows on the chair arms. She had hit close to the truth. She knew it. That swiftest of expressions had betrayed him. "Then you are infatuated with someone?"

Mr. Raven straightened to his full height and turned to the huge gilt mirror hanging above the mantel. He reached up to tidy his starched neckcloth, speaking over his shoulder. "You are very searching in your questions, Miss Weatherstone."

"Ah, but that is what old childhood friends do, Mr. Raven. They try to catch up on all that has occurred since the last time they saw each other," said Cassandra, teasing him just a little. It felt very good to turn the tables, if only this once. For the first time since she had entered the manor, she felt in full mastery of herself.

"Odd. I had thought that was what I was attempting to do when I first arrived. But you kept putting me off, Belle," said Mr. Raven swiftly.

Cassandra saw too late the trap that she had set for herself. She straightened primly, folding her hands in her lap. "We have already had this discussion, Mr. Raven. My reasons—"

"My assumption of your reasons," corrected Mr. Raven. "Since you actually had not been told about Sir Marcus's plans concerning a future between us, I now fail to understand why you have been so off-putting, *Miss Weatherstone.*"

Cassandra smiled at him, when what she really wanted to do was to wipe that arrogant expression from his face. She felt that he had pushed her into a corner, and her temper abruptly flared. "Very well, Philip. Let us take off the gloves altogether, shall we? You lived here at the Hall for a brief period. We were both children. You left the Hall, whereas I did not. You return with all expectation of being received with wholehearted joy and a degree of familiarity that would not be tolerated except in the most unconventional of houses. Forgive me, sir, but I was not raised to be a bumpkin nor a wild hoyden! Indeed, you are a stranger to me, and I have found your assumption of familiarity to be both uncomfortable and offending. There, sir, is plain speaking."

Mr. Raven's expression was startled. He let out his breath slowly. "Well, you have certainly learned to turn a neat phrase. I feel as though I have been finely drawn and quartered."

Cassandra raised her brows. "Then I trust the point is well taken."

"Exceptionally so, Miss Weatherstone," said Mr. Raven, grimacing. He made the slightest of bows to her. "I shall in future be more circumspect, I assure you."

"Thank you, Mr. Raven. It is all I ask," said Cassandra, inclining her head. She was trembling within from the risk she had run in addressing him so forcibly. Yet at the same time, knowing that she had scored a hit, she felt the euphoria of victory.

Mr. Raven was obviously about to reply when the drawing room door opened. He closed his mouth, tightening his lips.

Cassandra rose at the sight of her companion. Her triumph gave her more courage than she had had heretofore. "There you are, Biddy. Mr. Raven and I have had the most interesting conversation. I must tell you about it later." She pretended to ignore the gentleman's sharp glance. "How nice you look, Biddy. That is a pretty shade on you."

"Thank you, my dear," said Miss Bidwell, her gaze surprised. "But it is the same gown that I have worn for several years."

"Nevertheless, I have always thought it very attractive on you," said Cassandra imperviously.

"Belle, I was delayed in coming down because Steeves informed me that Sir Thomas has arrived. He is this minute up with Sir Marcus," said Miss Bidwell, glancing from Mr. Raven's remote expression back to her charge's heightened color.

"I am glad to hear it. Perhaps we shall hear good tidings before long," said Cassandra. "There is the bell. Shall we go in to supper?"

"My dear. Do you not wish to go upstairs and speak with Sir Thomas?" asked Miss Bidwell gently.

"I am certain that Sir Thomas will request to see me before he leaves," said Cassandra. "I see no point in lurking about the bedroom door until the physician exits."

Miss Bidwell bestowed a civil smile on Mr. Raven, who was obviously listening to the interchange with interest. "Pray excuse us for a moment, Philip."

When he bowed and turned away to walk to the farthest corner of the drawing room, Miss Bidwell turned again to Cassandra. She said in a lowered voice, "Belle, whatever has gotten into you? Surely you wish to go upstairs and ask Weems—"

"Weems will not allow me into the bedroom. I shall not kick my heels in the hallway like a recalcitrant child until he or Sir Thomas has the goodness to convey whatever news there might be," said Cassandra swiftly, her glance flashing. She could not believe that her sister was expected to behave in so juvenile a fashion. Perhaps it was good that she had traded places with Belle, she thought. It was obviously past time for Belle's household to begin treating her like a mature young lady. "I shall go in to supper in a civilized fashion and wait for Steeves to bring word that Sir Thomas is ready to speak to me."

She turned from her astonished companion and addressed her grandfather's guest. "Mr. Raven, I believe we are now ready to go in to supper. Will you join us?"

"Of course, Miss Weatherstone," said Mr. Raven, advancing to her side. "Allow me to escort you within."

With an inclination of her head, Cassandra laid her fingertips on the arm that he offered. As Mr. Raven escorted her into the dining room, Cassandra was aware that Miss Bidwell followed with disapproval radiating like a cloud about her. Cassandra glanced across the table at the elderly lady while Mr. Raven politely seated her. Miss Bidwell met her gaze steadily, her mouth pursed in a stern line.

Cassandra deliberately turned away. She would not allow herself to be treated like a naughty schoolgirl. That might have been what her sister was used to, but she was made of different stuff. She refused to be cowed.

The masquerade was all but over, and she would not be other than herself.

The problem with her sister's life, thought Cassandra, was that there were too many personages at the Hall who had watched her grow up. They had watched Belle become a young woman, Cassandra thought, but they had never allowed her to become an adult.

With that neat analysis, Cassandra turned her attention to getting through supper. For all of her newfound bravado, however, she could not help the way that her thoughts continually came back around to the old sick gentleman upstairs and what the physician might have to say about his condition.

The physician had not returned downstairs before the covers were turned down and coffee was being served in the drawing room. Miss Bidwell declined to partake and marched over to the settee in front of the fireplace, where she immediately picked up her tatting basket and started a new set of lace.

Cassandra understood that Miss Bidwell was still displeased with her. She did not attempt to cozen the elderly lady out of her sulks. Instead, she played hostess to her solitary guest and served coffee. It was a role that was not unfamiliar to her. She had often managed small talk with her uncle and aunt's friends, as well as with her own. She discovered presently that Mr. Raven was easy to converse with. He was an amusing companion, and she actually began to enjoy herself. It was scarcely surprising, however, she thought at one point. Not only was he an interesting conversationalist, he was a handsome gentleman, and she was thoroughly aware of it. Cassandra swiftly put an end to that line of reflection, telling herself sternly that it would not do to become too friendly with Mr. Philip Raven. Once the masquerade was done, she would likely never see him again. It occurred to her that that was not a particularly pleasing thought.

"Did you and Sir Marcus have a falling out?" asked Mr. Raven quietly.

"I beg your pardon?" said Cassandra, turning her

head to look at him. The question came quite out of the blue. They had been talking about books.

"I believe you understood me, Miss Weatherstone," said Mr. Raven.

Cassandra considered him for a moment. She quickly made up her mind. He had every right to know, after all. "Yes, we did. We had a terrible row as a matter of fact. It was over the discussion that he had had with you."

"I see." Mr. Raven considered his cup of coffee, then lifted it to his lips. When he had drunk and set it down, he said, "It appears that my presence here is the cause of all sorts of conflict."

Cassandra hesitated, then said straightforwardly, "I shall not deny it, sir. However, you mustn't blame yourself. My grandfather is responsible for his own words and actions, as am I."

Mr. Raven chuckled. His keen gray eyes were warm in expression. "I suppose that is to prick any overweening sense of conceit I might still possess. Since returning to the Hall, I have learned to my disconcertion that I am not at all as important as I thought myself to be."

"Oh, but you are, sir." A smile hovered about Cassandra's mouth. She had liked his self-deprecating humor and responded in kind. "At least—to my grandfather."

"You are a serious trial, Belle," he murmured.

When she cut a glance at him, he threw up his hand in surrender. "Very well! I shall abide by the guidelines that we have established. I shall not address you again by your given name until you give me leave."

She gently corrected him, with a smile. "*Unless* I give you leave, Mr. Raven."

"You are cruel, ma'am," said Mr. Raven, still smiling.

"Not at all. I am thoroughly conventional," said Cassandra. She lifted the pot. "More coffee, Mr. Raven?"

"Thank you, yes." When she had refreshed his cup, he remarked, "Somehow I did not expect the headstrong, free-spirited Belle Weatherstone I had known to become thoroughly conventional."

"One must expect change, sir," said Cassandra, only a little shaken this time by his comparison between herself and her sister. She was beginning to feel more comfortable in her role and bolder in expressing her own sentiments.

"You must be brutally frank with me, Miss Weatherstone. Do you believe that matters would be best served if I were to remove myself from the Hall?" asked Mr. Raven.

"No, of course not. You are Grandfather's guest. I have no right to make such a judgment," said Cassandra swiftly.

"Only consider a moment, however. Unless we have between us dissuaded him otherwise, Sir Marcus must still harbor hopes that we shall make a match of it," said Mr. Raven somberly. His gaze was keen on her face. "How do you perceive the situation?"

"My grandfather is very stubborn and obtuse about this matter," said Cassandra with a shake of her head. "I had no notion that he would refuse to consider an alternative."

"And what was the alternative if I may make so bold as to ask?"

"I wished to ask my uncle and aunt to sponsor me for a London season," said Cassandra. She shrugged slightly. "I am confident that they would agree, but my grandfather is adamant in his refusal to approach them."

"What objection could Sir Marcus possibly have?" asked Mr. Raven. "It sounds to me to be an admirable solution."

"My relations have not spoken to one another in many, many years," supplied Cassandra.

Mr. Raven frowned. "Light begins to come. I do seem to recall something about your uncle. Mr. Phineas Weatherstone, wasn't it?"

"Yes." Cassandra looked at him curiously. "Do you recall anything about why my grandfather and uncle came to be at such odds?"

"If I once knew, I have forgotten," said Mr. Raven. He regarded her unsmilingly. "So you asked Sir Marcus for a London season. A simple enough request on the surface. Every well-bred girl is supposed to have a proper come-out."

"I told Grandfather as much. He did not agree. And so, here we are," said Cassandra, turning her hands up and out.

"If I were to leave, then he surely could not hold to this hard line. Perhaps it is only my presence that encourages him in this phantasm," said Mr. Raven. "Perhaps if I left, you would be able to have your London season."

"My dear sir, I have been immured here all of my life. My grandfather has not made the least effort to introduce me to the world. Now he is old and ill. What would change?" asked Cassandra with a little laugh.

Mr. Raven did not reply. He merely regarded her with a thoughtful expression. Cassandra might have begun to be made uncomfortable by his unwinking regard, except that the butler entered with a gentleman in tow.

Cassandra rose swiftly. "Sir Thomas!"

Chapter Thirteen

The portly gentleman immediately came over to Cassandra and took her hand. He regarded her with sharp brown eyes. "How are you, my dear? I imagine that you are feeling some anxiety, so I must at once assure you that your grandfather is not in any immediate danger. I have bled him, and we must trust that will discourage the fever from returning."

"I am grateful, sir," said Cassandra, returning the friendly squeeze of his thick fingers. It seemed strange to be on such familiar terms with a virtual stranger, but she remembered that this gentleman had known her sister nearly all of her life. It would be considered very odd of her to behave any other way. And she was grateful to him. When Sir Thomas had been sent for, he had come away from his house party without delay.

Sir Thomas turned to Miss Bidwell, who had risen upon his entrance as well. "You, too, may rest easy, Miss Bidwell. The old tartar we both know so well is too stubborn to die just yet. In fact, I have faith that we shall see him back in the saddle before many more weeks are past."

"I am glad to hear it, Sir Thomas. Thank you for coming," said Miss Bidwell quietly. "You are a good friend to Sir Marcus."

The physician waved aside her accolade. "Nonsense. He would do the same for me if I discovered myself to be in bad straits." He glanced casually in Mr. Raven's direction.

Cassandra noticed it and supplied the required introduction. "Sir Thomas, I don't believe that you have met

Mr. Philip Raven." The gentlemen exchanged nods and shook hands. "Mr. Raven is my grandfather's godson."

"Yes, Sir Marcus has spoken of you, Mr. Raven. Indeed, if my memory serves me correctly, I once treated you for a childhood ailment," said Sir Thomas reflectively.

"Indeed you did, sir. I remember you very well," said Mr. Raven with a civil nod.

"Well! This is quite like old times, then. Sir Marcus would like to be up and about, naturally, but I have recommended to him the wisdom of remaining in his bed. There is time for all the rest when he is grown stronger," said Sir Thomas. "Belle, your grandfather was asking for you. He is asleep now, so do not disturb him tonight. However, I would like you to speak to him in the morning. He seemed peculiarly driven in his expressed desire to see you. Weems will let you know when he has awakened."

"I will do just as you have said," said Cassandra, nodding.

She intercepted a glance from Miss Bidwell, whose expression was slightly frowning. She thought that she had done something else to disrupt that lady's peace of mind and immediately sought an answer. "Biddy, is something bothering you?"

"Why, no, Belle. I just thought that you might wish to see your grandfather tonight. It seems so unlike you to put it off," said Miss Bidwell.

"Sir Thomas has just said that he is resting. It would be thoughtless and selfish of me, don't you think, to insist upon seeing him now?" asked Cassandra, putting up her brows in polite inquiry.

"Well, of course. But—" Miss Bidwell shook her head. There was a hint of confusion in her eyes. "You must do as you think best, my dear."

Cassandra inclined her head in acknowledgment. She turned back to the physician. "May I offer you refreshment, Sir Thomas? It is chilly out, and I thought perhaps you would like to fortify yourself with some hot coffee before your went out again."

"Why, that is very thoughtful of you, Belle," said Sir

Thomas with a faintly surprised note in his voice. "I would appreciate that very much."

He sat down, and Cassandra served him a cup of coffee that was generously sweetened. Sir Thomas drank with every sign of pleasure. "Thank you, my dear. It is just how I like it."

Sir Thomas turned to Mr. Raven. "Mr. Raven, I am glad that you have come to the Hall. Sir Marcus had confided to me several months ago that he had hopes of locating you. He wished you to come for a long visit. It is unfortunate that you have arrived at a time when Sir Marcus is unable to entertain you as he undoubtedly had planned."

"Indeed, Sir Thomas, I feel myself to be an imposition at such a time. I was just saying to Miss Weatherstone that it might perhaps be better if I were to withdraw until Sir Marcus is in better stirrups," said Mr. Raven.

"You mustn't go, Mr. Raven," said Miss Bidwell hurriedly. She threw a swift, censorious glance at Cassandra. "I know that Sir Marcus would not wish you to do so."

"I have told Mr. Raven the same thing," said Cassandra briefly. She smiled at Miss Bidwell's sudden surprised look. She had been quite able to interpret her companion's accusatory glance. Miss Bidwell had obviously thought that she had been trying for the last hour over coffee to persuade Mr. Raven to leave.

"Oh, don't run away on Sir Marcus's account, sir. Even if he were truly on his deathbed, he would want you here. It is my understanding that he has gone to some trouble in bringing you to the Hall, and I am confident that I know Sir Marcus well enough to reassure you that he would be very disappointed to learn that you had left before he had had an opportunity to have a proper visit with you," said Sir Thomas.

Mr. Raven bowed from his seat. "Thank you, Sir Thomas. You have relieved my mind." He met Cassandra's gaze briefly, as though in apology.

Cassandra understood that he would have preferred to withdraw from the Hall in light of their peculiar circumstances, but that he felt obligated to remain. "You are perfectly welcome to remain as long as you wish,

Mr. Raven," she said quietly. He bowed politely, but
with such a glance of irony that Cassandra had difficulty
keeping a straight face. She turned to Sir Thomas and
asked a question that had been burning on the tip of
her tongue for several minutes. "How is your house
party, Sir Thomas? Are you well satisfied with your
guests?"

"Indeed I am, Belle. It has been a pleasant interlude.
I shall be sorry when my guests all leave," said Sir
Thomas. "However, I expect that we shall have a full
house until after the new year. Perhaps . . ." His voice
trailed off as he contemplated Cassandra's attentive face.
He turned to Miss Bidwell. "Perhaps you might bring
Belle to supper one night, Miss Bidwell. I am certain
that she would enjoy the company. There is another
young lady in the party whom she would get along with
famously, I dare swear."

Cassandra looked at Sir Thomas, her expression
openly startled. How odd, she thought; the gentleman
wanted to bring her face-to-face with her sister. Cassandra wondered why Sir Thomas would want to do such
a thing. Surely, he knew that Sir Marcus was at outs
with his son, Phineas Weatherstone.

"That is a very kind invitation, Sir Thomas. Belle and
I would be only too happy to accept if Sir Marcus has no
objection," said Miss Bidwell, her own evident surprise
quickly covered with quiet civility.

"Oh, you may leave Sir Marcus to me. I will make it
all right. You are invited, too, Mr. Raven. That goes
without saying," said Sir Thomas. He got heavily to his
feet. "I must be on my way. It is a cold, dark night. My
coachman will need to light the lanterns to shine the
way." He made his good-byes, once again telling Mr.
Raven that he was glad to have met him again.

Cassandra went with Sir Thomas to the door. The physician kept up a steady stream of chitchat as he shrugged
into his greatcoat with the help of a footman and pulled
on his hat and gloves. He retrieved his black bag from
the porter before turning again to Cassandra.

"You have been abnormally quiet, Belle. I suppose I
must not be too surprised. Though you haven't admitted

it, you have been carrying a heavy burden these past months. However, you must trust me when I say that Sir Marcus is doing better than anyone could have expected," said Sir Thomas in a fatherly voice. "And it is now my guarded belief that we shall see a return of much of his former good health."

"I do not think that my grandfather shares your optimism, Sir Thomas. He says that he wishes to settle all of his business before he dies," said Cassandra with a tiny smile.

Sir Thomas snorted. "I can hear him say it, too, in that obstinate fashion of his. Pray do not worry overmuch, Belle. You know that whatever happens, even if the worst happens and I am proven wrong, I and Lady Kensing will stand your friends."

"Thank you," said Cassandra, tears stinging her eyes.

"Now do not go maudlin on me, Belle," admonished Sir Thomas, shaking his finger at her. "You must think of other things, such as coming to dinner and meeting my guests. You will like that, I know."

"Who are your guests? Do I know them?" asked Cassandra. She was willing to play the part that was expected of her. She knew that Belle would have been all agog at such an invitation, and so she opened wide her eyes and spoke in a slightly breathless fashion.

Apparently, her attempt at playacting was convincing, for Sir Thomas chuckled and shook his head. "You will meet them soon enough, my dear. And I suspect that you will be very surprised. However, that is for the future. I must send a note around to Sir Marcus—no, let me pen one now before I leave. That will be better."

Cassandra showed Sir Thomas into the library, where he would find writing supplies. She waited while he rummaged through the desk for paper and a sharpened pen and the inkwell. Sir Thomas penned the short note, signing it with a flourish. "There you are, Belle. The thing is as good as done," he said, sanding the sheet dry.

Cassandra accepted the note from him and folded it carefully. "I shall give it to my grandfather myself when I go up to see him," she said.

"See that you do. I will be gravely disappointed if I

do not see you a fortnight from now," said Sir Thomas
with a roguish wink.

Cassandra smiled as she thanked him. It would be her
sister, Belle, who would actually respond to Sir Thomas's
invitation, but he was not to know that. Cassandra escorted the physician to the front door once more and
this time saw the gentleman off. She turned back to the
drawing room, slipping the folded note into her dress
pocket.

Mr. Raven and Miss Bidwell had been making polite
conversation while they awaited her return. They broke
off when Cassandra entered the room.

"You were an inordinate time, Belle. Has Sir Thomas
gotten off all right?" asked Miss Bidwell, a hint of anxiety in her expression.

"Yes, of course. He merely wished to pen a note to
my grandfather before he left," said Cassandra.

"I see." Miss Bidwell looked as though she would
have liked to inquire further into the matter, but she
refrained. "I suppose that you will give it to Sir Marcus tomorrow."

"Yes," agreed Cassandra, smiling. She knew that her
companion was curious, but she thought it wouldn't do
Miss Bidwell any harm to wait to learn what Sir Thomas
had written. Caught up in the throes of excitement at
the unusual treat in store, her sister would naturally have
shown the note at once to Miss Bidwell; but that would
have been a childish thing to do. No, thought Cassandra.
She would hold the note that had been entrusted to her
hand until she was able to deliver it to the one to whom
it was directed. That was what any mature young lady
would have done and no one would expect her to do
less.

Cassandra realized that she was beginning to think of
her sister as being a bit backward for her age. Her sister
could not be held accountable, however. It was all due
to Belle's suffocating upbringing, of course. It was a
wonder that Belle was as strong-willed as she was, Cassandra thought, feeling the simmering of indignation. It
would harm the household not one whit to be taught a
lesson, and she was in just the position to do it. Perhaps

by the time that the masquerade was over, Belle would have to contend with less blind condescension.

Cassandra brushed aside the tiny part of her that was whispering caution. The course she had decided upon could well spell a greater risk of being unmasked as an impostor. But all believed her to be Belle, she argued to herself. No one at the Hall had any reason to believe otherwise.

"Well! I think that it is time for me to retire," said Miss Bidwell, turning to put away her tatting. Over her shoulder, she said shortly, "I shall require your escort, Belle."

"Of course. It is becoming rather late," said Cassandra quietly, accepting her companion's blatant tactic not to leave her downstairs unchaperoned in Mr. Raven's company. She certainly could not fault Miss Bidwell for holding to the conventions. She held out her hand to Mr. Raven. "I shall retire now, sir. If there is anything that you require, only make your request known to Steeves."

Mr. Raven took her hand and held it for a moment between his long fingers. "I wish that the evening had been longer, Miss Weatherstone."

Inexplicably, Cassandra felt her heart skip a beat. A depth in his low voice said more than the formal phrase. She looked up into his handsome face, meeting his gray eyes. The expression in them was one that she had not a great deal of experience in interpreting, but instinctively she knew that he was interested in her.

Cassandra felt the warmth of a blush steal into her face. Oh, this would not do at all, she thought hurriedly. She withdrew her hand from his. "That was a very pretty compliment, sir. I thank you for it," she said with dignity.

Mr. Raven bowed, the hint of a smile on his face.

"Come along, Belle," said Miss Bidwell in a sharp voice. She nodded to the gentleman. "Goodnight, Philip."

Mr. Raven bowed again. His expression had turned polite. He watched the ladies exit the drawing room.

Cassandra and Miss Bidwell traversed the hall and climbed the stairs, not exchanging a single syllable. Cassandra sensed that her companion was aggravated. Since she had no desire to open herself to a scolding, she kept her peace.

On the landing where they would go their separate ways, Miss Bidwell said stiffly, "Good night, Belle. I trust that you will sleep well."

"Thank you. I hope that you will do the same," said Cassandra before going into her bedroom. She closed the bedroom door quietly behind her.

Cassandra did not immediately go to bed, but stayed up reading by candlelight for an hour or more. When she did at last blow out the candles and climb into the cold bed, pulling up the coverlets, she had little difficulty in falling asleep.

She did not know how much later it was when she was shaken urgently by the shoulder and awakened out of a sound sleep.

Chapter Fourteen

"**M**iss! Miss Belle!"

Cassandra blinked owlishly at the light from a single candle, momentarily dazzled. She put up her hand and rubbed the sleep from her eyes. Then she recognized who it was that had wakened her. "Weems!" She bolted upright in the bed, sleep falling as suddenly from her as the coverlets. "What is wrong? Grandfather! Is he—"

"Don't you worry, miss. The master is fit as can be expected," said the valet reassuringly. However, his worn expression betrayed anxiety. "But he is asking for you, and he won't rest again until he sees you. I am afraid that he will fret himself into another fever if he goes on the way he is."

Cassandra reached for her wrapper, which she had draped over the end of her bed. "I shall come at once."

The valet waited patiently for her, then preceded her out of the bedroom and down the hallway. The sole candle threw odd shapes and shifting shadows across the paneling as they made their way toward Sir Marcus's rooms.

The valet halted and opened the door. He held the candle high so that its feeble light dispelled the dark in the dressing room. "Go on in, Miss Belle."

Cassandra passed through the dressing room and stepped into her grandfather's bedroom. She stopped and stared. All of the candelabras had been lit and positioned around the massive draped bed. Flickering shadows constantly shifted over the walls of the bedroom, creating a strange ghostly atmosphere.

The valet hurried past her to pull back the drapery

that hung down on the side of the bed and tied it back on the massive bedpost.

"Weems?" The voice was tired and querulous.

"I have brought her, my lord," said Weems quietly. He gestured for Cassandra to come closer. Obediently, she walked over to the bed.

"Belle? Is that you?"

"Yes, Grandfather." Cassandra sat down in the chair beside the bed and took her grandfather's hand. She was dismayed by the change wrought in him by the sickness. The candlelight threw Sir Marcus's face into sharp relief. His skin was stretched taut over his facial bones and he appeared gray. She felt a renewed surge of guilt for being angry with him. "Oh, Grandfather."

Sir Marcus gave a hoarse laugh. "Aye, I look like death warmed over, no doubt. I will be happy to shuffle off this mortal coil."

"Shakespeare," murmured Cassandra, drawing his hand up against her cheek. His skin felt like hot parchment. His signet ring was too heavy and loose on his shrunken finger.

Sir Marcus looked sharp at her. "Aye, Shakespeare. And what do you know of it, my girl?"

Cassandra realized her error. She had been at the Hall long enough to have found out that Belle had always been impatient of any sort of classical learning. Her sister would not have known even such a common reference. "Mr. Raven and I were discussing books earlier this evening," she said with a deliberately nonchalant shrug.

"Philip bored you to distraction, did he?"

Cassandra could tell that it was merely a rhetorical question, and so she said nothing. It was better to be silent, when what she wanted to say was that Mr. Raven had been anything but boring.

Sir Marcus shook his head. His eyes drooped half closed. "My godson was always a reader. He had a head for his studies. Unlike you, Belle."

Cassandra thought it was safe enough to agree with her grandfather's assessment. "Biddy has said that he was a much better student than I."

"Aye." Sir Marcus sighed. His heavy lids lifted slightly so that he looked straight at her. "Belle, I have been thinking upon what was said here earlier."

"Grandfather—"

"Pray do not interrupt me, Belle! It is a most annoying habit of yours, I assure you," said Sir Marcus fitfully.

"Yes, sir," said Cassandra, a smile trembling upon her lips.

He looked at her with suspicion for a moment, then seemed satisfied that she was actually awaiting what else he had to say. "Belle, I recognize that I have handled you wrong. You won't be driven. You never have been. You've too much spirit, more's the pity. I should have realized it at the outset, before I sent for Philip Raven."

Sir Marcus subsided, and his eyelids drifted low. Cassandra was afraid that he was falling asleep before he could finish what he wanted to say to her. She touched his hand. "Grandfather."

Sir Marcus roused himself, blinking in the candlelight. "Where was I? Aye, I recall now. Belle, I'll not force you to wed Philip."

Cassandra took a deep, shaky breath. This was what she had hoped to accomplish for her sister. She was grateful to have been able to turn Sir Marcus from his hardheaded course. Feeling that she should acknowledge what had been told her, she said, "I am sorry to disappoint you, Grandfather."

"You haven't, my dear. Never think that. I should like to propose a compromise, however. Now don't fire up at me before I've told you what I have in mind, Belle," said Sir Marcus, lifting his hand to stem what objections he obviously expected. "I've given your expressions of concern over this match grave consideration. I have come to recognize the force of some of your arguments, at least."

"I am glad," said Cassandra. She meant it, too. She had been so horribly disillusioned in her grandfather, and now he was restoring himself in her eyes—at least, to some extent. He had mentioned a compromise, after all. "What is this compromise that you propose, sir?"

"It is a small matter, Belle. I merely wish you to spend time with my godson. I want you to get to know one another more fully. If you still do not care for the notion of a match afterward, then I shall not say another word to you about it," said Sir Marcus. "That is fair enough, is it not? Will you do that much for me, Belle? For my sake?"

Cassandra thought about it briefly, turning over her grandfather's proposal carefully in her mind. She could find no hidden flaws in it. Surely, there could be no possible objection her sister might have against such an inoffensive request. She was not obligating Belle to a betrothal, after all. "Very well, Grandfather. I will do as you ask."

"You are a good girl, Belle." Sir Marcus patted her hand. He eased himself back more comfortably on his pillows with a sigh. "Now I may rest easy. Weems!"

The valet appeared seemingly from nowhere. With a gesture, he silently indicated that the interview was over. Cassandra rose. "Good night, Grandfather," she said quietly.

The valet escorted her out of the bedroom. Weems handed a lighted candle to her. As he showed her out the door into the hall, he said, "Thank you, miss. He will rest now, as he said."

"I am glad that I was able to help, Weems." Cassandra went off to bed feeling much better about her, or rather, her sister's, relationship with their grandfather. It was just a pity that Sir Marcus didn't know her for herself, thought Cassandra with regret.

At breakfast, Cassandra was joined by Miss Bidwell. The elderly lady was attired in a demure cap and a dark gray gown. There was not a bit of ornament in her dress, and Cassandra thought that her companion looked unusually austere. Miss Bidwell greeted Cassandra with unwonted reserve. "Good morning, my dear."

Cassandra perceived that she was still out of favor with her companion. She decided to ignore Miss Bidwell's obvious displeasure in her. She nodded and said very civilly, "Good morning, Biddy. I trust that you slept as well as I did."

"Yes, thank you for inquiring," said Miss Bidwell with restraint. She told the footman that she wanted just tea. When she had been served, she dismissed the manservant and waited until they were alone in the breakfast room before she addressed Cassandra again. With raised brows, she said, "I understand that you and Sir Marcus have come to an agreement of sorts."

Cassandra looked at her in surprise. "Why, yes. Grandfather sent for me late last night, and we talked. How did you know? Have you been talking to Weems?"

"Certainly not! I do not discuss Sir Marcus's activities with his valet," said Miss Bidwell. She poured cream into her tea and stirred it vigorously. "I have myself visited with Sir Marcus this morning."

"A bit early for it, surely," said Cassandra, glancing over at the mantel clock. It was just past nine in the morning. She thought that her grandfather must have had a very short night's rest, since he had sent for her in the predawn hours and then had wakened again to send for Miss Bidwell.

Miss Bidwell gave the slightest nod. "It was, indeed. However, Weems informed me that Sir Marcus should not be put off, and so I went along before breakfast. Belle, Sir Marcus has told me that he has your assurance that you will cooperate with his wishes."

Cassandra thought she needed to be certain that Miss Bidwell understood exactly what had been discussed between herself and her grandfather. She looked levelly at Miss Bidwell. "I merely agreed to get to know Mr. Raven a bit better. That is all, Biddy."

"Yes, of course. That is perfectly understood. Belle, Sir Marcus made a request of me that I felt I could not refuse," said Miss Bidwell. She cleared her throat. "I daresay you shan't care for it, but it is certainly meant for your own good. I thoroughly agree with Sir Marcus that it is necessary. I am to act as your chaperone while Philip Raven is here at the Hall."

Cassandra looked at the elderly lady in quiet surprise.

She had assumed that function was already being filled by her sister's companion. "Why, of course."

Miss Bidwell mistook her statement for sarcasm. "Belle, pray do not be cast into the sulks," she begged. "I know it is not what you like. You do not like to be hedged about, as you have often enough told me. You must realize, however, that in this instance I must abide by Sir Marcus's command."

"Biddy—"

"Pray let me finish, Belle. I agreed with Sir Marcus that even though you and Philip were children together, circumstances have changed. You are a young lady now, and Philip is an eligible *parti* in the eyes of the world. I would be shirking my duty as I know it if I were to leave you and Philip to your own devices," said Miss Bidwell.

Cassandra tried to reassure the lady, who was obviously laboring under some emotional upset. "Biddy, understand. I do understand. And I shall be as decorous as anyone could wish, I assure you."

Miss Bidwell nodded, though there was still a tightness in her expression. "You have not heard the rest, Belle."

Cassandra's heart sank as she began to dread whatever the condition was even before it was spoken. Miss Bidwell's attitude hinted so strongly that she would dislike it.

"Sir Marcus has voiced his concern that you are of an age when it will be frowned upon by the neighbors if you are allowed to ride without supervision," said Miss Bidwell. She cleared her throat. "He . . . he told me that he is giving orders that you are to be accompanied by a groom from now on when you go out riding."

Cassandra was at once relieved. Her sister had told her that the groom could be trusted. However, she was thoroughly cognizant of the part that she had to play and so no hint of her true emotion could be revealed. She said hastily, "A groom? What nonsense! I have always ridden when and where I chose. I'll not have it."

"Belle, I have been entrusted with Sir Marcus's orders, and I have no choice but to see that they are carried out," said Miss Bidwell sternly.

"I have agreed to all the rest, but this last—! Biddy,

I cannot have a groom following me about everywhere," exclaimed Cassandra.

"I believe that Sir Marcus has already sent a message round to Young John," said Miss Bidwell. "I am sorry, my dear, but the matter is already closed."

Cassandra struggled to maintain her facade of outrage when what she really felt was relief. "I cannot be expected to give up all of my freedom!"

Miss Bidwell threw up a hand, a pained expression on her face. "Pray, Belle! Pray do not be difficult. I ask only for your cooperation in what can justly be termed our present difficult circumstances."

"I perceive no difficulty, Biddy, none whatsoever. I simply refuse to be hedged about like this," said Cassandra, forcibly voicing her opposition to the plans made for her. Her sister would have been heated by such unwelcome restrictions, she knew. And Miss Bidwell had just told her what Belle would have said. "I shall speak to Grandfather about it if I must."

"Belle, you mustn't. Sir Marcus must be allowed to rest without new anxieties thrust upon him," said Miss Bidwell in swift alarm. "Surely, you must see that your best course is to submit—"

"Nonsense, Biddy. This is simply my grandfather's way of having things his own way. He has unleashed you and the rest of the household to see to it that I do just as I ought, in hopes that Mr. Raven shall find me to be an acceptable, proper bride. I am not so dense that I do not understand that. Really, Biddy, I would have thought you, at least, to be above such subterfuge," said Cassandra heatedly.

"Belle!" Suddenly, there were tears in Miss Bidwell's eyes. "You have been angry with me. You haven't confided in me as is your wont. I have felt it keenly, believe me. Pray do not be angry with me anymore. I cannot bear it."

Cassandra was taken aback. She had no idea what Miss Bidwell was referring to, except that she had not shown Sir Thomas's note—which she still needed to deliver to her grandfather—to the lady. Miss Bidwell was the one angered the day before. She simply had not

reacted to it. A light dawned in Cassandra's mind. That
was it, of course. Miss Bidwell had expected her—
Belle—to try to assuage the lady's displeasure. When
she had not, Miss Bidwell had interpreted her continued
civility as anger. Cassandra instantly felt sorry for the
elderly lady. Miss Bidwell had been confused when Cassandra had not reacted as her sister might have done in
the same circumstances. "I am not angry with you,
Biddy. I know well enough that you find your position
as my companion onerous at times."

"Oh, no, no!" exclaimed Miss Bidwell, pulling out a
delicately embroidered handkerchief from her pocket
and dabbing at her eyes. Her spectacles bounced on her
nose as she pushed them up. "Scarcely onerous, dear
Belle. It is just that I feel my duty so strongly and so
many times I am unable to . . . that is to say, I fear
that you have been raised so unconventionally that . . .
oh dear!"

Cassandra could guess what the elderly lady was trying
to say. She had noticed at first meeting that her sister
was more plain-spoken and spirited than herself, and she
had envied Belle for those qualities. However, she could
well understand how her sister must have frustrated a
high stickler like Miss Bidwell. She said dryly, "Perhaps
you shouldn't say anything else, Biddy."

"I suspect that you are correct, my dear," agreed Miss
Bidwell, giving a last sniff. "I seem to have lost the art
of diplomacy altogether. Oh, my! It is all so very awkward!"

"What is awkward, Biddy?" asked Cassandra, toying
with her toast. She really wasn't as hungry as she had
thought, she decided. This whole affair had overset her
appetite. She could easily accept Miss Bidwell's chaperonage, for that would scarcely differ from her aunt's
close watch over her. Besides, with Miss Bidwell constantly in company with her, it would be much more
difficult for Mr. Raven to speak to her on any but the
most mundane topics. He would not be as able to trot
out memories of which she had no recollection.

"Why, Philip Raven, of course. Really, Belle! One

would think you had not a wit of sense," said Miss Bidwell with asperity, putting away her damp handkerchief.

"Oh—Philip Raven." She smiled at Miss Bidwell. She was fairly confident that she and Mr. Raven had come to an understanding. That fact, coupled with her interview with her grandfather that morning and Miss Bidwell's announcement that she would be chaperoning them closely, had completely lessened her anxiety of being exposed by the gentleman. "As far as I am concerned, there is nothing at all awkward attending Mr. Raven's visit. He is my grandfather's godson and guest. That is a perfectly legitimate reason for his presence here."

"Belle, you haven't forgotten why Sir Marcus sent for him! And why Sir Marcus wants me to strictly chaperone you," said Miss Bidwell, raising her brows.

"Of course not." Cassandra took a sip of tea before she continued. "Biddy, I have agreed to get to know Mr. Raven better. I have not agreed to anything more. In short, Biddy, I have not the least desire to wed Mr. Raven, and so I refuse to acknowledge any awkwardness attending our association."

"Bravo, Miss Weatherstone."

Chapter Fifteen

Cassandra looked around quickly. She saw that Mr. Raven was lounging in the doorway of the breakfast room. He had apparently opened the door so quietly that neither she nor Miss Bidwell had heard him come in. "Mr. Raven!"

"The same." He bowed, then strolled toward the table. His bottle green frock coat showed to advantage his broad shoulders, and his fawn breeches molded to his muscular thighs. His boots were polished to a high gloss and reflected the morning light as he moved. "Forgive me, ladies. I could not but help to overhear at least part of your conversation." He looked faintly amused, but there was speculation in his eyes as he glanced at Cassandra.

Cassandra felt heat steal into her face. Her embarrassment at being overheard speaking so openly about the gentleman was not mitigated by Miss Bidwell's scrambling apology.

"Philip, how very disconcerting for you, to be sure. I pray that you will forgive us!"

Mr. Raven raised his hand. "Really, there is no need to apologize, Miss Bidwell. Miss Weatherstone's forcibly expressed opinion merely confirms my own inclinations."

Miss Bidwell was completely disconcerted. "Indeed," she faltered.

"Oh, yes. I do not wish a match between myself and Miss Belle Weatherstone any more than she does. I am actually rather relieved to discover her true feelings," said Mr. Raven blandly.

Miss Bidwell was stupefied at the gentleman's bluntness. "I . . . I see." She rolled her eyes toward her charge.

Cassandra was unaware of Miss Bidwell's mute appeal. She watched Mr. Raven with the faintest of frowns between her brows.

Mr. Raven strolled over to the sideboard loaded with covered dishes and began filling a plate with steak and kippers and eggs. Over his shoulder, he said, "It is better to have all of the cards on the table at once, don't you agree, Miss Weatherstone?"

"I agree completely, Mr. Raven," said Cassandra slowly. She searched his face as he came over to the breakfast table and sat down. She had detected an odd tone in his voice as he posed his question. "Shall you think me overly bold in asking you to declare your cards, sir?"

"Belle!" exclaimed Miss Bidwell, aghast. "I am not at all certain that this is a proper conversation to pursue."

"Rest easy, Miss Bidwell. Miss Weatherstone is completely in her rights." Mr. Raven smiled at Cassandra. "I should prefer it, actually. However, I suspect that you may not wish to reciprocate."

Cassandra inclined her head. She felt a small thrill of fear and anticipation. "You are quite right, sir. I do not wish it."

"Every young lady is entitled to her secrets," said Mr. Raven thoughtfully.

"I can assure you that my charge has no secrets, Mr. Raven," said Miss Bidwell stiffly.

"You devastate me, Miss Bidwell. I had quite hoped to discover an elusive mystery attached to her," said Mr. Raven quietly.

"There is nothing elusive or mysterious about me," said Cassandra with a small shrug, quite in her best imitation of her sister. For a split second, no more, it had flashed across her mind that Mr. Raven suspected her of not being who she was purporting to be. But that was impossible. There was absolutely no way that he could know, she thought. Strangely enough, she felt a twinge of disappointment.

"No, of course not. The Belle Weatherstone I knew

as a boy was always completely straightforward with her thoughts, and she could never sit still for anyone or anything," said Mr. Raven, his keen gray gaze resting on Cassandra's face.

Cassandra gave a quick smile. "As you say, Mr. Raven." She again had the oddest sensation that he was questioning her identity.

"This is an inappropriate conversation, Philip," said Miss Bidwell firmly. She stood up. "I think it high time for Belle and myself to retreat and leave you to enjoy your breakfast in solitude. Come, my dear."

"Please stay, Miss Bidwell," said Mr. Raven. His smile was persuasive. "You are Miss Weatherstone's chaperone, and in light of what has already been said, I believe it to be necessary to smooth out any remaining questions that either of us may harbor."

"Biddy," murmured Cassandra, glancing across at the elderly lady.

"Perhaps that is true," said Miss Bidwell reluctantly. She sat back down and folded her hands on the tabletop. "Very well, Philip. You may proceed."

"Thank you, Miss Bidwell," said Mr. Raven, making a short bow from the waist in deference to the lady. "I have always respected your wisdom and never more than now, when Miss Weatherstone and I are caught in what could easily be considered a compromising situation."

"Oh, my presence must surely dispel any such unworthy suspicions," said Miss Bidwell with an abrupt nod of reassurance.

"I rely upon you completely, ma'am," said Mr. Raven. "Your untarnished reputation must lend us protection from the servants' gossip."

Cassandra listened with amused respect as Mr. Raven exerted his quiet charm to smooth over her companion's ruffled feathers. Miss Bidwell's countenance was not nearly so forbidding as it had been just seconds before.

Mr. Raven turned back to Cassandra. "I was actually quite glad to hear you express your sentiments a moment ago, Miss Weatherstone. As it happens—and I realize that I must be categorized as ungentlemanly for saying so—I feel just the same as yourself."

"As we have already established," murmured Cassandra.

Mr. Raven inclined his head. "Quite. I do not have a desire to wed. Frankly, I am uncertain of my feelings about such a step just now. And there are sundry other reasons, too, that I must take into careful consideration before making such a commitment."

"Do those reasons have anything to do with your business interests on the Continent?" asked Cassandra.

He looked startled, then slowly smiled. Again, there was a measure of speculation in his eyes as he looked at her. "As it happens, yes. Unfortunately, I am not at liberty to discuss those things with you. You will, I trust, accept my assurances on that head."

"Naturally," said Miss Bidwell, inclining her head. "I am certain that you are a man of some affairs, Philip."

"Yes," agreed Mr. Raven, without enlargement.

Cassandra had her own suspicions what the gentleman's affairs might entail. A wife, for instance. He had certainly been startled enough when they had talked previously, and she had made mention of a romantic attachment. It had almost seemed that he had felt guilty at denying that any such tie existed. "What of Sir Marcus's wishes? Do they count for nothing, Mr. Raven? You are his godson, after all."

Miss Bidwell turned completely around to regard her charge. "Belle, have you lost your senses? One does not question a gentleman in such a forward manner."

Cassandra ignored her companion's astonished interposition. "Well, Mr. Raven?"

Mr. Raven gave a half shrug as he cut the tender beef on his plate. "What can I say that will not sound either ungrateful or mean-spirited? Sir Marcus made his wishes plain to me; that is, it would give him the greatest satisfaction to know that you and I were to make a match of it, Miss Weatherstone. As you know, I have had to refuse his request. I trust that I was able to do so with enough diplomacy as to spare his feelings somewhat."

"Perhaps you were too diplomatic, Mr. Raven," said Cassandra tartly. "We both are aware that my grandfather is an obstinate old man. He does not easily give up his notions. Only witness his latest request, which is that I make myself very agreeable to you. He has ensured the proper atmosphere of courtship by ordering my companion to chaperone us as strictly as though we were attending a Bath soiree."

"This is plain speaking, indeed," said Mr. Raven, putting down his knife and fork. He lounged back in his chair, one browned hand wrapped loosely round his mug, an amused expression on his face.

"Quite; uncomfortably so," snapped Miss Bidwell, shooting a reproving glance at Cassandra.

"Mr. Raven spoke a moment ago about laying our cards on the table. Very well, let us do so," said Cassandra. She leaned forward and earnestly met the gentleman's eyes. "Mr. Raven, we are in the unenviable position of dancing to my grandfather's piping. He wishes for us to become betrothed. We have agreed that is not an option for either of us. However, I have given my word to my grandfather that I will make an attempt to know you better. He naturally hopes that in the process I will learn to love you and withdraw my objections to his plan."

"Naturally, you are adamantly opposed to obliging him," said Mr. Raven, looking at her very closely.

Cassandra smiled, her eyes never wavering from his intent gaze. "But of course, Mr. Raven."

Miss Bidwell made disapproving sounds, but neither principal paid any heed to her. They continued to examine each other's face.

"No doubt that sword of Sir Marcus's is intended to cut two ways, Miss Weatherstone, for I assume that familiarity is supposed to engender fonder emotions in me as well," said Mr. Raven. A tremor of laughter came into his voice. "I must give credit where it is due. You have managed to strip aside all convention, haven't you?"

"You did say that you recalled that I was one for plain speaking, did you not?" asked Cassandra with a fleeting smile. She felt both daring and frightened at her boldness with Mr. Raven. She had never before discussed anything so openly with any gentleman, including her uncle. Generally, she had always expressed any concerns that she had with her aunt, knowing full well that lady would relay them to her uncle. Apparently, her sister operated quite differently with those in her life, for Miss Bidwell did not seem at all surprised at the completely unconventional turn of the conversation, but rather, resigned.

"And of course Miss Bidwell is supposed to provide just the proper amount of restriction to our interaction, in order to manufacture that piquancy that accompanies a true courtship," said Mr. Raven, flashing a grin.

"Yes," said Cassandra, sharing her own smile with him. "And since my grandfather knows very well that I cannot stand to be hedged about in any way, I would have felt obliged to go counter against Biddy's very proper chaperonage and meet with you on the sly."

Mr. Raven's brows rose. "An interesting proposition, I must say," he murmured.

Cassandra instantly felt uncomfortable and disconcerted. He had taken her up so swiftly. It alarmed her. His gaze was penetrating and speculative. She dropped her gaze to her hands.

"I find this entire conversation preposterous!" said Miss Bidwell, her color considerably heightened. Behind her spectacles her eyes expressed her outraged feelings.

"Just so, Miss Bidwell," said Mr. Raven gently.

Miss Bidwell's posture was very erect. "Belle, I assure you that I would never push you so hard that you would wish to flaunt my authority to such an outrageous degree."

"I know that you would not. Just as I would not go so far as to indulge in clandestine meetings," said Cassandra hurriedly with a swift glance at the gentleman who was still watching her.

"A pity," said Mr. Raven regretfully.

Cassandra threw a repressive look at him. She might be heavily embroiled in deception and subterfuge, but at least she knew right from wrong in this instance. "Really, Philip."

Mr. Raven's swift grin flashed white against his browned face. "Have I been elevated? Am I now to be 'Philip'?"

Cassandra sighed, relinquishing the struggle. She was quibbling over shades of convention when what she should really do was question her own standards. "Oh, very well. You may call me 'Belle.' But I warn you, it is only to satisfy my promise to Grandfather. It is not at all because I wish to further any familiarity between us."

"That is quite understood. Believe me, my decision concerning Sir Marcus's request was never a reflection upon you or your many estimable qualities, Belle," said Mr. Raven.

"I should think not!" interposed Miss Bidwell, taking instant umbrage.

"Thank you, Philip. I accept your rejection of my hand in the spirit in which it was given. I, too, have no personal objection against you," said Cassandra.

As they smiled at each other, Miss Bidwell shook her head in total disbelief. "I shall say it now. I am positively appalled at modern manners. One could be forgiven the impression that you were both back in the schoolroom and have just made up a silly quarrel!"

"We always did come to cuffs, didn't we? As I recall, it was generally Belle's fault," said Mr. Raven, in a reflective tone.

Cassandra merely raised her brows and looked at him. She wasn't about to rise to the bait, especially considering that she had no memories to draw from. Miss Bidwell unwittingly delivered her.

"Belle, you need not answer that. Really, Philip! I had expected better of you," said Miss Bidwell, almost scolding. "Pray do not expect me to negotiate peace out of whatever squabbles arise between you. I didn't do it then, and I have no intention of doing so now."

Cassandra looked at Miss Bidwell with surprise. "Why, Biddy, that is precisely what I hope you will not do. We shall get along famously if you will simply chaperone us in a quiet, unobtrusive fashion."

"Quite right. We don't wish any unwanted piquancy added to our so-called courtship," said Mr. Raven. He was smiling. "Or otherwise we might learn to like each other."

Miss Bidwell threw up her hands.

Chapter Sixteen

The weather took a decided turn for the worse just as Young John the groom had gloomily predicted. Before morning, thunderstorms roiled angrily overhead. All day a steady downpour beat against the sturdy walls of the manor and the countryside round about. That afternoon the deafening thunder crashed continually, accompanied by brilliant flashes of lightning.

Cassandra stood in the east end of the gallery and watched the heavenly display in awe. Water sheeted against the leaded panes, and the roar of the storm battered against the walls. The candles that lit the long gallery were eclipsed by the dazzling bolts that split the black skies.

She did not notice that she had company until she heard his voice. "Belle, what are you doing?"

Cassandra turned, her face lit up. "Oh, Philip! I do so love a good storm! Isn't it magnificent?" she asked, turning once more to the uncovered windows.

There was a moment's stunned silence. "Yes, it is magnificent."

They stood together for a long time, watching the fury of the elements. Then Cassandra turned again to him with a sigh. "It doesn't appear as though it shall abate for several hours."

"No, I should think not. Will you walk with me?" asked Mr. Raven, holding out his elbow.

Cassandra accepted his escort, tucking her hand inside the crook of his elbow. She smiled up at him. "However did you manage to find me without Biddy trailing along?"

"Miss Bidwell sent me to look for you, as a matter of

fact. She thought you might be alarmed by the fury of
the storm," said Mr. Raven. He glanced down at her.
"Are you not afraid?"

Cassandra shook her head. She said cheerfully, "No,
why should I be? I am inside where it cannot touch
me. It is rather like watching a spectacular theatrical
production. I have heard that there is a very good pre-
sentation of the Battle of Trafalgar in London. I should
so like to see it."

"Perhaps you will one day," said Mr. Raven, smiling.

"I do hope so. Have you ever really looked at all of
these portraits? Since reading my grandfather's family
history, I have been fascinated by them," said Cassandra. She nodded at those that they were slowly walking
past. "That one is my great-great-grandmother. A fright-
ful old dragon, is she not? Yet she was reputed to be a
charitable lady of great compassion. And that one
there—can you guess his secrets by looking at him?"

"I haven't a clue. Why don't you tell me," said Mr.
Raven, glancing down at her with a half smile on his face.

"He was accused of ridding himself of two wives and
a bitch dog by poison," said Cassandra, dropping her
voice for effect.

- Mr. Raven cocked a brow. "A bitch dog? One must
naturally inquire why."

"Oh, it is said that the poor creature made too much
noise," said Cassandra. She impishly smiled up at her
companion. "He is said to have explained away the
deaths of his wives for the same reason."

Mr. Raven gave a shout of laughter. "A character,
indeed." He opened the door leading out of the gallery
and ushered her through it. Her fringed shawl slipped
off one elbow to trail on the floor. He caught it back up
for her. Cassandra thanked him matter-of-factly, not giving a thought to the intimacy of the exchange.

"Now where are you taking me?" asked Cassandra
curiously, as Mr. Raven once more took her arm.

"I am obediently fetching you back to the drawing
room, where our dragon of a chaperone anxiously awaits
us," said Mr. Raven, companionably matching his steps
with hers.

Cassandra chuckled. "Oh, yes, I had forgotten. Biddy does take her commission far too seriously, don't you think?"

"Does she? I am beginning to suspect that she is not near strict enough," murmured Mr. Raven, looking down into her face.

Cassandra caught her breath at the exceedingly warm expression in his eyes. "Philip, I—"

Mr. Raven stopped and turned toward her, catching one hand in his. He turned her hand over and raised her open palm to his lips. For a brief moment his lips pressed warm against her sensitive skin. Her fingers curled involuntarily in shock.

Mr. Raven straightened and looked down into her stunned eyes. A smile touched his mouth. "Sh, don't say a word. We are playing at a game, you and I. Let us go on pretending."

Cassandra's heart was beating fast. She stared up into his inscrutable eyes, wondering wildly what he was thinking. "Pre . . . pretending?"

Mr. Raven settled her hand back into his bent elbow, his own fingers warmly covering hers. He began walking again. "Why, yes, Miss Weatherstone. Sir Marcus and Miss Bidwell must continue to be encouraged in their hopes that we will make a match of it. Do you mind it that I flirt a little with you?"

"Oh, no. That is . . . oh no, not in the least," stammered Cassandra, her head in a whirl.

"You see, I felt that it might take a bit of practice," said Mr. Raven matter-of-factly.

"Oh, I see," said Cassandra, only partially reassured. The kiss that he had pressed to her tingling palm had seemed very real to her. Her fingers still curled when she thought of it.

Mr. Raven introduced an innocuous topic, and she was able to respond without discomfort. But she did not forget that totally disconcerting kiss.

It rained for days. The date of Cassandra's rendezvous with her sister came and went. There was never any question of riding out to the crofter's cottage. Cassandra knew that she could never have made it there and back in such violent weather. She very much doubted that her sister, even as intrepid as she knew Belle to be, would have braved the persistent downpour, either. In any event, she couldn't have saddled the gelding without the groom's help, and she suspected that Young John would have refused to oblige her under such drenched conditions.

With hardly a twinge of anxiety, Cassandra resigned herself to keeping up the pretense of being her sister for a while longer. It wasn't so terrible, really, she thought. She was able to visit with her grandfather several times, though never at a very long stretch.

Sir Marcus seemed determined to husband his strength. Cassandra was glad to see that her grandfather was making progress. His voice was becoming stronger. He was more alert, and he was able to sit up for longer periods. Weems continued to fuss over his master, but the valet's anxious expression was not nearly so pronounced.

Cassandra was learning to love the irascible old gentleman. She found that she was becoming more and more reluctant to face the inevitability of leaving him. She knew that when she returned to her uncle and aunt, it was highly unlikely that she would ever see Sir Marcus again. More than once, Cassandra nearly blurted out her true identity to Sir Marcus, but there was always something that held her back.

Cassandra took note that she was not the only visitor to Sir Marcus's rooms. Mr. Raven spent hours closeted with Sir Marcus. She knew, because Weems told her, that they sometimes played chess or backgammon. She wondered occasionally what they found to talk about together, but neither gentleman ever volunteered any clues. However, she suspected that the visits were not always amenable, for once she went in directly after Mr. Raven had left, and she had found her grandfather preoccupied and fretful. Sir Marcus demanded that she bring his writing board and supplies to him, and when she had done so, he had told her to go away in an abrupt fashion that surprised her.

Afterward, she had closely questioned Weems, but all the loyal valet would say was that Sir Marcus had been made irritable by something that Mr. Raven had conveyed to him. Cassandra learned later that a letter was sent out in the post to Sir Marcus's man of business, Mr. Petrie-Downs.

One evening after coffee, Cassandra brought up the subject to Mr. Raven. "I wonder what could have caused my grandfather's moodiness these past two days? Have you any notions, Philip?"

Mr. Raven's expression did not change, though his gray eyes flickered. "Perhaps Sir Marcus simply hates being an invalid. It must be very frustrating to be unable to do those things that one is used to doing."

"Quite so." Miss Bidwell nodded. "Sir Marcus was always an active gentleman. There was never an endeavor too difficult for him, and now for all intents and purposes, he is bedridden. That is an extremely unpleasant reality, I am certain."

"Perhaps that is it," said Cassandra noncommittally. She briefly met Mr. Raven's eyes before she bent her head again to her embroidery.

Despite Cassandra's intuitive feeling that something was being hidden from her, she had never been happier. Mr. Raven proved himself a consistently pleasant companion. They walked in the gallery in the cold mornings, talked in the afternoons and played backgammon in the evenings. Under the benign yet watchful eyes of Miss Bidwell, they spoke often and at leisure about everything under the sun. When the weather cleared at last, she and Mr. Raven rode together, always sedately accompanied by the groom, Young John.

Cassandra did worry about how she was to get in touch with her sister. She had not yet been able to manage going off on her own without either Mr. Raven or the groom in company. She could only bide her time until the opportunity presented itself. Not for the first time, Cassandra wondered at her own and her sister's naivete. They should have made some sort of arrangement for communicating if one or the other was unable to ride out to the crofter's cottage. However, neither of them had really thought through all of the contingencies of the masquerade.

However, Cassandra spent considerably less time reflecting upon her problem than she might have otherwise if a certain gentleman had not been at the Hall. For the first time in her life, she was the sole object of a gentleman's notice. Even though she knew that Mr. Raven was merely humoring Sir Marcus, that did not stop her enjoyment. She, too, was humoring her grandfather and never had her word of honor been more pleasant to fulfill. She hoped that Mr. Raven was feeling as entertained as she was. It would have been a pity if the gentleman was actually bored in her company, she thought.

However, never by word nor gesture did Mr. Raven intimate that he had had his fill of her company. Quite the contrary, as a matter of fact. He seemed to like it that they had been thrown together through Sir Marcus's obstinate whim.

Mr. Raven referred hardly at all anymore to his and Belle's childhood, for which Cassandra was grateful. That was the one true anxiety that she had, for she was woefully ill-equipped to respond to oblique references that would assuredly have made perfect sense to her sister.

Instead, Mr. Raven's conversation was filled with interesting sidelights about himself and his life in the army, his travels and the news that was in the newspapers. Cassandra responded with her own little anecdotes and expressed her opinions on the news and literature. She had always loved to read, and it was obviously a passion that Mr. Raven shared. They discovered a mutual interest in history, particularly in the classical ages of Rome and Greece, and debated often some obscure point of times past. Sometimes she caught an odd or arrested look in his eyes, as though he had been taken aback by some stray thought, but Cassandra was never made uncomfortable in his presence. In fact, her initial wariness had completely dissipated, until she had almost forgotten that she was in actuality masquerading as her sister.

Once, she started to tell Mr. Raven about someone

she knew in Bath. He listened with an intent expression, then asked, "Tell me, Belle, when did you go to Bath? I was under the impression that you had never traveled away from the Hall."

Cassandra was startled. She knew at once that she had made a major blunder. "Why, I haven't been to Bath. Did you think that I had?" She managed a credible laugh. "I must be a better storyteller than I imagined. I don't know Mrs. Knapes personally. I simply know of her through my sister's letters. Cassandra is such a vivid writer that one could almost believe that one is in the same room with her!"

She knew that she was beginning to sound as though she was babbling, so she stopped, drawing a steadying breath. She tossed a glance up at Mr. Raven's face. "I am sorry if I did not make myself clear. Of course I have never spoken to Mrs. Knapes myself."

"I see. I had forgotten that you had a sister. A twin sister, I believe?"

"Yes; of course you never met Cassandra, have you? She was never at the Hall," said Cassandra with a slight pang at the truth of it.

"Whom does your sister live with?" asked Mr. Raven.

Cassandra looked up at him, frowning a little at what she was beginning to think of as an interrogation. "Cassandra resides with my uncle and aunt."

"That is a bit odd, surely, for twins to live apart?"

"Oh, perhaps it is. We are used to it, however. No doubt you will recall hearing something about the circumstance?" asked Cassandra, trying to draw him out without revealing her own ignorance.

"I seem to have a vague memory, now that I chance to reflect a little. Did I not ask you once how you came to be your grandfather's ward?" asked Mr. Raven.

"Very possibly you did. My parents were killed in an accident when we were quite small. My sister and I were separated, one to live with my Uncle Phineas and Aunt Margaret and the other to live with Grandfather," said Cassandra.

"It must be very difficult for you," commented Mr. Raven.

"I don't know," said Cassandra, smiling. "My sister and I correspond on a regular basis, though we have never had occasion to visit."

"Do you miss her—your sister?" asked Mr. Raven, watching her face.

"Of course I do." Cassandra smiled at him again. "I trust that I shall see her again quite soon, though."

"I trust that your hope is not misplaced," said Mr. Raven gravely.

Chapter Seventeen

When she was not with Mr. Raven, Cassandra found enough to occupy her time and thoughts in the running of the household. After their initial astonished skepticism, the housekeeper and steward had developed the habit of coming to her with any questions. Cassandra began to pay the household bills in her grandfather's behalf and even perused the monthly accounts more than once.

She no longer felt any moral discomfort in managing her grandfather's affairs. It would have been Belle's place to step in, though it was doubtful to Cassandra that Belle would actually have exercised her right.

However, Cassandra felt that as long as she was supposed to be her sister, she would do what she knew she ought. When Cassandra recalled how petrified she had been upon having to open that first letter addressed to her grandfather, she had to smile at herself. Now it all seemed quite natural to her to sit at Sir Marcus's desk and attend to estate business.

One afternoon, Miss Bidwell walked in on Cassandra when she was working at her grandfather's desk. Cassandra looked up inquiringly. Miss Bidwell stood at the door, her hand still on the knob, and an expression of surprise on her face. "Oh! I am sorry, Belle, I did not realize that you had come into the study. Er . . . what are you doing, my dear?"

"I am going over the ledgers for this month's expenses," said Cassandra absently. She dipped a pen in the inkwell and made a careful entry.

"Belle, are you quite all right?"

Cassandra looked up, surprised by the worried tone

in Miss Bidwell's voice. "Why, of course. Why do you ask?"

Miss Bidwell advanced on the desk. Her eyes behind her spectacles held an expression of bewilderment and anxiety. "It is just that— Belle! I have never known you to take an interest in anything having to do with the running of the household. Indeed, when I recall how I despaired of ever instilling in you the simplest lesson, I cannot but wonder."

"Wonder what, Biddy?" asked Cassandra quietly. She watched her companion's face. Her heart was beating fast, for she thought that this might very well be the moment that she had both dreaded and anticipated.

Miss Bidwell made a helpless gesture. "I don't know. Such thoughts have gone through my mind. I really don't know what to think. It is just that you have changed so. I don't know what to make of it, my dear."

Cassandra smiled a little. "Is it so strange that I should wish to keep busy just at this time, Biddy? Or that your lessons did not fall on completely deaf ears?"

"No, no, I suppose not. Well! I shall just leave you to it, I suppose." Miss Bidwell turned away and started toward the door. As she reached it, she exclaimed, "Oh, I had almost forgotten why I came in! Weems said that Sir Marcus wished for his favorite snuff to be brought up. He recalled that he left it here in the study. Have you seen it, Belle?"

"Why, I don't believe so. Where would it have been?" asked Cassandra.

"No doubt in the desk, don't you think?" said Miss Bidwell, coming again toward her.

Cassandra opened the desk drawers one after the other. She had no idea if the canister of snuff was in the desk or not. She had made it a point not to rifle through more of Sir Marcus's things than she thought she ought. The ledgers were one thing, but the contents of the desk quite another. She was beginning to feel nervous with Miss Bidwell watching her every move, and was relieved when at last she stumbled on the sort of canister that she was looking for. "Here it is, I am sure of it."

Cassandra picked up the canister. A piece of paper

that was sticking to the bottom of it fluttered loose and fell to the desktop.

"Thank you, my dear. Though I do not approve of taking snuff as a general rule, perhaps Sir Marcus will find some pleasure in his former habit," remarked Miss Bidwell as she bore away the canister. Before she closed the door, she said, "I shall see you at supper, of course."

"Of course," agreed Cassandra. The errant paper had fallen across the ledger pages that she was working on. She picked it up, intending to put it back into the drawer from which it had come. She chanced to glance at it, however, and stopped, looking again at what was written on it. There was her name, and the handwriting was unmistakably that of her uncle.

Cassandra read further, her brow furrowing. It was a letter, written by her uncle some months previous and addressed to Sir Marcus. As she made herself mistress of its contents, Cassandra's mouth dropped open. "Oh, my goodness," she whispered. "Uncle Phineas mentions my come-out this spring, hinting that Aunt Margaret could bring Belle out, too. I wonder if that means—"

Cassandra turned the sheet over, but there was nothing else written on it. "Surely Grandfather answered the letter. He must have. And denied his permission, for Uncle Phineas would have told me if he had been able to arrange for Belle and I to come out together."

She looked across the study at the portrait of Sir Marcus that hung above the mantel of the fireplace. She addressed her grandfather's likeness with gathering indignation. "Why, you had the perfect opportunity to help Belle. If you had asked, they would have agreed to sponsor Belle. But you didn't ask, did you? You couldn't bear the thought of being under obligation to your son and his wife, whom you detest. Poor Belle!"

Cassandra thrust the letter back into the drawer and started to slam the drawer shut. Then she stopped, thinking hard. It wouldn't do any good to give the letter to Belle. That would only serve to wound her sister, when Belle was brought face-to-face with proof that their grandfather had cared so little about pressing for her future happiness. However, she herself might be able to use it as ammunition with Sir Marcus. Perhaps if she confronted her grandfather about the overture that was made by her uncle, Sir Marcus might be shamed into admitting that it was possible for Belle to be properly sponsored into society. He couldn't tell her again that there was no one appropriate to bring Belle out, thought Cassandra angrily.

As she recalled the consequences of her last disagreement with Sir Marcus, she shuddered. It was not pleasant to consider, but if she was to help her sister, then she simply had to stiffen her resolve. "I must choose my time more carefully," she said aloud.

Cassandra retrieved the letter and folded it up so that she could slip it into her pocket. She shut the ledger and stepped away from the desk. She no longer felt like looking at rows and columns of figures.

Cassandra glanced at the ormulu clock as she left the study. It was too early, really, to change for supper, but she thought she would go up to her bedroom anyway. She had much to think about, not the least of which was the struggle she had with her feelings toward her grandfather. She loved him now, but that did not blind her to the notion that he was a very selfish, obstinate old man.

She had been envious of Belle, but now Cassandra was not so certain that she was. She had admired Belle's independent spirit and her frank manners, and she still did. However, Cassandra rather thought that when they had been parted to live in separate households, she had gotten the better portion.

"Belle, where are you?"

Cassandra looked round, startled. She had been so sunk in thought that she saw she had actually passed Mr. Raven in the hall without ever seeing him. "I . . . I'm sorry, Philip. I did not notice you."

"So I saw. You never heard a word I said until just now," said Mr. Raven, regarding her with some amusement.

Cassandra flushed. She felt that she had been unpardonably rude. "Pray forgive me. I fear that I was miles away in my reflections. Is there something you wanted?"

"It wasn't important. However, perhaps I should ask you if there is something that I may do for you?" Philip caught up her hand, the pressure of his fingers both warm and secure. Very quietly, he said, "Belle, you seem troubled. Can I help?"

Cassandra was both touched and shaken by his gentleness. She shook her head. "No, there is nothing you can do. It was nothing, really. Just a silly megrim. Has Biddy sent you to hunt me down again?"

Mr. Raven looked around the deserted hall. With a conspiratorial look, he said, "Actually, I have been looking for you myself. I am going mad from inactivity. Will you save me and come out riding?"

Cassandra felt some of the tension drain out of her. "Oh, yes! I would love it above all things."

"Good. I shall await you in the gallery. A quarter hour?"

Cassandra nodded. "I shall be there." She winged her way upstairs to her bedroom to change into her habit, her state of mind quite altered. She put the incriminating letter in with her underthings for safekeeping. She would not think any more about it just then.

Cassandra made short work of changing into her habit. Gathering up her whip, she went quickly through the quiet house toward the portrait gallery.

When she pushed open the door and entered, she saw that Mr. Raven was already waiting for her. He wore a plain coat of excellent cut and well-fitting breeches that were smoothed into white-topped knee-boots. In one gloved hand he carried a quirt.

Mr. Raven came to her and took her arm. "We are going out the east wing. I requested that Young John leave our horses there."

Cassandra glanced up at his lean profile as they walked swiftly out of the gallery. "What is behind all of this bother, Philip?"

He glanced down at her as they went down the stairs that led out of the manor onto the expanse of lawn. "Can't you guess? I have been wanting to be alone with you all day."

Cassandra looked down, feeling ridiculously pleased.

She said nothing more. When they emerged out of the
side door of the manor into the chilly day, she looked
around for the horses. There were only two tied nearby,
cropping at the browned grass. "I don't see Young
John," she remarked.

"No, I have bribed him to remain behind," said Mr.
Raven matter-of-factly. He put his hands around her
waist and lifted her easily up into the saddle. Then he
stood looking up at her, his gloved hand lying flat against
the gelding's shoulder close to her knee. "Do you
mind?"

Cassandra's cheeks were warm. She felt breathless
from the giddy feeling of simply being lofted atop the
horse as though she were featherlight. She adjusted her
riding skirt, avoiding his gaze. "Oh, not in the least. I
enjoy riding without an escort, as you must know."

"Quite." Mr. Raven walked off a few paces to his own
horse, put his foot into the stirrup and swung up onto
its back. He gathered the reins between his gloved fingers. "Shall we?"

Cassandra flashed a smile and spurred her horse. She
glanced back over her shoulder at the manor, feeling a
sense of freedom. It was glorious to be out away from
those oppressive walls.

Cassandra and Mr. Raven rode for a long time. They
talked earnestly about anything that came to mind. Cassandra scarcely noticed where they were going. The wind
blew fractiously, yanking at her hat and veil with icy
intent and eventually chapping her cheeks. Cassandra
gradually began to realize that she was chilled through.
Even her fingers inside her gloves were growing numb.

"You look cold, Belle," remarked Mr. Raven suddenly.

"I am, rather," admitted Cassandra. Her teeth had
begun to chatter, and she had to clench her jaw to con-
trol it. "But I am enjoying myself so much."

He was frowning. There was concern in his gray eyes
as he studied her. "I must get you back. I don't wish
you to catch a chill."

"I think if I was just out of the wind for a bit, I would
be all right," said Cassandra.

"We should head back. I think if we ride in that direction, it will be quicker," said Mr. Raven, nodding to his left. He threw a concerned glance at her and reached out to touch her arm. "It will be cross-country. Can you manage?"

"Of course I can," said Cassandra stoutly, even though her heart sank at the thought of what might lie ahead of them. Ditches and fences to be jumped and rugged stands of trees that would catch at her clothing as she passed under them. She knew that her sister would never have blinked at the prospect, however, and so she did not murmur.

Several minutes later, they found themselves in a shallow valley. The wind moaned low across the dead grassland, but its force was abated. Cassandra realized that she wasn't being beat by the wind any longer, and she straightened in the saddle. "Thank God, it's stopped," she said.

"There is something that we haven't seen before," said Mr. Raven, pointing with his whip.

Cassandra looked round to where he was pointing, and her smile froze. Her companion was pointing at the old crofter's cottage and the rough stable. She wondered at once if her sister was there, or whether there was any sign that they had left of their last meeting.

"That? Why, it is just an old abandoned crofter's cottage, Philip," she said.

"So it is. It is also out of this cold. Come, Belle," said Mr. Raven.

Cassandra had no choice but to follow him. She stared around as they approached the cottage from the back. The wind was moaning low through the shallow valley. It gave her the shivers just hearing it.

Mr. Raven had dismounted and gone to an unshuttered window of the cottage. He bent and peered inside for a moment. "There doesn't appear to be anything or anyone here," he said, straightening. He turned toward her. "I wouldn't like to trust us to the flooring inside. It looks rotten as can be. Let's have a look at the stable."

"I don't think anyone has lived here for ages," said Cassandra hastily. "Do let us ride on, Philip."

He paid no heed, but strode to the stable's entrance. When he came back round the corner, he walked over to where she still sat on her horse. "Come, Belle, let me help you down." He grasped her round the waist.

Cassandra protested even as she felt his strong hands lifting her. "But I don't wish to—" She slid down into his arms, and suddenly became speechless as she met his gaze. Heat climbed into her face. "Put me down," she said breathlessly.

He flashed a grin. "In a moment." He swept her up higher against his chest and strode off with her into the stable. When they were inside, he set her on her feet. With one arm still about her shoulders so that she was standing close to him, he said, "There you are, my lady. You'll be warmer in a few minutes."

Cassandra stared up at him. She had caught hold of his neck for security when he had swept her up, and now her arm was trapped between them. She could feel the firmness of his shoulder beneath her gloved fingers.

Mr. Raven muttered something under his breath. He brought his other hand up and caught her chin between his fingers. Then he bent his head to take sudden possession of her cold lips. His mouth was firm and unyielding. It was a hard, passionate kiss.

When Mr. Raven raised his head, he was breathing harshly. He stared down at her shocked face. "I believe I have run mad," he said quietly.

Cassandra shook her head, too bemused to respond. Her only coherent thought was that he had been right. She was already warmer, considerably so. If this was Mr. Raven's notion of how to succor a lady in distress, it was highly effective.

Mr. Raven released her. He stepped back. "I apologize," he said stiffly. "It was not my intention to insult you."

"You haven't insulted me," whispered Cassandra, her eyes still on his.

Mr. Raven did not reply, only stared down at her with a naked expression. Cassandra felt a blush coming swiftly to her cheeks, and she turned away, pressing her gloved hands to her face. "Oh! Oh, I don't know what to think!"

Behind her, Mr. Raven said with deliberation, "I think that we need Miss Bidwell."

"Yes, yes, perhaps we do," allowed Cassandra, her heart still beating fast. She turned around, to find that he was still watching her. "I don't believe that we either of us meant this to happen."

"No, I certainly did not," said Mr. Raven shortly. He took a swift step toward her, then stopped. His hands clenched. "I wish nothing more than to kiss you again. But I cannot, for if I do I will not want to stop."

Cassandra swallowed. She had never heard such words in her life. She was at once frightened and thrilled. "Philip, you must not say such things. You know that you must not."

Mr. Raven laughed, though without amusement. "You are undeniably correct, Miss Weatherstone."

"Pray—!" Cassandra threw out one beseeching hand toward him. The cold distance in his voice had cut her to the quick. "Pray do not! Do not go away from me like that."

"I should never have come back," said Mr. Raven, turning aside to catch hold of the stall railing. "It was too soon. There are things left unresolved, things that—" He straightened with a sigh. "You would not understand."

"Has it anything to do with your wife?" asked Cassandra quietly. She was breathing very shallowly, dreading his answer.

Mr. Raven reacted as though struck. Astonishment spread over his face, and his nostrils flared. "Sir Marcus told you? He told you about . . . about Sophia?"

Cassandra turned her back to him so that he could not see her expression. She thought she would suffocate. She forced out a reply. "I did not know her name."

Her arm was caught, and she was swung around. Cassandra glanced up, startled, into his intent eyes. Then she turned her face aside, afraid of what he might have seen. Apparently, it had been enough. His grip eased, though she was not let go.

"You little devil. You've tricked me, haven't you? You knew nothing about her," said Mr. Raven very softly.

Cassandra cast a quick glance upward. His expression was harsh. "I surmised there might be a woman. I did not know anything else for certain."

Mr. Raven sighed. "I shall have to tell you the whole."

"No! I don't wish to hear it," said Cassandra swiftly.

"Nonetheless, hear it you will," said Mr. Raven, a grim set to his mouth. He led her over to a dry water trough and overturned it. "Sit down there. Please, Belle. I have never asked you for anything so seriously in my life."

Cassandra could not withstand his plea, though it had made reference to a history that she did not share. Without a word, she drew her skirts around her and sat down.

Mr. Raven said nothing for a moment, seeming to be at a bit of a loss where to begin. Then drawing a breath, he said, "You must understand that I never meant to wed. It simply happened, being the result of a mad series of circumstances."

"Do you love her?" blurted Cassandra.

"No! At least, not in the sense that you mean." Mr. Raven shook his head, his jaw working. "I am beginning badly. I met Sophia after the siege of Badajoz. I saved her from a pack of soldiers."

Cassandra stared at him, not fully comprehending. "I don't understand."

"The city was being sacked, Belle! There was looting and murder and death on every side. Sophia was not the only female dragged screaming out of her hiding place into the roads," said Mr. Raven harshly.

"You mean—" Cassandra swallowed.

"Yes. They were going to rape her. I stopped it. I killed the two of them, just as the last one managed to put a bayonet in me," said Mr. Raven. His voice became flat and unemotional. "A priest came to aid us. He helped us to safety, and I lost consciousness for a time. I think from loss of blood. Afterward, he urged me to marry Sophia. I appeared to be dying, and he told me that shortly it would not matter to me who bore my name. But for Sophia, it meant protection. As an officer's wife, she would be entitled to protection and could be gotten safely out of Badajoz."

"But you did not die."

"No." Mr. Raven sighed. "My batman found me and carried me back to our lines. He nursed me back to health. I remembered what I had done, that I had married Sophia. My batman set inquiries afoot, but no one knew where she had gone. All that was known was that the priest had accompanied her."

"Did you never find her?" asked Cassandra.

"Not at once. Not for three years," said Mr. Raven shortly.

Cassandra had a startling revelation. "Your business interests on the Continent that kept you there after you had sold out of the army."

"Quite." Mr. Raven sat down on the trough beside Cassandra and turned his head. He gave her a self-mocking smile. "You will never be able to guess where she had gone."

Cassandra shook her head. "No, I have no notion. A young girl alone except for a priest. Did she have family?"

"I was able to track down a distant cousin who survived the war. He could tell me little, except that Sophia's father had once written to him that she wanted to become a nun. He showed me the letter," said Mr. Raven. "It was all the clue that I had. That, and the priest's name. But eventually I found her. She had taken orders."

"Oh, my goodness." Cassandra could scarcely grasp the significance of all that he had told her. One thing was perfectly clear, however. He was married to a nun. "Philip, I don't know what to say. What are you going to do? Are . . . are you going to bring Sophia back to England?"

"I talked at length with Sophia." Mr. Raven laughed quietly at his recollections. "My appearance was a grave shock to her. She had had no notion that I had survived, you see. It created a difficulty for her. As a married woman, she could not remain in orders; but she did not wish to leave the nunnery. She had the life that she had always wanted."

"What can be done, then?" asked Cassandra. Without being conscious of it, she had laid her hand on top of his arm.

Mr. Raven covered her fingers with his other hand. "We have petitioned for annulment. It has been more than a year now. I am awaiting confirmation that our petition has been granted."

Cassandra thought about what she had been told. She remembered after one of Mr. Raven's visits how irascible her grandfather had been. Sir Marcus had insisted upon having his writing supplies and sent her away. "So you told Grandfather about Sophia," she said slowly. "And he has written to Mr. Petrie-Downs concerning the matter. I suppose he hopes that some acquaintance of his will be able to exert some influence."

"Did he do so? I hope that Sir Marcus does know someone who has access to the right ears in the Vatican," said Mr. Raven. He rose to his feet, pulling her with him. "And now you know my idiotic story. You seem to have warmed up. Shall we return to the Hall?"

Cassandra nodded. She walked with him out of the stable, her thoughts keeping her silent. She allowed him to lift her into the saddle and thanked him. Before he could turn away, however, she stayed him by catching hold of his coat sleeve. "Philip, you are a good man. I . . . I honor you for it."

Mr. Raven smiled crookedly at her, an unreadable expression in his gray eyes. "Thank you, Miss Weatherstone. Would that I was not quite so noble." With that cryptic remark, he turned away and got up onto his own horse.

Chapter Eighteen

Cassandra and Mr. Raven did not discuss his private life again. It was a subject that by mutual agreement they simply did not touch on. Cassandra thought about Mr. Raven's unusual predicament often, however. She hoped for his sake that there would come some word soon from Rome that would make him a free man once more.

In a way, a bond had been formed between them that otherwise could not have existed. Cassandra at last had a tiny bit of shared history with Mr. Raven, and it allowed her to be more comfortable in his presence than she had ever been with another person in her life.

When the wind was too harsh to allow her and Mr. Raven to ride, Cassandra was perfectly content to work on a piece of embroidery as she sat in front of the warm hearth. Mr. Raven often joined the ladies, either reading or conversing quietly.

Miss Bidwell watched and listened without comment, only smiling at a particularly spirited exchange between the two. Occasionally, her expression was thoughtful as her gaze rested on Cassandra's head as the younger woman plied her embroidery needle smoothly through the cloth.

One afternoon on a particularly blustery day, the doors to the parlor were opened wide by the butler. Sir Marcus was carried in a chair by his valet and a stalwart footman into the room. The ladies and Mr. Raven at once jumped up from their seats.

"Grandfather!" exclaimed Cassandra. "Whatever are you doing downstairs?"

"I've surprised you, haven't I? I've surprised you all,"

said Sir Marcus in a hoarse voice. He slapped one hand against the arm of the chair. "Put me down! I wish to sit over there in that wing chair. I'll not stay in this invalid's lift a moment longer, I say."

"As you wish, my lord," said the valet, nodding across the old gentleman's head at the footman. "Careful, Timothy. We'll put it down right next to—"

"No, Weems! I shall walk to the wing chair, I tell you," snapped Sir Marcus. "Put me down here, now, this instant!"

While Cassandra and her companions stood looking on with stunned concern, the valet and footman did as they were told. They lowered the chair to the floor. Weems took hold of his master's elbow and levered him to his feet. Sir Marcus grunted from the effort and clutched the footman's arm for support on the other side.

"Sir Marcus!" Mr. Raven leaped forward. "Let me help you, sir!"

"Thank you, Philip." Sir Marcus relinquished his fast hold on the footman's sleeve and grasped Mr. Raven's strong arm. With the help of his godson and valet, he managed a few very careful steps to the wing chair that was situated in front of the cheerfully crackling fire. He was lowered into the chair and sank back with a weary sigh. "I'm as weak as a newborn babe," he complained.

"It is to be expected, my lord," said Weems repressively.

"You're a deuced excuse for a nursemaid and no mistake," growled Sir Marcus.

"As you say, my lord," said Weems, not at all perturbed. The valet spread a wool blanket over his master's thin knees and retreated.

"Well! Here I am downstairs at last," said Sir Marcus. He glanced around the parlor complacently. His gaze fell on his granddaughter. "Are you not happy to see me up and about, Belle?"

"Indeed I am, Grandfather. I am just so astonished, however. Sir Thomas held out little hope of you leaving your bed for . . . for some time," said Cassandra, stammering a little because she did not wish to reveal how pessimistic the physician had been. She threw a glance at her companions. "I had no idea that you were so much better."

"I suppose that is why you keep staring at me as though I were some apparition," said Sir Marcus.

"We are all of us not unnaturally astonished, Sir Marcus, but nevertheless well pleased," said Miss Bidwell. "Belle has had more faith in your rallying than anyone, I think."

"Belle knows me too well to believe that I would die on her, at least before I had made things right," said Sir Marcus. He turned to Mr. Raven. "And you, Philip? Have you nothing to say for yourself?"

"I, too, can only express my pleasure to see you out of your sickbed, sir," said Mr. Raven with a slight bow.

Sir Marcus shook his head. "You're still a dull stick, Philip. I am pained to have to say it, but there it is. I would have thought that being in the army would have broadened your outlook and given you some flair."

"It was not flowery speeches that I exchanged with the French, sir," said Mr. Raven dryly.

Sir Marcus threw back his head and laughed. His eyes rested warm on his godson. "No, of course it wasn't. Bullets did well enough, eh? Now, what do you think of the Hall? It is a snug property, is it not?"

"Indeed, what I have seen of the estate is quite impressive. Belle and I have ridden over most of it," said Mr. Raven.

"I have no doubt of that. Belle has always loved to ride," said Sir Marcus. "There was a time that I could not keep her from trotting off at first light and not returning until dusk. I trust that you are a bit more circumspect these days, Belle."

"Of course, Grandfather. Philip and I have enjoyed several sedate rides together with a groom in tow," said Cassandra lightly. She would not mention the ride that she and Mr. Raven had taken alone, which had led to Mr. Raven's astonishing confidences. She had sat down again and picked up her embroidery hoop. She began stitching, pulling the satiny thread taut with each smooth insertion.

"Aye, the escort rankles, doesn't it? Never mind, it is for your own good," said Sir Marcus. He paused, intently eyeing her. "What is that you are doing, Belle?"

"I am embroidering a chair cover for the dining room, Grandfather," said Cassandra calmly. There was a moment's silence. She looked up when she felt herself to be under close observation. Her grandfather was staring fixedly at her. "Is there something wrong, sir? Shall I call Weems?"

"No, no. There's nothing wrong," said Sir Marcus hastily, waving his hand at her. "Why don't you entertain Philip for me? Miss Bidwell, pull your chair closer. I wish to speak with you for a moment."

"Of course, Sir Marcus," said Miss Bidwell in a slightly surprised tone. Mr. Raven moved the lady's chair next to Sir Marcus's, and she thanked him. Then she sat down, folded her hands primly in her lap and bent her head to listen to a low-voiced question from Sir Marcus.

Mr. Raven strolled over to the sofa upon which Cassandra was seated. He sat down on the end and picked up her basket of threads. Idly, he looked through them. "This is a pretty shade. What secrets do you think they are sharing?"

"Oh, I should think that my grandfather wants a report of how things go with us," said Cassandra calmly, biting off her thread. "Could you hand me that other pink, please? Yes, that is the one. Thank you!"

Mr. Raven set aside the basket. He raised one arm and laid it across the back of the sofa, angling his body so that he better faced her. "And how does it go with us, Miss Weatherstone?"

Cassandra smiled at him. "Why, very well, I think. We can neither of us be accused of shirking our duty."

"That is true. We have practically lived in one another's pocket these past several days," said Mr. Raven thoughtfully. "We have gone along surprisingly well. There has not been one cross glance or word between us."

"You sound surprised, Philip. Have we changed so much, then?" asked Cassandra teasingly.

He looked at her, smiling. "Yes, yes, I think that we have. I like you better than I ever thought possible."

Cassandra felt a blush stealing up into her cheeks. She cast her eyes down at her stitchery. "Surely not. You knew me well enough before."

"No, I don't think that I did," said Mr. Raven quietly. "There is something very different about you, Belle. Something that I haven't quite put my finger on. I shall reason it out eventually, I suppose."

Cassandra looked up quickly. She felt an uncomfortable rush of dismay and delight. Her heart was beating unnaturally fast. "You . . . you confuse me, sir. You speak in riddles that I don't understand."

Mr. Raven frowned. "I am not certain that I understand it myself."

"Belle!"

Cassandra started at Sir Marcus's summons. "Yes, Grandfather?"

"You will be happy to know that I have decided in favor of Sir Thomas's invitation," said Sir Marcus.

"Invitation?" faltered Cassandra. Her thoughts were still on Mr. Raven's words. She was relieved that the unnerving conversation with Mr. Raven must necessarily be at an end. She felt that the gentleman's perceptive nature was bringing him uncomfortably close to the truth, and she wasn't certain how she should handle it.

"Listen to the girl! As though she did not know what I was talking about!" exclaimed Sir Marcus. "Aye, Belle, Sir Thomas's invitation, which you had Weems bring in to me several days past."

"Oh, that! I had quite forgotten it," said Cassandra. "What did Sir Thomas have to say, Grandfather?"

Sir Marcus snorted in disbelief. "Merely that he wishes you and Philip and Miss Bidwell to attend a soiree tomorrow evening. I have just been telling Miss Bidwell that I think that you should go. I have already sent a note round to Sir Thomas that he may expect you."

"Tomorrow evening?"

The possibilities tumbled through Cassandra's mind. She felt relief that she would see her sister. They simply had to make some plan to meet privately. But almost instantly she realized that that was a moot point. She and Belle would be seen together for the first time by Uncle Phineas and Aunt Margaret. Almost certainly she would be recognized by her aunt and uncle, and they would realize that they had been duped. She hoped that her aunt and uncle would not be too angry with her. What explanation could she possibly give that would soothe their hurt and affronted feelings? A surge of homesickness swept through her. Oh, how she longed to see them again! She must look her best when she saw them again.

"Whatever am I going to wear?"

Cassandra did not realize that she had spoken her question aloud until Sir Marcus and Miss Bidwell started laughing.

"Isn't that just like a woman? Always wondering what she is going to put on," said Sir Marcus, still chuckling. "It is a good thing that we are not like the female of the species, eh, Philip?"

"Quite. However, in this instance I must sympathize with Belle. I brought little in the way of evening togs," said Mr. Raven.

"I shouldn't worry overmuch, Philip. Sir Thomas is a country doctor, not a courtier. He'll not expect London finery, I daresay," said Sir Marcus.

Mr. Raven subsided, a skeptical brow raised.

Cassandra recalled very well what her aunt had packed for her to wear to Sir Thomas's house party, and there was nothing in Belle's wardrobe that was going to be adequate. "Sir, I beg to differ. Sir Thomas has several guests to his house party. It is likely to be a more formal affair than you envision. I . . . I suspect that I haven't anything to wear that will measure up."

"I must agree with Belle, Sir Marcus. We must work on the assumption that Sir Thomas may have some influential personages staying with him. Belle has a gown that may be passable, given the addition of a few tucks of lace and ribbons. We shall have to go into the village to the shops and engage a seamstress," stated Miss Bidwell.

Sir Marcus stared at the elderly lady. His bushy brows

contracted until they almost met over his large nose. "Is that what you think, ma'am?"

Miss Bidwell gave a single nod. "Indeed it is, Sir Marcus."

"Then take Belle in at first light. I shall stand the cost for whatever you think is necessary, Miss Bidwell," said Sir Marcus decisively.

"Thank you, Grandfather," said Cassandra.

He shook a bony finger in her direction. "Aye, you've managed to wrap me round your finger yet again, miss! This is a high treat. You'll scarcely sleep a wink for excitement, I'll warrant. Belle, I'll have your promise now that you will behave yourself with all propriety."

"Of course I shall, sir," said Cassandra, smiling at him.

Sir Marcus nodded. "Very well. I shall trust you. And you, Miss Bidwell! You'll turn her out every inch a lady, I know."

"Indeed I shall, Sir Marcus," said Miss Bidwell, nodding.

"I'll want to see you before you go, Belle," said Sir Marcus.

Cassandra promised to come see him before she left for the soiree.

"Now I am tired," said Sir Marcus, deflating abruptly. He stirred fretfully in his chair. "Pull the bell, Philip. I want Weems. Tomorrow, Philip, I wish to go over some estate matters with you."

"I am completely at your disposal, Sir Marcus," said Mr. Raven with a bow.

Chapter Nineteen

At first light, Miss Bidwell knocked on the door and entered Cassandra's bedroom and ruthlessly drew back the bed draperies and the window curtains. Sunlight streamed into the room. Cassandra threw her arm over her eyes, muttering incoherently.

"Come, Belle, it is time to get up. I have already asked that Young John bring round the gig," said Miss Bidwell, bustling over to the wardrobe. She looked through the several gowns that were in the wardrobe and selected a green merino and a matching corded pelisse. "You'll need to dress warmly. It is snowing a little, I think. Now I am going downstairs to ask that some hot tea and biscuits can be served to us before we go."

Cassandra sat up, yawning. "I shall be with you directly, Biddy."

"See that you are. I have the gown that we decided upon last night folded in a hatbox in my bedroom. I shall take it downstairs with me so that we shall not have to come back up," said Miss Bidwell. She glanced around, folding her hands before her. "I trust that I have remembered everything."

"I am certain that you have, Biddy," said Cassandra with a smile.

Miss Bidwell shook her head regretfully. "I only wish that I had known earlier about this soiree. Of course Sir Marcus has no notion of what it will take to make that gown presentable in such a short time." Miss Bidwell walked over to the door. Opening it, she admonished, "Now don't fall back to sleep, Belle. We have much to do and very little time in which to accomplish it."

Within an hour, Cassandra and Miss Bidwell climbed

up into the gig to set off for the village. Miss Bidwell was also attired warmly in a heavy pelisse and velvet bonnet. She had insisted that Cassandra bring a muff to warm her hands and that a heavy wool rug be wrapped snugly over their laps.

"I am aware that you are not particularly susceptible to the cold, Belle, but humor me in this. I shall feel more comfortable if we both keep as warm as possible," remarked Miss Bidwell as she took up the reins.

"Very well, Biddy," said Cassandra docilely. She had no objection to make, for she was grateful for the comfort provided by the muff and rug. It was a cold, damp day, the kind of weather that so readily chilled one to the bone.

The drive to the small village proved to be a pleasant jaunt. The countryside was serene and peaceful, the barren branches of the trees seeming to be waiting for the cloaking of winter.

As they drove down the village's one thoroughfare, Cassandra looked around curiously. She had not been at Sir Thomas's house long enough to have enjoyed any possible excursions into the small town, and so she had never been there. The village appeared to be a quaint, bustling place, and she liked it immediately.

However, as she and Miss Bidwell executed their errands, the charm of her first visit quickly wore off. She was continually greeted by different personages, who spoke to both her and Miss Bidwell in a friendly, familiar fashion. It was a bit nerve-racking, not knowing anyone's name and having to pretend otherwise. Cassandra felt as though her mind was doing cartwheels in her efforts to be so like her sister that no one could suspect otherwise.

Cassandra was certain that she had offended at least one lady simply because she had not greeted the lady at once, as her sister would have done upon coming face-to-face with the woman. She had lingered a step or two behind Miss Bidwell to peer closely into an apothecary shop when the lady spoke to her. Cassandra tried to smooth over the awkward moment by claiming that she had been woolgathering and offered her apology. The lady nodded, but slanted a backward glance at Cassandra as she went on her way.

After that disconcerting experience, Cassandra stayed close beside Miss Bidwell in hopes that she could pick up clues from her companion's demeanor and greetings whenever they chanced to meet other acquaintances.

The village boasted just one true dress shop. Miss Bidwell showed the gown in the hatbox to the seamstress and asked the woman's advice. After much discussion, they agreed that several knots of ribbon and a new ruching of lace would refurbish the gown nicely on such short notice. The woman promised to have the gown ready by five of the clock, which would leave ample time to dress for the soiree. It was agreed that a messenger would deliver the gown up to the Hall.

"I only hope that it turns out as well as I have envisioned," said Miss Bidwell with the slightest air of anxiety as they emerged from the shop.

"I am positive that it will," said Cassandra soothingly. She honestly had not a notion how talented the seamstress might be, but judging from her sister's wardrobe the woman was not completely inept. "She seems to know her business. If it isn't just what we want, then I can certainly do some last-minute basting of lace."

Miss Bidwell stopped short on the walkway to glance at her. "You, Belle? Surely, you jest."

"No, I am learning to be quite handy with a needle, actually," said Cassandra with studied casualness. Once more she had inadvertently revealed too much of herself. She grasped the elderly lady's elbow, and in an attempt to distract her, she admonished, "Biddy, do come on! That gentleman wishes to pass, and you are blocking his way."

Miss Bidwell murmured an apology and walked on toward the gig. She cast an anxious glance at Cassandra. "Belle, are you quite, quite sure that you are all right? I think it is wonderful that you are so willing to help, of course. However, you are not precisely well versed in such matters, are you?"

"Oh, I may not have been in the past, but I am learning quickly. You are well enough acquainted with me to know that I am equal to any challenge," said Cassandra cheerfully, hardly turning a hair. She caught up her skirt and stepped up into the gig.

"Quite true," murmured Miss Bidwell, throwing her a glance as she, too, got up into the gig. Miss Bidwell took up the reins and gave the horse its office to go.

When they had returned to the Hall, Steeves conveyed the message that Sir Marcus had sent down word that he wished to speak with his granddaughter directly upon her return. Cassandra at once exchanged a worried glance with Miss Bidwell. She finished stripping off her gloves, turning her gaze anxiously to the butler. "I trust that he is not—"

"Not as I know, miss. Mr. Raven said nothing about the master being ill," said Steeves, taking her gloves as well as her muff. He also accepted Miss Bidwell's gloves.

Cassandra had already started up the stairs. She paused, her hand on the banister as she looked down at the butler. "Mr. Raven?"

"Yes, miss. Mr. Raven was closeted with Sir Marcus all morning. He is now in the drawing room," said Steeves.

"Thank you, Steeves. I shall see Mr. Raven presently, I suppose," said Cassandra.

"I shall inquire after tea, Belle," called Miss Bidwell.

"Yes, of course." Cassandra hurried up the stairs, wondering if Mr. Raven had had news in the morning post. It was the first thing that had flitted into her mind to explain why Mr. Raven had been in with her grandfather for such a long time.

Mr. Raven would naturally have informed Sir Marcus of such an item of importance. However, Cassandra very much doubted that Sir Marcus would volunteer anything about it to her, for she was supposed to know nothing about Mr. Raven's private affairs.

She hoped that Sir Marcus would not keep her long. She was anxious to go down to the drawing room and discover for herself if the long looked-for papal letter had come at last.

Cassandra went along to her grandfather's rooms and knocked on the door. It was opened promptly by the valet. She said cheerfully, "Good day, Weems. How is my grandfather?"

"He is as well as could be expected, miss."

At Cassandra's look of inquiry, the valet amplified. "The master had Mr. Raven up to go over several estate matters. Sir Marcus has been tired out by the unusual exertion, miss."

"I see. Then I shall not stay with him long, Weems," said Cassandra.

The valet nodded his approval and ushered her into the bedroom. Cassandra went toward the canopied bed. She saw that her grandfather was sitting up against a bank of embroidered pillows. At first glance it appeared that Sir Marcus was asleep, but then he stirred, seemingly at some little noise that she had made.

"Ah, Belle. You are back at last," a pleased note in Sir Marcus's voice. "Has your shopping trip proven to be worthwhile?"

Cassandra dropped a kiss on his wrinkled forehead. It was the first time that she had ever felt emboldened enough to take such a liberty. "Yes, I think so. We shall see what the seamstress does with the lace and ribbon that we gave her for refurbishing my gown."

"You could appear at a ball dressed in rags, Belle, and you would outshine every one of the others," said Sir Marcus with fondness.

"Why, thank you, sir," said Cassandra, rather touched. "However, I rather think that you are biased in your granddaughter's favor."

Sir Marcus chuckled. "Aye, I am that. Belle, I requested you to visit me because I have something for you. Weems, bring me that box."

The valet approached, carrying a tarnished silver jewel box. He set it down carefully on the bed within Sir Marcus's reach and opened the ornate lid. Inside was an impressive array of old-fashioned gold and silver pendants and bracelets and necklaces and rings. The precious stones set in several of the costly pieces sparkled in the light.

"Oh!" exclaimed Cassandra involuntarily.

Sir Marcus reached into the jewel box and fumbled

until he was able to grasp a long length of translucent pearls. The pearls rattled against the edge of the box as he lifted them out. "These belonged to your grandmother. They were my first wedding gift to her. I wish you to have them. Wear them tonight."

Cassandra was overwhelmed and dismayed. Her first thought was that Sir Marcus should be handing them to her sister, not to her. "My dear sir! I cannot possibly take them."

"What nonsense! Take them, I say! I wish you to have them," thundered Sir Marcus, his face turning a shade darker.

Cassandra reluctantly accepted the long strand of perfectly matched pearls. They slipped smooth as pale silk through her trembling fingers. She knew that she was holding a small fortune in her hands. "Oh, they are so beautiful."

Sir Marcus nodded, obviously satisfied with her reaction. "And they will look beautiful on you, Belle. You will come show me how they look before you leave this evening."

"Of course I shall," said Cassandra, her smile trembling on her lips. She wished fervently that it could be she, Cassandra, who could express her gratitude for such a magnificent gift. It was so very hard, especially just now, not to be known for herself.

"Weems, take the box away." Sir Marcus waited until the valet had picked up the box and exited the bedroom into the dressing room. Sir Marcus turned again to look at Cassandra, and he reached out to grasp her wrist. "Belle, are you feeling quite the thing?"

Cassandra was startled. "Why, of course I am. Why-ever do you ask?"

"I have been hearing odd things. Not bad things necessarily, but odd," said Sir Marcus.

"How do you mean?" asked Cassandra, sitting very still. She could feel her heartbeat quickening, and hoped that Sir Marcus could not detect it fluttering in her wrist.

"Why, that you have taken over some of the steward's duties with the bills. That you take an interest in the preparation of menus and housekeeping. That you read!" Sir Marcus was staring intently at her, as though he could draw answers from her eyes. "Belle, you must tell me. Have you been feeling unwell lately? Is that why you have been less energetic than your usual wont? I never knew you in all of your life to sit of an evening and embroider. You have told me often enough how those things bored you to tears. Tell me the truth, girl! Are you sickening?"

"Sickening!" Cassandra blurted the word out with amazement. "Of course I am not!"

"Then what is it? Pray tell me," begged Sir Marcus. "You know that I will do anything for you. Only tell me what I must do to make you better."

"I am not sickening, Grandfather, really! If . . . if I have seemed different somehow, more subdued, then I must put it down to your own health, sir," said Cassandra, her mind working as quickly as it was possible. "I have been greatly concerned about you. Biddy may tell you so and Steeves and the rest. Why, I have been doing and saying all sorts of things that are out of character. But it is only because of my anxiety over you, sir, nothing more. I am trying to occupy my mind so that I do not think about it so often."

"But . . . reading, Belle? You have never enjoyed reading, except for those silly novels that you and Miss Bidwell have such a fondness for," said Sir Marcus, his bushy brows lowered. "And I haven't any of those in my library, I know."

Cassandra wondered how many of the household had reported on her "odd" behavior to Weems, and thus to Sir Marcus. She could not help what had already been said about her. She would simply have to carry on in her stumbling way.

"I had never before come across such a fascinating book, you see," said Cassandra. She folded her hands demurely in her lap, the warmed pearls pooled under her palms. "It is called *A Faire History of the Weatherstone Family of Great Britain.*"

A light flared in Sir Marcus's winter-blue eyes. He shifted against his pillows, his gaze never leaving her face. "You found that, did you? And you say that it is fascinating?"

"Quite fascinating. I never knew before what a ramshackle lot we are," said Cassandra dryly.

Sir Marcus gave a gruff laugh. "Aye! You have the right of it, my dear. Very well, I am satisfied. I shall let you go along now, Belle. I am tired. Philip and I went over all of the estate earlier, and my eyes feel like dry marbles in my head."

"What sort of business did you discuss with Philip, sir?" asked Cassandra delicately, wondering if her grandfather might divulge just the right thing that she was hoping to learn.

Sir Marcus looked at her from under lowered brows. "Now what manner of question is that, my dear?"

"Why, a perfectly ordinary one, I should think," said Cassandra with the lightest of shrugs.

"You're curious about whether or not we discussed you, aren't you?" asked Sir Marcus bluntly.

"Not precisely," said Cassandra. She could scarcely say more, for she simply couldn't announce that it was Philip Raven's personal affairs that occupied her thoughts lately. Sir Marcus would not unnaturally leap to the conclusion that she—or rather, Belle—was more than passing interested in Mr. Raven. And that would not do.

Sir Marcus sighed. "Very well, Belle. I shall tell you all. I went over several matters having to do with the estate, things that must be seen to and that I cannot expect anyone else to do for me. Philip is my godson. I wish him to be fully familiar with all of my holdings. As I recall, we did not discuss you to any degree."

Cassandra was suddenly struck by the oddity of what Sir Marcus had said, or perhaps more important, what he had not said. "Grandfather, are you making Philip your heir?" she asked slowly, for it had occurred to her that Sir Marcus had all along been quite insistent that Mr. Raven learn all there was to know about the Hall and its environs.

"If I am, what is that to you?" asked Sir Marcus, lying

back on his pillows, seemingly at his ease, but with his blue eyes fixed intently on her face.

"What of your son, my Uncle Phineas?" asked Cassandra, point-blank.

Sir Marcus's hollowed cheeks flushed. "I have told you not to mention that name to me."

"I shan't, at least just now when I know you are wearied," said Cassandra, nodding her understanding. She smiled at her grandfather. "It would not be a particularly good time, would it?"

The anger drained from Sir Marcus's expression. "Aye, you know just how to humor this old man, do you not? But I shall not discuss my private affairs with you, Belle, so don't think it."

"We shall see," said Cassandra, undeterred by his stern warning. She felt that her sister would not have left it so easily. "What of Philip's business interests on the Continent? Shall that interfere with your plans for the Hall?"

"I hope not. Of course not." Sir Marcus scowled. He shifted as though one of his pillows had slipped and was digging into his back. "Don't bother me anymore with foolish questions, Belle. I am deuced tired, and you make my head ache."

"Shall I call Weems?" asked Cassandra, rising. She knew that there was no more to be gotten out of her grandfather. She held the string of pearls clasped loosely in her hand.

"Aye." Sir Marcus's lids had fallen shut, but suddenly he opened his eyes again. "Do not forget. I wish to see you in all your finery this evening before you go."

"I shan't forget," promised Cassandra. She slipped the pearls into her pocket and went to tell the valet that Sir Marcus needed him. Then she left and traversed the hallway to her own bedroom.

Chapter Twenty

When she had entered and shut the door to ensure her privacy, Cassandra walked over to stand in front of the cheval glass. She withdrew the length of pearls from her dress pocket and held them up to her throat and studied herself. The luminous pearls looked magnificent against her creamy throat. She loved them.

Cassandra stared a moment longer into her own wide hazel eyes. Then she lowered her hands and looked at the pearls laying in her palms. Her grandmother's pearls that had been saved for Belle, and she was to wear them instead. And she did not feel in the least guilty; on the contrary, she actually envied her sister.

"I am beginning to despise myself," she whispered.

Cassandra turned away from the mirror and found a drawer that she could put the pearls in, wrapped safely in her silk stockings. She paused, then reached out to open another drawer. Cassandra withdrew the folded paper that she had put away. She read it again before folding it back up and placing it back in the drawer. It was not the right time, she thought. Not yet, at any rate.

Cassandra left the bedroom and went downstairs. She inquired of a footman if Mr. Raven was still in the drawing room. She nodded at the servantman's answer.

Cassandra entered the drawing room. "There you are, Philip." She glanced around to see that he was alone, and shut the door. "I am glad to see that Biddy is not here. I wish to speak privately with you."

Mr. Raven set aside the morning papers and gestured to the wing chair opposite him. "Pray sit down. I must admit that you have roused my curiosity."

Cassandra walked over and seated herself. "Philip,

you were with my grandfather all this morning, I am
told. I know that the post was taken up to Sir Marcus
yesterday before I saw it. I thought perhaps that he
wished to tell you that he had gotten some word about
your affair. Or that you had yourself received a notice
of some sort."

Mr. Raven shook his head, his brows drawn together.
"Unfortunately, no. That was not the reason for Sir Marcus's request to see me this morning."

"I had so hoped, for your sake," said Cassandra, sighing. She looked across at him, curious. "Philip, were you
aware that Sir Marcus is making you the heir to the
Hall?"

Mr. Raven stared at her for several seconds. His expression was unreadable. "I suspected it, but I was not
certain. He has not told me directly so, nor did he completely deny it when I inquired. Are you certain? He
would have to completely disown Mr. Weatherstone if
that is truly the case."

"I am not positive. However, I am fairly confident that
it is so," said Cassandra with the slightest of shrugs to
express her helplessness. "He will not hear of anything
said to him about my uncle."

"I am distressed to know that there is such a depth
of bad feelings between Sir Marcus and Mr. Weatherstone. I must make clear to Sir Marcus that I will not
accept an inheritance that cuts out the legitimate succes-
sion," said Mr. Raven forcibly.

"I doubt that there is anything you might say that will
have the least effect," said Cassandra, shaking her head.
"I very recently discovered that my grandfather had a
letter from my uncle. It was a civil letter, requesting
permission to allow myself and my sister to visit together. From all that I can deduce, Grandfather denied
his permission. He will not have anything to do with my
uncle, even for our sakes."

"I am sorry. It is a harsh blow, I know," said Mr.
Raven.

"I shall not let it lie," said Cassandra quietly. "I
cannot."

"What do you intend to do?" asked Mr. Raven, his gaze riveted on her face.

"I don't know as yet," said Cassandra, sighing. "I fear pushing the matter too strongly with my grandfather, for I don't wish to throw him into such a passion that he will make himself ill again. Yet I must make some attempt to persuade him to listen to reason."

"Forgive my blunt speaking, but it is my feeling that Sir Marcus uses his state of health as a sort of blackmail to cow his household into submission," said Mr. Raven quietly.

Cassandra looked at him intently for a moment before she nodded. "Yes, so I have thought also."

"You told me once that Sir Marcus is master of his own emotions. I have yet to hear that his heart has been unduly affected by his illness, so I do not believe you need fear that he will be carried off by a seizure of some sort," said Mr. Raven. "I do not presume to be a physician. However, I can say with confidence that after spending several hours with him over the span of these last weeks, I do not believe Sir Marcus is in any immediate danger of dying."

"Truly? Or do you say that simply to relieve the worst of my anxiety?" asked Cassandra.

"Believe me, Belle, I have seen the spectre of death in men's countenances on too many occasions not to recognize it if it were haunting Sir Marcus," said Mr. Raven.

Cassandra felt a lightening of the oppression of her spirit. "Thank you, Philip," she said gratefully. "You have not only relieved my mind of its most pressing fear, but encouraged me, as well."

Mr. Raven leaned forward from his chair and captured one of her hands between both of his. Very softly, he said, "I am most happy that I have been able to do so."

Cassandra felt the security of his strong clasp. When she looked into his gray eyes, she read compassion and something else in his expression. There was a keen interest, a warmth in the depths of his eyes that sent a tingle along her spine. She was all of a sudden keenly aware of the intimacy of their pose. She blushed. "Philip—"

The door opened, and Miss Bidwell entered. Cassandra started and quickly pulled free her hand. Mr. Raven casually sat back in his chair. Miss Bidwell's spectacles gleamed in the light as she looked swiftly from one to the other. "Here you both are! I have been looking for you, Belle. You must excuse us, Philip. We have a great deal to do yet if Belle is to be ready for this evening."

Mr. Raven politely stood up to acknowledge the lady's entrance. "Of course, Miss Bidwell."

"Come along, Belle."

Cassandra hesitated, looking at Mr. Raven. She didn't wish to leave the drawing room, for she had the oddest sensation that something of importance had almost been said.

"Belle, you must know that I cannot allow you to have private *tête-à-têtes* with Philip," said Miss Bidwell a little sharply. She was still standing at the door with her hand on the knob.

Cassandra's ingrained training responded to her companion's reminder. "Of course not. You are right. Forgive me, Biddy." She rose at once and walked over to join Miss Bidwell at the door. She glanced back over her shoulder.

Mr. Raven nodded to her, and she felt warmed by the amused understanding in his eyes. She said demurely, "I shall see you again later, sir."

Mr. Raven bowed politely. There was a flare in his eyes that had nothing to do with the civilities. "I look forward to it."

Miss Bidwell waited until she and Cassandra had passed out into the hall and she had closed the drawing room door before she spoke again. "My dear Belle, you know better than to encourage a gentleman. I don't care that it is only Philip Raven, whom you knew as a child. It simply isn't done. What were you thinking of?"

"I wasn't encouraging him," protested Cassandra, startled.

"My dear, when a gentleman looks just *so* at a young lady, and she speaks just *so* to him as she is walking out the door—" Miss Bidwell shook her head. "Your headstrong ways have never been in more evidence, my dear."

Cassandra flushed. "Really, Biddy! We were just talking. It is not as though you caught him making love to me."

Miss Bidwell turned red from embarrassment and annoyance. "Belle! What things you do say! I trust that you shall be more circumspect in your speech and manners at the soiree tonight."

"You needn't be anxious on my account, Biddy. I shall behave with complete propriety," said Cassandra, thoroughly irritated. It irked her that she was being cautioned and scolded in such a manner.

"Pray see that you are. I should dislike to have to inform Sir Marcus that you had disappointed our trust in you," said Miss Bidwell tartly.

Cassandra drew a slow breath to stop herself from saying something that she might later regret. "What is it that you wished to see me about, Biddy?"

"Oh, yes. I had all but forgotten," exclaimed Miss Bidwell. "Come upstairs, Belle. I have questioned the housekeeper and discovered that one of the newer maids has had some experience in hairdressing. I thought it would be interesting to allow her to experiment a little this afternoon to see if there is a new way that you might like your hair done for this evening."

Cassandra's irritation at once began to dissipate. Despite how overbearing Miss Bidwell could be at times, it was perfectly obvious that the lady cared very much for Belle Weatherstone. "That was considerate of you, Biddy," said Cassandra. "I shall be glad to see what the maid can do."

She accompanied Miss Bidwell upstairs to her bedroom. The maid was already waiting for them, and Cassandra obediently sat down on a stool in front of the cheval glass.

Chapter Twenty-one

It was a cold night, brilliantly moonlit. Cassandra and Miss Bidwell sat in the carriage, hot bricks on the floor to warm their feet and rugs covering their laps. Mr. Raven sat opposite, their escort to Sir Thomas's soiree. There was little conversation as the carriage rolled forward into the night, each occupant seemly preoccupied with their own thoughts.

Cassandra was feeling some apprehension mixed with her anticipation of the evening party. It was certainly ironic that she was being taken to Sir Thomas's residence to meet her sister, who was pretending to be her. Of course, she could say nothing about it to her companions. Sir Thomas had not divulged to anyone who his guests were. Cassandra was positive of that. Otherwise, she felt certain that Sir Marcus would have said something and, knowing what she now did about her grandfather's acrimony toward her uncle, she thought that he probably would have refused to let her attend the soiree. Though it was difficult, Cassandra had to pretend ignorance of Sir Thomas's guest list.

Cassandra had a strong suspicion that Sir Thomas had not announced the inclusion of the party from the Hall to his other guests. As she envisioned Belle's face when her sister saw her walk into the ballroom, she could not help smiling. Her sister would naturally be stunned and taken aback to see her, and to be introduced to Miss "Belle" Weatherstone. Cassandra only hoped that she and Belle could both maintain their composures. It was certain to be a strange moment, especially with Uncle Phineas and Aunt Margaret looking on.

Cassandra hoped that her aunt and uncle would not be too angry with her.

"Did you say something, my dear?" asked Miss Bidwell.

"What?" Cassandra looked over at the lady with surprise, before realizing that she had actually given a little laugh. "Oh, I was just thinking about this evening's entertainment, Biddy. It . . . it will be a vastly interesting evening, I am persuaded."

"Yes, it will. You will be in company for the first time, Belle, so do, pray, mind your manners," said Miss Bidwell sternly.

"You needn't be anxious on my account," said Cassandra, her lips twitching. It was obvious to her that Miss Bidwell was uncertain what to expect from her, or rather, from Belle. She was confident that Miss Bidwell would have no cause for complaint, for she was not entirely without the social graces.

Cassandra realized that Mr. Raven's gaze was on her, and she smiled at him.

He returned her smile before addressing Miss Bidwell. "Pray do not fear, Miss Bidwell. I shall set myself to take good care of our fledgling."

Miss Bidwell did not appear to be particularly reassured. However, she managed a polite nod of acknowledgment. "Thank you, Philip."

The carriage arrived, and they descended from it to enter the well-lit house. In the front entrance hall their wraps were taken. Then they were shown upstairs to the ballroom, where the butler announced them to the assembled company. However, it was doubtful that more than a handful of individuals heard their names over the loud babble of conversation, laugher and music. However, Sir Thomas and his wife, Lady Kensing, had apparently been awaiting their arrival and came up at once to greet them.

"Miss Weatherstone, Miss Bidwell. And Mr. Raven! We have been expecting you. How happy we are that you have been able to attend our little function," said Lady Kensing warmly. Her ladyship looked intently at Cassandra's face, and a tiny smile touched her own countenance. "It has been a long time, Belle. You have

grown up to be an uncommonly pretty young lady. I
may call you Belle?"

"Of course," said Cassandra, inclining her head
graciously.

After greeting them all, Sir Thomas tucked Cassandra's hand into his bent elbow. "You must not mind it
that I bear you off on the instant, Miss Belle. There is
someone here that I should like you to meet."

"How very kind of you, Sir Thomas," said Cassandra
with a mischievous smile, at once leaping to the conclusion that Sir Thomas meant to reunite her with her family. She caught Miss Bidwell's startled expression as their
portly host bore her off.

Sir Thomas escorted Cassandra purposefully through
his guests, briefly introducing her as he went. Cassandra
watched as the polite expressions altered, becoming startled. There were astonished gasps, and the din of conversation gradually died away to a mere murmur. Cassandra
felt increasingly uncomfortable as she became aware that
she was some sort of unexpected attraction.

One gentleman went so far as to catch hold of Sir
Thomas's sleeve. "Oh, I say! Who did you say she was?"

"In a moment, Blackburn, in a moment," said Sir
Thomas genially, freeing himself and leading Cassandra
on.

Cassandra had briefly met most of the house party
before the masquerade and it was disconcerting to say
the least to return in the guise of another. Sir Thomas's
houseguests had had ample time to become acquainted
with her aunt and uncle and the other Miss Weatherstone. As for Sir Thomas's neighbors, naturally they
were acquainted with the fact of Miss Belle Weatherstone's existence at the Hall, but until this moment
Cassandra doubted that any had realized the striking resemblance between the two young women in their midst
that evening.

Sir Thomas triumphantly brought Cassandra up to a
small group. A singular stillness had fallen over the ballroom as all attention was focused on them. "Here we
are! Phineas, Margaret, allow me to present a young
neighbor of mine."

Mr. Phineas Weatherstone and his wife turned. Their civil, smiling expressions underwent radical change at first sight of Cassandra.

Cassandra, beginning to move forward with every expectation of welcome from her aunt and uncle, was completely taken aback by their reaction. They stood stock-still, staring at her. Amazement and disbelief were openly seen in their faces. She was shocked that they did not know her.

Cassandra started to address them as she always had done, but then she heard a murmuring of whispers around the ballroom. Instantly, she realized how imprudent it would be to unmask herself in company. There would be immediate scandal. The tale would be too delicious not to carry on to London. As much as she wanted to declare herself to her aunt and uncle, she could not. It would harm them, holding them up to the ridicule and comment of the world.

Sir Thomas looked from one to the other of the elder Weatherstones, watching their frozen features. "The young lady requires no introduction, of course."

"No, no, she does not," said Mr. Weatherstone stiffly. He glanced around the ballroom as though searching for someone.

Mrs. Weatherstone made a strange gurgling sound and put her gloved hand up to her mouth, her dismayed gaze fixed on Cassandra's face. Her own countenance had paled, so that the alabaster of her skin was in sharp contrast with the deep sea green of her gown.

Cassandra was profoundly disturbed and disappointed. She had assumed that her aunt and uncle would recognize her as Cassandra. After all, she had resided with them for nearly all of her life. She had expected both recriminations and a glad reunion, not this blank astonishment.

When Cassandra saw their faces, she had to catch herself up. She almost trembled with the effort. She had felt such a strong wave of homesickness at the sight of them that she had almost run into their arms. She had sorely missed them.

But of course, they had not missed her. After all, they had had a Cassandra with them.

All Cassandra could do was to continue to play her role. Cassandra was beginning to wonder if she would ever have her own life back.

"Good evening," said Cassandra formally, inclining her head.

Mr. Weatherstone gave a bare nod. However, Mrs. Weatherstone recovered sufficiently from the shock that she was able to give a weak smile. She held out a limp hand in greeting. "My dear. It . . . it has been such a long time since we last met."

Cassandra shook her aunt's hand. Her eyes went to her uncle's watchful face. He was unchanged. He appeared well and as always he was attired impeccably. It made her heart glad to see him, to see them both. She replied in a neutral tone that concealed her own strong emotions. "Yes, it was the day that my sister and I were separated. We were quite small at the time."

A tremor passed through Mrs. Weatherstone. She turned, seeking her husband's support. Mr. Weatherstone took his wife's arm before addressing Cassandra. "You must forgive us if our greeting has been somewhat . . . distant, Belle. It was such a profound shock to see you. Sir Thomas did not warn—prepare us. Is my father with you this evening?" Once more he scanned the ballroom, a frowning expression in his brown eyes.

"Sir Marcus has been very unwell of late and is just now beginning to recover," said Cassandra. She saw that Miss Bidwell and Mr. Raven were coming up, and she felt immense relief. It was such an unexpectedly awkward and difficult moment. She was glad to be able to fall back on the familiar civilities. "I am accompanied this evening by my companion, Miss Bidwell, and Sir Marcus's godson, Mr. Philip Raven."

Sir Thomas made the introductions. He seemed impervious to any undercurrents. Mr. Weatherstone shook Mr. Raven's hand, studying him. "I seem to recall your name, sir."

"Do you? I don't think that we have ever met," said Mr. Raven.

"No; perhaps it is only that you are my father's god-son," said Mr. Weatherstone.

"No doubt," agreed Mr. Raven.

Mrs. Weatherstone and Miss Bidwell had begun with a stilted conversation, but they quickly discovered common ground and began chatting more comfortably together. Mrs. Weatherstone turned to her husband. "Phineas, Miss Bidwell tells me that she once resided in Bath."

"Indeed. You have family there, Miss Bidwell?" asked Mr. Weatherstone politely.

"I did once, sir. They are all gone now," said Miss Bidwell. "I have always hoped to return, however, for I enjoyed the town very much. Often I have considered taking Belle with me. She would like the shops and such."

"Quite," said Mr. Weatherstone. He turned again to Cassandra and his eyes considered her. "I am surprised on more than one head, Belle. I would have assumed that my father would not have allowed you to come tonight when he knew that we should meet."

Cassandra glanced at Sir Thomas, before remarking to her uncle, "I do not believe that Sir Marcus was informed that you would be among Sir Thomas's guests, sir."

"I'll warrant that he did not," agreed Mr. Weatherstone. A faintly amused expression crossed his face as he glanced at their host. "You have managed to surprise us all, Sir Thomas."

"I had hoped to," said Sir Thomas with a smile. "It seemed such a pity not to bring the two young ladies together when they chanced to be in the same neighborhood. I trust that you will eventually forgive me for my meddling, Phineas."

"No doubt I shall," said Mr. Weatherstone, his expression relaxing even further as he chuckled.

"My dear Belle. What a positive start you gave me," said Mrs. Weatherstone in a friendly tone, taking hold of both of Cassandra's hands. "You can have no notion how very like Cassandra you look."

"Oh, but I can, ma'am," said Cassandra with a small

laugh. The exquisite irony of the situation appealed
strongly to her sense of humor.

Mr. Raven had been listening, and now he interposed
a question. "Forgive me, Mrs. Weatherstone, for inter-
rupting. Are you perhaps speaking of Miss Weatherstone's sister?"

"Why, yes. You haven't met Cassandra yet, have
you?" said Mrs. Weatherstone, looking curiously at him.

"I have not had that pleasure, no," said Mr. Raven,
bowing. He glanced in Cassandra's direction as he
straightened.

"Where is Cassandra?" asked Mr. Weatherstone,
looking around. "She was here but a moment ago."

"Are you looking for me, Uncle?"

Cassandra turned around, as did everyone else. There
stood her sister, Belle. From beside her, she heard an
audible gasp from Miss Bidwell. Cassandra smiled impishly, her eyes on her sister's face. "Hullo, Cassandra."

"My goodness. It is *you*!" exclaimed Belle, her eyes
rounding with astonishment. "I couldn't be certain, for
I never expected— But it *is* you!"

"Yes, Sir Thomas orchestrated a surprise meeting of
the family," said Cassandra, sending a quick smile at the
portly gentleman. "Was it not brave of him?"

"What a charming idea," exclaimed Belle, throwing
her arms about Cassandra for a quick hug. As she drew
back, her hazel eyes turned brimful of mischief. There
was a wealth of meaning in her voice. "I am so very
happy to see you. I have such things to tell you."

"And I, you," said Cassandra, holding tight her sister's
hands. She pressed Belle's fingers to let her know that
she needed to talk to her.

"Well! They don't seem to be such strangers after all,"
said Sir Thomas with a pleased chuckle. "I say, I don't
believe I have ever seen such a stunning pair of young
ladies."

"No, indeed," said Miss Bidwell, somewhat faintly.
She kept staring at the two young women as though she
had difficulty believing her eyes.

"It is extraordinary," said Mr. Raven, looking from

one to the other. There was a considering expression on his lean face.

Belle glanced at him. She seemed about to say something directly to him, then stopped. She addressed no one in particular. "I fear that the gentleman is unknown to me."

"This is Mr. Philip Raven, Sir Marcus's godson. Mr. Raven, my niece, Miss Cassandra Weatherstone," said Mr. Weatherstone.

Belle gave her hand to Mr. Raven. She looked up into his face with a glinting smile. "Sir Marcus's godson? I feel that I know you already, Mr. Raven."

He bowed, but his gaze never left her laughing countenance. He said slowly, "It is a rare pleasure, Miss Weatherstone."

"And this is Miss Bidwell, Belle's companion," said Mrs. Weatherstone, supplying the last introduction.

Belle turned to Miss Bidwell. She hugged that lady, which obviously astonished Miss Bidwell very much. Belle shook her head, laughing at herself ruefully. "How very happy I am to see you, Miss Bidwell! You cannot imagine. My sister's letters mentioned you quite frequently. You must forgive my familiar behavior on that head."

"I am glad that I am at last able to make your acquaintance, Miss Cassandra," said Miss Bidwell with a pleased smile. "I must say that you are very much like your friendly letters."

"Am I?" Belle slid a mischievous glance in Cassandra's direction. "It is a pretty compliment."

"But quite true. Your letters are utterly fascinating. Biddy and I positively hang upon every word," said Cassandra, tongue in cheek. She was rewarded when her sister went into a peal of uninhibited laughter.

Mr. Weatherstone shook his head, an unreadable expression on his face. "You are in rare form tonight, Cassandra."

"But I am positively agog with excitement, Uncle Phineas! I have long wished to talk with my sister," said Belle with a flashing smile.

"Then why don't you two run along, my dear?" said

Mrs. Weatherstone, smiling. "You must have much to catch up on."

"Oh, indeed," said Belle.

Mrs. Weatherstone nodded civilly at Cassandra. "It is good to see you again, my dear."

"Thank you, ma'am," said Cassandra quietly. She ached to say more, to tell about everything she had experienced to the woman who had virtually been a mother to her. However, she knew quite well now that she could not do so. Instead, she submitted to Belle's insistent pressure on her arm and went off with her sister.

Chapter Twenty-two

Belle drew Cassandra aside to a window alcove where they could have a private conversation even though they were still in full view of the ballroom. Many sets of eyes followed the pair of young ladies, so incredibly alike in face and form, with only differences in hairstyle and gown to set them apart.

A loud buzz of astonished conversation arose, and several people approached Sir Thomas and the Weatherstones. The two young ladies paid no heed to the attention that they were generating. All of their focus was concentrated upon each other.

"I am so sorry not to have met you when I said that I would. The storm—" Belle shuddered.

"Yes, I know. It would have been marvelous indeed if even a duck was out in that," said Cassandra.

"Oh, Cassandra! I was so very astonished, but amazingly glad, too, to see you here tonight," whispered Belle. "However did you manage it?"

"It was not I, but Sir Thomas. He hatched a little plot all his own. He asked our grandfather to allow me—you!—to attend the soiree this evening. Naturally, Grandfather knew nothing about Uncle Phineas and Aunt Margaret being amongst the guests," said Cassandra, also speaking in low tones. She glanced about them to be certain that there was no one within hearing.

"Of course he didn't," agreed Belle. "He would never have allowed me—you!—to come if he had." Belle paused, a contemplative expression on her face. "However, Cassandra, there have been various comments from neighbors about how much I resemble Belle Weatherstone. One of them at least surely remarked on the resemblance to the servants. I am all but persuaded that Grandfather must have heard something through the grapevine."

"Then why did he not say anything to me? Why did he allow me to come tonight?" asked Cassandra.

"I don't know. That is what is so odd," said Belle, frowning. "He has never socialized to any great degree and has not been keen on my doing so, either. I don't understand."

"Perhaps I do, however. Grandfather was receptive because he wants you to spend time with Philip Raven. What better way than to send you off to a soiree in his escort?" said Cassandra. She gave a small smile. "Even if it meant allowing you to come face-to-face with Uncle Phineas and Aunt Margaret and me."

"I own, I was astonished to see Philip. I almost said something to him, but caught myself in the nick of time. I don't think that I have ever seen Biddy turned out half so well. And that gown—surely it is one of mine?" said Belle, inspecting her sister's attire with interest.

"Yes, Miss Bidwell had it refurbished so that I could make a presentable appearance in the exalted company tonight," said Cassandra. She touched the string of pearls about her neck. "And Grandfather presented these to me today. He wished you to wear them this evening. I felt so guilty about taking them, Belle!"

"My word! What is happening up at the Hall? Grandfather has never been so considerate or generous to me before. Is Grandfather in his right mind?" asked Belle, half seriously.

"Yes, I think so. At least, he must be if you do not find it strange that he is determined to promote a match between you and Philip Raven," said Cassandra.

"Is that what you meant when you said that Grandfather wanted me to spend time with Philip?" Belle's hazel eyes suddenly kindled. "Has he never let go of that nonsensical notion? Wait until I see him. I shall comb his hair for this, I swear."

"I *am* glad that you feel that way, Belle," said Cassandra, relieved to find that her instincts concerning her sister's preferences had been correct. "I have had a falling out with Grandfather over his matchmaking. I did not think that you wished to wed Philip Raven."

"Certainly not! Oh, if you have put an end to that nonsense, I shall be eternally grateful to you," exclaimed Belle. "But wait, didn't you just say that Grandfather wanted me—you!—to spend time with Philip?"

"Yes," sighed Cassandra. "You cannot imagine how awkward it all is. Grandfather is very stubborn, isn't he?"

"He is an obstinate old stick," said Belle roundly. "What did he say?"

"Let us say Grandfather struck a bargain with me—or you, actually."

"What sort of bargain?" asked Belle, eyeing her sister somewhat suspiciously.

"He asked that you spend time with his godson so that you can get to know each other better. I agreed to it, and so did Philip," said Cassandra.

"Philip? You call him 'Philip'?" asked Belle with surprise.

Cassandra felt heat steal into her face. "I couldn't very well hold him to a formal footing since we are supposed to have spent part of our childhood together, could I?"

"No, I suppose not," agreed Belle. "I am surprised, really, that Philip consented. He was never one to simply go along. He just refused to do whatever he didn't want to do in that quiet way of his and then there was no moving him."

"Perhaps that is what he did with Sir Marcus. Perhaps that is why our grandfather came up with this arrangement," said Cassandra thoughtfully. Of course it was a bit more complicated than that, in light of Mr. Raven's unusual matrimonial entanglement, but that was not a topic for discussion for the present.

"What do you mean?"

"Philip refused to fall in with Grandfather's wishes and offer for you," said Cassandra baldly. "I think now Grandfather hopes to soften Philip's position with his policy of having us live in one another's pocket."

"Well, it shan't matter how much time I spend with Philip, I would never change my mind," declared Belle.

"Why? Have you a dislike of him?" asked Cassandra curiously.

"Oh, no, of course not! Philip and I were the best of friends. It is just that I know we wouldn't suit. We are simply too different. We would drive each other mad within a year," said Belle cheerfully. "Besides, I haven't seen anything of the world or been courted or . . . or anything!"

"Why, what have you been doing all of this time in my shoes?" asked Cassandra teasingly. "It doesn't sound at all as though you have put the time to good use!"

Belle laughed. "Oh! I know what you are thinking. I *have* had such fun, and Uncle Phineas and Aunt Margaret are such dears, though they can be a bit too hovering, can they not? But a single house party is not at all like a London Season. And I do so long to have one!"

"I suggested to Grandfather that Uncle Phineas and Aunt Margaret could bring you out," said Cassandra. At her sister's surprised and hopeful expression, she shook her head. "No, he has not consented. In fact, that is why we had such an awful falling out. He made himself ill, too. He is quite all right now, though! I felt so guilty, however."

"Oh, you mustn't let Grandfather's crotchets bother you," said Belle, waving her hand. She smiled tremulously, a sudden sheen of moisture in her eyes. "Cassandra, it was so brave and . . . and unselfish of you to suggest such a wonderful thing!"

"I just thought what fun it would be to take London by storm together," said Cassandra with a laugh.

"Yes, wouldn't it just!" exclaimed Belle, her eyes gleaming with enthusiasm. "No one could hold a candle to us, could they? Only consider the stares that we are getting tonight!"

"Oh, here comes Philip Raven. And there is another gentleman bearing down on us as well," said Cassandra, somewhat dismayed.

She had not even begun to pour out all of her thoughts and concerns to her sister. There was their uncle's letter to Sir Marcus and their grandfather's reception to it. They needed to put their heads together, too, about what to do about bringing the masquerade to a close.

It had become abundantly clear to Cassandra that it would be more and more difficult to change places the longer it went on. Her aunt and uncle had not known her at once, and certainly she could not simply step into her own shoes at the house party at this late date and expect to know everyone in the house or what had gone on since her absence.

"I must say, I am favorably impressed by Philip. He has become quite a handsome fellow," said Belle, watching the gentleman's approach. "How odd! I would never have thought he would turn out half so well. He was a bit of a stick-in-the-mud, always talking about books or history."

"He still does. That is, talk about books and such," said Cassandra, diverted at once from her concerns.

"Does he really? How utterly boring. Didn't I say just a moment past that we would never suit?" said Belle, shaking her head.

With Mr. Raven's approach, Cassandra knew that their hurried *tête-à-tête* was over, and she feared that she might not have another chance that evening to say anything of importance. "Belle! I've got to talk to you again. About us," she said urgently.

"Yes." Belle looked round hastily. Seeing that both gentlemen were coming into earshot, she whispered, "Then meet me at the crofter's cottage tomorrow! At the same time!"

Cassandra nodded, before turning with a welcoming smile to Mr. Raven. "Philip, here is my sister. Wasn't I saying but a day or two ago that I wished that I had the opportunity to be with her? And here we are!"

"Indeed, it must be a very exciting reunion for both," said Mr. Raven, returning her smile. He regarded her keenly for a long moment, in such a way that made Cassandra instantly wonder what thoughts were going through his mind.

Mr. Raven did not enlighten her. He turned and greeted Belle politely. She inclined her head, shooting up a mischievous glance at him from under her lashes.

"I am quite glad to have made your acquaintance, Mr. Raven. I hope that I may claim close enough acquaintance to dispense with formalities?"

"Of course, Miss Weatherstone," said Mr. Raven with a smile and bow.

"Pray call me Cassandra. And of course I must call you 'Stubby,' mustn't I?" said Belle with a gurgling laugh and upswept glance.

Mr. Raven appeared stunned. Cassandra's eyes flew to his face, and she felt her heart thump. Belle had used the old childhood nickname that she had had for him, the very one that she had not known about until he had revealed it to her.

"Oh, I say! Miss Cassandra, pray introduce me," said the other gentleman, taking hold of Belle's hand while his gaze traveled with admiration and wonder to Cassandra's countenance.

Belle flashed a smile. "Benny, this is my sister, Miss Belle Weatherstone. She resides with our grandfather up at the Hall. Belle, pray allow me to present Mr. Benjamin Salter. He is Lady Salter's nephew."

Mr. Salter bowed to Cassandra. "I am humbly pleased to make your acquaintance, Miss Belle. I am in awe of the double portion of beauty and grace that we have been honored with this evening."

"Thank you," said Cassandra, somewhat taken aback by the gentleman's fulsome address.

The two gentlemen exchanged names and civil pleasantries. Then Belle was claimed by Mr. Salter for the upcoming dance, and she went off with only a single backward wave for Cassandra.

Mr. Raven turned to Cassandra, remarking gravely, "Your sister is quite memorable."

"Yes, she is very amusing and spirited," said Cassandra, looking after her sister with mingled fondness and dismay. Belle was playing her role without reflection or caution, she thought. She still couldn't believe that Belle had mentioned Mr. Raven's childhood nickname. She wondered how else her sister had been so reckless. Cassandra hoped that Mr. Raven had forgotten her sister's blunder, but she was quickly disabused of her frail optimism.

"I had not expected to hear that old nickname after all of these years," said Mr. Raven, looking intently at her. "Especially from a young lady whom I have just met."

Cassandra smiled quickly, a little nervously. "I am sorry. I suppose that I must have shared the nickname with Cassandra in one of my letters. It . . . it really doesn't fit you now, does it? I trust you are not offended."

"Not offended, no." Mr. Raven regarded her for another long moment. Then he seemed to dismiss the subject. "Miss Bidwell sent me in search of you, Belle. Would you care for some refreshment or would you like to dance?"

Cassandra looked at him in real surprise. "Why, Philip, are you asking me to dance?"

"I did promise to take faithful care of you," he said, smiling at her.

Cassandra dropped her gaze. She felt a glorious feeling of happiness rising up. "Yes, so you did. I should like to dance, I think."

"I am at your command," said Mr. Raven, and held out his hand to her.

She laid her gloved fingers in his hand, and his strong fingers closed over hers. Cassandra allowed Mr. Raven to lead her out onto the gleaming dance floor. A last set was just forming up for a country dance. Cassandra glanced around curiously. Her sister and Mr. Salter were in another set. Belle was talking animatedly with her partner, and Cassandra smiled. Her sister was obviously not the least shy in company despite her sheltered upbringing.

Cassandra could not help but notice that she kept meeting long stares from others around her and Mr. Raven. She responded to several civil greetings from complete strangers. "It seems that my face has given me an instant introduction to everyone," she murmured to her companion. "It is really quite awkward."

Mr. Raven laughed. "Yes; I can imagine that it does

feel very odd. However, I understand the curiosity your arrival has aroused. I was myself quite knocked for a loop when I saw Miss Cassandra Weatherstone."

The music struck up, and within moments the lively pattern of the dance separated them. When they came back together briefly, their hands linked, Mr. Raven remarked, "You are not very like your sister in personality."

Cassandra, turning with him in a full round, looked up at him in sharp surprise. "Am I not?"

Mr. Raven met her eyes, his own gray gaze keen. "No, I think not."

They separated, each turning to a new partner in the dance. Cassandra could not stop thinking about what had been said. She wondered what Mr. Raven had meant by his statement. She and Belle were so much alike. How could he say otherwise and so flatly? She was almost afraid to ask him, but her curiosity could not be denied.

When they came together again in the dance, she asked, "Philip, what did you mean when you said that my sister and I are not alike? We are twins, after all."

"True, but from the little I have seen of Miss Cassandra Weatherstone this evening, it leads me to believe that her nature is bolder than yours. Your manners are more refined and more gracious," said Mr. Raven. He smiled across their linked hands at her. "I approve of the difference, Belle."

Cassandra was left bereft of words. She could only respond with a faltering smile. She wanted to defend Belle, and herself, too. Belle was high-spirited, certainly, but she was not a hoyden. As for the rest, she should have been able to receive Mr. Raven's compliment as herself, not in her role as Belle! She was utterly confused and annoyed. Never had it seemed more irksome to be going by her sister's name.

The quick movements of the country dance brought them together again. "You are angered," murmured Mr. Raven, looking at her.

Cassandra instinctively shook her head, before realizing that it was true. "No . . . yes! I don't know what to say!"

"I perfectly understand," said Mr. Raven. "Your loyalty to your sister is admirable. I apologize if it seemed that I was insulting of her."

Cassandra threw an upward glance into his face as they passed each other in the round. She was still upset, though she was uncertain why it was so. "I ask that you not speak of it again, Philip."

He inclined his head, a faint smile on his face. "Of course."

Immediately after the country dance, Cassandra was introduced to another gentleman by Lady Kensing. Mr. Raven bowed and retreated, leaving Cassandra looking after him. She had only a moment to indulge her regret, however, for her new partner promptly whisked her onto the dance floor.

The gentleman at once said, "I say, Miss Weatherstone, I hope you don't mind my saying so, but you look extraordinarily like Miss Cassandra."

Cassandra stared at her new dance partner in surprise. Surely, he was not as dense as his observation seemed to indicate. "Yes, I know."

The gentleman shook his head. "Extraordinary! Utterly extraordinary."

Chapter Twenty-three

As the evening progressed, Cassandra had no more time for reflection. Her hand was solicited for every dance. She was practically mobbed by the gentlemen, both old and young. It seemed everyone was fascinated that there were two identical Miss Weatherstones, and neither she nor Belle were ever without a dance partner.

Cassandra noticed that Belle seemed to be on an easy footing with most of the guests, and she felt a mild twinge of envy that she could not abandon herself equally to the enjoyment of the evening. However, her nerves were constantly being fretted by the tension of sustaining her role.

Cassandra recognized some of the guests from her short time as part of the house party, but others she discovered to be Sir Thomas's neighbors. Naturally, alarm became her companion, for she felt put out of countenance when these personages claimed also to be neighbors of those residing at the Hall. Over and over again, Cassandra had to assume that she was supposed to share a common history with these people until something in their conversation proved otherwise.

Cassandra became profoundly relieved that Sir Marcus apparently had a reputation for being something of a recluse because none could claim more than a passing acquaintance with Miss Belle Weatherstone. Still, she could feel the strain beginning to take its toll. Never would she have believed that she would find herself placed in such awkward circumstances.

Her eyes once more sought out her sister, who was obviously enjoying herself, and Cassandra sighed. Cassandra felt that Belle had the easier part. After all, Belle didn't have to know anything about any of these people and could develop a relationship at her leisure.

Cassandra fielded innumerable questions about herself and Sir Marcus and the Hall in general. Cassandra found it difficult to believe how nosy some individuals could be. It was all solicited with a polite smile and civil manner, of course, but the crux of the questions was a rampant curiosity.

Cassandra might have felt completely beleaguered, except for the presence of Mr. Raven. He always seemed to appear at her elbow at the most crucial moments. Cassandra was fervently glad of his unobtrusive support. She wondered whether he had any idea how she was depending upon him.

Almost without exception, each person who spoke to Cassandra made some comment on how extraordinarily alike she and the other Miss Weatherstone were. Cassandra became quite tired of it, but all she could do was to smile and civilly agree.

Inevitably, there came an instance when Mr. Raven was absent. Cassandra was rapidly sinking before the onslaught of a particularly inquisitive lady when she was rescued by her uncle. "Belle, might I interest you in a lemon ice?" asked Mr. Weatherstone.

"Yes, please." Cassandra nodded to the lady and took her uncle's arm with gratitude. As they walked away in the direction of the refreshments, she said with heartfelt relief, "Thank you, sir."

Mr. Weatherstone chuckled as he glanced at her. "I observed that you were beginning to look a trifle hunted in Mrs. Webster's company. The lady can be quite overwhelming, as I well know. I have taken to ducking into the billiards room whenever I chance to see her coming down the stairs."

Cassandra gave a gurgle of laughter and looked up at her uncle with open affection. "I have not a doubt of it, sir."

There was a startled expression on Mr. Weatherstone's face as he continued to stare at her. A puzzled question seemed to form in his eyes, only to vanish. Then he smiled, quite warmly. "My dear niece, have I told you yet what a great pleasure it has been to me to meet you tonight?"

Cassandra was disconcerted. It had been so like her uncle to watch out for her, as he always had. She had forgotten, just for an instant, that he believed her to be her sister. It was dismaying to realize that he had come to her rescue, not out of affection, but because good breeding had demanded it.

She felt her throat constrict with sudden tears. "Th . . . thank you, Uncle Phineas. You can have no notion what it has meant to me to see you and Aunt Margaret. I . . . I wish . . ." Cassandra stopped, averting her face, afraid that if she said anything more that she would disgrace herself by bursting into tears.

Mr. Weatherstone obviously thought that he understood the source of her surge of emotion. He pressed her fingers in reassurance. "My dearest Belle. I, too, wish that we had been closer. I had hoped to bridge the breach between Sir Marcus and myself, but unfortunately that has not come about."

Cassandra at once looked up. She clasped both hands about his arm. "Oh, pray do not give up, sir," she said earnestly.

Mr. Weatherstone studied her face. "Does it mean that much to you?"

Cassandra nodded. "Oh, yes. I can't imagine losing everything that I have gained."

"You humble me, Belle. Very well, I shall set aside my pride for your sake and that of your sister. We must see what can be done," said Mr. Weatherstone.

At dinner, Cassandra was placed at the farthest end of the table from her sister, an attentive gentleman on either side of her.

She glanced the length of the table and saw that Mr. Raven was one of her sister's dinner partners. For some unfathomable reason, she felt her heart skip a beat. As she observed them, she could not help but be a little envious of Belle's apparent ability to engage in vivacious conversation with anyone she chanced to meet. Certainly Mr. Raven was listening to her with an intent look in his eyes, and he laughed more than once.

When it came time to leave, Cassandra was glad. She was exhausted. The evening had been a huge disappointment to her, and she had developed the headache from the tension of maintaining the masquerade in public. She wanted nothing so much at that moment than to have her own life back and to return to quiet Bath with her aunt and uncle.

It did not help matters that Miss Bidwell marveled over and over about the remarkable resemblance between the two sisters. "I don't believe that I have ever seen anything quite so amazing. Your gestures and your facial expressions were positively identical to each other. If you had been attired just alike, why, I believe that no one could have told you apart," said Miss Bidwell finally.

"An interesting observation, Miss Bidwell," murmured Mr. Raven.

Miss Bidwell's words had hit uncomfortably close to the truth. Cassandra at once felt the familiar sense of alarm. "Pray do stop going on about it, Biddy," she begged. "It is all I heard all night. 'Why, Miss Weatherstone, how much you look like your sister.'"

In the yellow gleam of the coach light, Miss Bidwell appeared surprised. "My dear Belle! I had no notion that it bothered you so. I am certain that I would not have mentioned it at all if I had but known."

"It was vexatious after a while, is all," said Cassandra lamely. She knew that she had sounded peevish so she reached out to squeeze her companion's hand. "I am sorry, Biddy. I never meant to snap at you. I am behaving badly. I have the headache, and it makes me short-tempered."

"My poor dear. I don't believe that you have ever suffered from the headache before in your life," said Miss Bidwell with instant sympathy.

Cassandra sighed. Once again she had done something out of character. She did not reply. She was simply too tired to try to explain away the mistake. She leaned her head back against the squabs, hoping that the conversation was over.

"I hope that you are feeling better tomorrow, Belle.

I thought it might be a good day for a ride," remarked Mr. Raven.

Alarm again instantly shot through Cassandra, and her entire body tensed. She was supposed to meet with her sister at the crofter's cottage. "No! I—" She bit back what else she was going to say, flabbergasted at how easily self-betrayal had nearly undone her.

"What were you going to say, Belle?" asked Mr. Raven.

"Nothing. Nothing at all," said Cassandra. "I simply don't wish to discuss the morrow just now."

"Just as you wish," said Mr. Raven quietly.

The remainder of the drive back to the Hall was silent. Cassandra bade her companions a swift good night and hurried up to her bedroom. She took off the string of valuable pearls at once and put them away, feeling as though she never wanted to gaze on them again. The beautiful pearls had become a symbol of her entrapment in her sister's life.

Cassandra was struggling with her gown when a knock sounded on the door and Miss Bidwell entered.

"Here you are, my dear. I have mixed up one of my headache powders for you to drink. It will enable you to sleep," said Miss Bidwell, setting the glass down on the bedside table. She came over to help with the buttons on Cassandra's gown. "Let me do this. You are all thumbs tonight, Belle."

"Thank you, Biddy." Cassandra stood still while the elderly lady expertly undid the buttons and she was at last able to step out of the gown. She felt that she had to say something to explain herself. "I don't know what is wrong with me. I can't seem to think straight tonight."

"Is it any wonder? I know that it was quite a shock for me to see Mr. and Mrs. Weatherstone and Cassandra, so I may well imagine how you were affected," said Miss Bidwell.

Cassandra forbore to tell her companion that she had had previous knowledge of their attendance. "I don't think it was that, really. I think it was just being in the same room with my sister after all of these years and having everyone staring at us so and whispering about us." Part of the distress that had so tangled her emotions and thoughts boiled over. "Oh, Biddy, I disliked it immensely. I felt as though we were some sort of freak show!"

"I do not find that surprising in the least." Miss Bidwell helped Cassandra into bed, smoothed the covers, then handed the glass to her. "You and your sister should have been raised together. Then there would not be occasion for such rude curiosity as you were made to suffer tonight. Oh, it is true you would still have garnered interest. However, on the whole, people would have been used to seeing you together. And you and your sister would have been immune to the looks and comments by the time that you entered society."

"Yes, I suppose that is true," said Cassandra with a sigh. It was really of little help to her to think about the might-have-been, but she knew that Miss Bidwell was doing her best to comfort her.

On the thought, Cassandra obediently drank the potion. She grimaced at the taste as she handed back the glass. "That is horrible, stuff, Biddy."

"Be glad that your constitution does not require you to take it very often," said Miss Bidwell. She bent to blow out the candle and then went to the door. "Good night, my dear."

"Good night, dear Biddy."

Twenty-four

Early in the morning, Sir Marcus summoned his granddaughter. Cassandra knew that he would naturally wish to be told everything about the soiree. Anticipating her grandfather's interest, and feeling that there could be no better time to confront him, Cassandra slipped the letter written by her uncle into her pocket before she entered her grandfather's rooms.

Cassandra greeted her grandfather with a kiss on his heavily lined cheek. She greeted him cheerfully. "Good morning, sir. I trust that you are feeling well this morning?"

Sir Marcus waved aside her solicitude. "I am as well as can be expected." He was propped up in a sitting position against several pillows. "Come sit down in the chair beside me, Belle."

Cassandra obeyed. She thought that he appeared to be in better health than he had in some time, though his dressing gown almost seemed to swallow his frail frame. She was encouraged that she had indeed chosen the proper time to bring to his attention the contents of the letter from her uncle.

"Did you enjoy yourself yesterday evening, Belle? Was it as grand as you thought it would be?" asked Sir Marcus

"The evening met all of my expectations and exceeded them," said Cassandra, quite truthfully. She would not confide in her grandfather that she was referring more to her acute disappointment than to any pleasure that she had taken in the evening. That information would not at all suit her purposes, as long as she remained in her role as Belle.

Sir Marcus gave a graveled chuckle. "Aye, I imagine that your eyes nearly popped from your head as you craned your neck to see everything. You are unused to being amongst such giddy entertainments. I trust that you behaved yourself as a proper lady."

"I couldn't have been more proper, sir," assured Cassandra with an understanding smile.

"I shall consult with Miss Bidwell to be completely reassured on that head," said Sir Marcus, chuckling again. "But come, tell me all about it. I trust that Philip made an adequate escort. He should have, after spending these years past in Wellington's army. I have heard that the officers are a polished lot when doing the pretty in company."

"Philip was quite attentive, Grandfather," said Cassandra. She added candidly, remembering, "In fact, I do not know that I would have fared half so well without his support."

Sir Marcus looked at her from under his brows, mild surprise in his expression. "I am glad to hear it. I wish you and Philip to come to like each other very well, Belle."

"I know you do, Grandfather. However, you must know that your hopes of a betrothal between us are slim, at best," said Cassandra, bracing herself mentally for her grandfather's displeasure. "If there was nothing else standing against it, there is still the small matter of his marriage."

Open astonishment crossed Sir Marcus's face, before his expression turned bland. He plucked absently at a loose thread in his coverlet. "Told you about that, did he? I wonder why."

"Perhaps because he wished everything to be perfectly open and aboveboard between us," suggested Cassandra.

Sir Marcus snorted and left off fussing with the coverlet. His jaws worked with his irritation. "It was a foolish thing to do. How are you to fall in love with the man knowing that he is wed, I should like to know? What was Philip thinking?"

"I imagine that he was thinking it was an impossible situation," said Cassandra dryly.

"Nonsense! He'll be free soon enough, I'll warrant. I have friends in strategic places. I wrote them on his behalf. Philip shall not have to languish forever," said Sir Marcus staunchly.

Cassandra shook her head. "My dear sir, can you not see that it does not matter? I have not changed my mind, nor shall I. Indeed, I have come across something that gives me hope that I shall be able to realize at least one of my dreams."

"What is that? What are you talking about, girl? I can't make heads or tails of it," said Sir Marcus with impatience.

"Just this, sir." Cassandra withdrew the letter from her pocket and unfolded it. She did not give the creased sheet to her grandfather, but held it up where he could see it. "I came across this in your desk when I was searching for your snuff canister. It is a letter from my uncle, in which he civilly requests that my sister and I be allowed to meet with each other. He hints that he would like to foot a London Season for—"

"Enough! Enough, I say! I'll not hear another word," exclaimed Sir Marcus, throwing up an authoritative blue-veined hand. "I have told you already what my position is concerning this matter, Belle. I'll not have it brought up again."

"I am sorry for it, sir. Truly I am. But you must see that I cannot let it rest. You told me that you knew no one to sponsor me. That is not true, Grandfather. My uncle and aunt will be glad to step in, I know it. And this is what I wish for more than anything else," said Cassandra.

"Your wishes in this matter are unimportant, Belle," said Sir Marcus angrily. "It is what I wish that will be done."

"No, sir, that is not the case." Cassandra folded the letter back up and slipped it into her pocket. She stood up. "If you will not consent, I shall myself petition my uncle and aunt to take me on. Also, I shall tell Philip at once that I reject any offer that he may ever make to me. And that will not suit you at all, will it?"

"I shall not have you defy me in this fashion, Belle!" thundered Sir Marcus. His face had reddened, and he was breathing rather quickly. His long, skinny fingers clenched and unclenched on the brocaded coverlet.

Cassandra's heart melted. "I am sorry, Grandfather, I truly am. I hope that you do not make yourself ill over this again."

His wintry eyes blazing, Sir Marcus hurled back her concern. "Be damned to you!"

"There is nothing more to be said," said Cassandra quietly. She tried not to feel hurt by her grandfather's rejection, but it was extremely difficult to keep her perspective. She was doing this for her sister. Cassandra started to leave the bedroom, then turned back to look straight into her grandfather's angered red face. "By the by, Uncle Phineas and Aunt Margaret and my sister are amongst Sir Thomas's guests. I saw them all last night, and they were very well disposed toward me. They shall receive me, Grandfather, I know it."

"Belle! Don't dare to leave this house! Damn that interfering physician! *Belle!*"

Ignoring her grandfather's tantrum, Cassandra let herself out of the room. When she passed the valet, Weems threw her a reproachful glance as he scurried into the bedroom in answer to his master's agitated shouts.

Cassandra went directly downstairs to the drawing room, where she was certain she would find Mr. Raven. She was shaking. Tears had spilled over onto her face, and she wiped them hastily away before pushing open the door. She entered hurriedly. "Philip."

Mr. Raven rose upon her entrance, at once thrusting aside the newspapers when he saw her face. "Belle! What is wrong? What has happened?" He strode over to her, his expression one of deep concern.

As he reached her, Cassandra gave her hands to him. "My very dear friend, I know that we are to ride together this morning, but will you excuse me? I have had a most unpleasant interview with my grandfather and I should like to be alone for a while."

"But of course." Though Mr. Raven gave his consent readily, he retained hold of her hands. "Can you tell me what has passed between you and Sir Marcus? Perhaps I can do something to help."

Cassandra shook her head and smiled tremulously. "There is nothing that you can do. It was an old argument, and I very much fear that it has turned out little better than before. However, I do thank you for your solicitude. Now I must go."

"Belle." Mr. Raven tightened his fingers about her hands. He said with quiet intensity, "You must know that I would do anything for you."

Cassandra looked up quickly, startled. What she saw in his expression sent heat surging into her face.

Mr. Raven took her other hand and so held her, looking down at her with a close-held mouth. His gray eyes were fixed on her face. "If I were free . . . If I could speak, then—" he compressed his lips, as though biting back the words.

Cassandra thought she knew what he would say if he could, and her heart soared. "Philip. Dear Philip."

Slowly, his gaze still fastened on her face, Mr. Raven raised first one hand to his lips and then the other. The warmth of his kisses pressed against her skin sent her pulses racing, and Cassandra trembled. She stared up into his face, enmeshed by the blaze of passion that flared in his gray eyes.

A blinding revelation struck her with such force that she audibly gasped. "I . . . I must go!" She tugged free and hurried from the room.

As she ran upstairs to her bedroom and slammed the door behind her, Cassandra could think of nothing else but that incredible and unexpected ardency in Mr. Raven's eyes. She pressed her palms against her hot cheeks. "Oh, what have I done? What have I done?"

All without knowing, she had fallen in love with Philip Raven. If she had truly seen what she thought she had in his gray eyes, then he was in a fair way to being in love with her, as well.

"Not with me! With Belle!" cried Cassandra despairingly.

She thought she could not stand it a moment longer. She was to meet Belle that very hour. She would change places with her sister at once.

Cassandra ripped off her day gown and attired herself hurriedly in her riding habit and boots. She left the bedroom and ran down the backstairs, emerging from the manor without anyone being the wiser.

She strode quickly across the yard out to the stables. When the groom came up to her, she said, "Young John, I shan't require your escort this morning. Just bring me Rolly."

"The master ordered that I accompany ye, miss," said the groom. He peered at her. "Howsomever, it may be that ye are wishful of meeting Miss Belle?"

Cassandra stared at the old groom, standing very still. "How . . . what are you talking about?" she said sharply.

"I've known almost from the beginning, miss. Rolly told me," said Young John simply.

Cassandra sighed in surrender. "I was afraid of that. Rolly doesn't love me as he does her. Yes, Young John, I am supposed to meet my sister at the old crofter's cottage."

"Miss, is she all right?" asked Young John hesitantly.

"She is perfectly well. She is pretending to be me at Sir Thomas's house party," said Cassandra.

The groom nodded, satisfied. "I'll be bringing Rolly out to ye, miss."

Within minutes, Cassandra was cantering alone away from the manor. A fine drizzle began to blow in gusts across the dead fields. Cassandra was made uncomfortable by it as her clothing became damp, but she did not turn back.

When she topped the rise overlooking the shadow valley, she saw a chestnut horse being led into the dark stable. She breathed a sigh of relief. Belle had already arrived.

Cassandra spurred her mount forward and rode down to the stable. "Belle!"

Her sister appeared at the entrance. "Be quick, Cassandra! You will be soaked before you know it."

Cassandra slid off of the gelding. She landed in a

muddy puddle with a small splash that splattered her skirt. "Yes, I know. We shall both be the worse for this outing, I daresay."

"Not I! I am never ill," declared Belle, reaching out to take the gelding's reins from her. "Oh, Rolly, I have missed you so." The gelding whickered and nudged against her with his soft nose. Belle laughed and reached into her pocket. "Yes, I have brought you a carrot. Here you are, sir!"

Cassandra tried to shake the folds out of her heavy damp skirts. Her jacket felt clammy against her skin, and through it she could feel the chill in the air. But none of her physical discomforts were as important as the agitation that exercised her mind. "Belle, we must change places at once."

Belle, holding the carrot for the gelding, looked over at her in surprise. "What . . . now?"

"Yes," said Cassandra firmly.

"But, Cassandra, you can't have considered. We can't simply trade clothing and ride away, not now. Why, you haven't the least notion what friendships I have formed or whom I have discussed any number of things with," said Belle reasonably. She brushed her hands together. "It would be better to wait until the house party is over. Indeed, that is quite what I had in mind to tell you last night, but I did not have the opportunity."

Cassandra's heart sank, and along with it her spirits. Belle was expressing precisely what she had begun to realize at the soiree. As she had watched her sister moving amongst Sir Thomas's other guests, Cassandra had seen how familiar Belle's standing was with most of them. It would not be an easy task to fit into the house party again; in fact, she knew that it would be impossible to do so. Belle had been a guest for too long for there not to be some comment if Miss Weatherstone were to suddenly become forgetful of names and conversations.

Yet Cassandra felt pressed to convince her sister that it had to be done. "Belle, there are reasons. I cannot remain at the Hall. Pray believe me when I say that I cannot do it any longer."

"Why, what is this? Cassandra, you are shaking like a

leaf. What is wrong?" asked Belle in quick concern, having taken her sister's hands in her own.

Cassandra swallowed. "Belle, I . . . I've had a terrible fight with Grandfather again. I found a letter from Uncle Phineas asking him to allow us to be together. Grandfather refused his request, and in the process rejected the possibility of Uncle Phineas and Aunt Margaret bringing you out for a Season along with me."

Her sister's fingers tightened painfully around Cassandra's hands, then eased. "I see. It is little more than one could expect from Grandfather, however," said Belle in a harder voice than usual.

"I am sorry, Belle. I have tried," said Cassandra, blinking back tears.

Belle was searching Cassandra's face. "But that is not what has truly overset you, is it? Tell me the truth, Cassandra."

Cassandra shook her head, almost unable to keep her countenance. "Oh, don't ask me. Pray don't ask me."

Finally, as Belle continued to press her, Cassandra admitted in a low, despairing voice, "I've fallen in love with Philip!"

Chapter Twenty-five

Belle stared at her incredulously. "You've fallen in love with Philip?"

Cassandra gave a small hiccoughing laugh. "Is it so incomprehensible?"

"Oh, no! Of course not," said Belle hastily. "It is just that—"

"I know! You and Philip would not suit. But that doesn't mean that he and I would not," said Cassandra, a trifle crossly.

"Quite true. Indeed, now that I reflect upon it, you and Philip are obviously made for each other," said Belle with a quick smile. "I couldn't be more delighted, Cassandra. You must be ecstatically happy."

Cassandra groaned and shook her head. She tightened her hold on her sister's hands. "Oh, Belle. You don't understand at all!"

Puzzlement crossed Belle's face. "But this is marvelous news, Cassandra! I don't understand why—"

Cassandra tore free her hands. "But don't you see? I've been you all of these several weeks! How am I to tell him about what we've done? What can I say that will not sound totally reprehensible?"

"Oh." Belle studied her sister. "You haven't said so, but you think that Philip cares for you, too."

Cassandra wiped her eyes, angry at herself for crying. "Yes. At least, I suspect that he does. He has never said anything. But it's the way that he looks at me sometimes. Some of the things he says have made me think that—" She stopped, biting her lip. "Belle, if Philip is in love, he thinks it is with you."

Belle stepped back a pace, shaking her head. "Not with me, I assure you."

"Well, no," admitted Cassandra. "But he thinks that I'm you, so it comes down to the same thing."

"Oh, my. It is rather a coil," said Belle, frowning.

Cassandra laughed a little hysterically. "Do you think so?"

Her sister looked at her reproachfully. "Cassandra, you really must get hold of yourself. One could believe you to be the center of a Cheltonham tragedy."

Cassandra started to retort, before honesty compelled her to take a long, close look at herself. She sighed, brushing her gloved fingers across her forehead. She had the beginnings of a headache again. "I am sorry, Belle. It is just that I don't know what is to be done."

"And so you wish to run away." Belle nodded. "Perfectly understandable. But that is just what you must not do. You shall have to tell Philip, of course. Perhaps I should pen a note to him, too. I can have one of the grooms run it over to you at the Hall, perhaps in the guise of an invitation to visit me—you!—in Bath." She rolled her eyes. "I tell you frankly, Cassandra, I never expected this masquerade to be so complicated. There are times that I don't know who I really am."

"I completely understand," said Cassandra with heartfelt agreement. She sneezed violently.

"Bless you," said Belle absently. "Now, how to word it? I hope that Philip will understand why we felt that we had to do this. I trust that he will not be offended at your deceiving him."

"My deceiving him! What about you, I should like to know? I haven't been in this all by myself," said Cassandra with some heat.

"Well, of course you haven't. However, it is you who are in love with Philip, and he with you. I suspect that my part in this will be far less important to him than your own," said Belle.

Cassandra was deflated. "You are right, of course. Oh, Belle! What if he is angry with me—with us? What if it gives him a complete disgust of me? What will I do then?"

"Let's not think about those things unless they happen," begged Belle. "What we must concentrate upon is
bringing Philip up to scratch so that he will make you
an offer."

"An offer?" Cassandra stared at her sister. Suddenly,
the full weight of her situation came over her. She felt
the blood drain from her face. "Belle—" She swallowed.
"Belle, Philip is already married!"

Belle stared at her in momentary incomprehension.
Then she demanded, "What! What do you mean that
Philip is married?"

"Just that," said Cassandra simply.

"I don't believe it," exclaimed Belle.

"But it is true. It happened in the war." Cassandra
sighed, brushing the back of her hand across her forehead. "I suppose that I must tell you everything."

"I should say so," said Belle, putting her hands on
her hips.

Cassandra started in a stumbling fashion to relate
what Philip Raven had told her.

When Belle had heard Cassandra out, she could only
shake her head in disgust. "What a ninny. What an abso-
lute ninny Stubby has been."

"You mustn't call him that. He instantly picked up on
your old nickname for him at the soiree," said Cassandra
quickly. "I thought he might tumble to the truth about
us at any second."

"Well, perhaps it would have been for the best," said
Belle flatly.

"You can't have thought it out, Belle. Imagine the
talk! The scandal—poor Uncle Phineas and Aunt Margaret," said Cassandra.

Her sister waved her hand and made a frustrated
noise. "Oh, I know that we would have created a scandal
if anyone had realized we were masquerading as each
other yesterday evening. However, it would certainly
have gotten us over the one hurdle."

"Yes, I shall still have to talk to Philip," said Cassandra, accepting it finally. She shivered and wrapped her
arms around herself. "I know that I shan't enjoy it."

"Only an idiot would think otherwise," said Belle

roundly. She took a turn about the stable. "I don't know what can be done about the other, Cassandra. About Philip's marriage, I mean."

"Oh, what's to be done except to wait? But at least, if Philip isn't completely put off by my confession, he and I can wait together," said Cassandra.

"What about coming-out for the Season? What about Aunt Margaret's plans for you?" asked Belle curiously, turning to stare intently at her sister.

Cassandra shook her head. She wrung her hands in an unconscious gesture of indecision. "I don't know. I can't say just now."

"Cassandra, how long are you willing to wait?" asked Belle intently. "I've heard that it sometimes takes years for an appeal to be heard in Rome."

Cassandra looked at her sister. She didn't have an answer. Her heart urged her to say that she would wait forever, if that was what it took. Her head said otherwise. It wasn't practical to wait forever. She could decline into an old maid and be a demand on her uncle's bounty for the remainder of her life.

However, Cassandra could not imagine wedding anyone else but Philip Raven. She could not go with logic, not when her heart hurt at the very thought of losing him. "I want Philip," she whispered.

"Oh, Cassandra! I don't know what to say. I am so sorry."

Belle swooped over to Cassandra and hugged her. There were tears in her own eyes. "I . . . I'll write the note explaining everything and send it over to the Hall as soon as I may. I hope that will make all right with Philip."

"What about our grandfather? Do you wish me to say anything to him?" asked Cassandra, dashing her hand across her eyes to wipe away the tears. The pounding in her head was becoming vicious.

Belle shook her head. "No, not just yet. We can't trade places again until the house party is over, which will be in another fortnight. I shall meet you here then."

"Yes."

Belle turned quickly away and went to her mount.

Cassandra mutely watched her sister untie the reins. There seemed to be nothing more to be said.

Before leading the chestnut out into the sheeting gray rain, Belle looked back. "Cassandra, it will be all right. You'll see. Everything will work out just as it is supposed to, I promise."

Cassandra nodded, a smile wavering over her lips. She watched her sister disappear into the weather. Then she gathered the reins to her own mount. The gelding followed her obediently out into the rain and stood stoically while she mounted from the standing block behind the crofter's cottage.

Icy water trickled down Cassandra's face and inside her cravat. She gathered the leathers and turned the gelding. She was fast becoming soaked. It would be a most unpleasant ride back to the Hall, she thought dimly.

By the time that Cassandra rode into the stable yard, she could scarcely think or see. The din in her head was monstrous loud, and the blinding, pulsating lights that interfered with her sight hurt her eyes. She practically fell off of the gelding and stumbled over the long hem of her skirt. The aged groom caught her before she actually fell forward onto her knees.

"Miss! Are ye hurt? Were ye thrown?"

Cassandra heard the alarm in the old groom's voice. She clutched his arm for support. Her legs didn't seem to want to bear her weight. "It . . . it is all right, Young John," she murmured, and felt herself reeling into a darkening swoon.

It seemed but a moment before Cassandra felt herself swung up into a powerful embrace. A dearly familiar voice whipcracked over her head. "The door, Young John!" There was the sensation of movement before rain was striking her face. With an inarticulate protest she hid her face against a strong shoulder, the damp fabric of a man's coat rubbing against her cheek.

She recalled nothing else until she felt herself lowered onto a bed. Cassandra tried to rouse herself, pushing up on her elbow. "What—?" She looked up, but she could make out nothing through the pounding but some moving shadows. She put a hand to her pounding temple. "Oh, my head."

"The maid and I will take care of her now, Philip, rest assured." A door closed, and there was the rustling of skirts.

Cassandra fell back against the soft pillow. She knew that voice. She puzzled over it until she had it. "Biddy," she sighed.

"Yes, I'm right here, dear Belle. We are going to get you out of those wet things now."

"My head, Biddy. It hurts so."

"I'll give you a powder in just a few moments, my dear."

Later, Cassandra would recall nothing more than a brief struggle as her soaked riding habit was removed before she was allowed to rest, warm and dry in her nightclothes. A horrid-tasting draft was poured down her throat. Then she fell back down in the black well and knew nothing more.

Cassandra was dreaming luridly. She was caught fast. She had been thrown by Rolly into a deep ditch. She had to climb out. It was raining and the water was rising. She had to get out.

Half conscious, Cassandra mumbled feverishly. There was light somewhere. It hurt her eyes, and she squeezed her lids shut, uttering an incoherent protest. Suddenly, she sensed that she was not alone. She tried to wake up. She knew that she was not awake. She had been dreaming. Perhaps she was still dreaming. The bed was going around and around. She had to hold it still. She clutched the bedclothes, trying to stop the awful spinning.

Sir Marcus's voice rolled over her in deeply disturbed tones. "I don't mind telling you, Philip, that I am worried. It is unlike Belle to be ill. I've never known her to be sick a day in her life."

Mr. Raven's calm voice answered. "Sir, this is not Belle."

Cassandra stopped struggling against the lethargy that threatened to overcome her. Acute dismay shot through her. He knew, and he probably hated her. She started to tremble.

The dark well was opening up beneath her again, and Cassandra did not try to stop herself from falling. She allowed herself to spiral once more into unconsciousness, thankful for her escape.

Chapter Twenty-six

Cassandra wakened, her head clear. She moved it experimentally. There was no more pain, thankfully.

"Oh, miss! You're awake! I'll run and get Miss Bidwell!"

Cassandra turned her head and saw the maid's flapping skirts disappearing through the door of her bedroom. The door was left ajar. She was puzzled why the maid had been in her room. Then she remembered having been ill. She had begun remembering other things, too, when the door was thrust fully open.

Cassandra looked across the space of the bedroom apprehensively to meet Miss Bidwell's inscrutable gaze. The elderly lady advanced toward the canopied bed, her hands folded before her. Cassandra cleared her throat. "Biddy, I—"

"There is no need for you to say anything, Miss Cassandra," said Miss Bidwell. She bent to place a cool palm on Cassandra's forehead. "The fever has broken, just as I had hoped last night that it would. You gave us quite a scare, my dear."

Cassandra's heart had plummeted upon being addressed by her rightful name. "Does everyone know? Who I am, I mean?"

"Indeed we do." Miss Bidwell's expression was noncommittal. "It was a thoughtless and reprehensible trick that you and your sister have played. However, it is over now, I am happy to say."

Cassandra felt tears pricking her eyes. After coming to know and love her sister's companion, it hurt unbearably to be treated with such civil indifference. She felt that she deserved it, though. "I am sorry, Biddy. It . . .

it wasn't meant to drag on as it did. I simply wished to meet my grandfather and—" The tears overflowed at the unresponsive expression on Miss Bidwell's face.

Miss Bidwell's countenance at once underwent transformation. She sat down on the bed and gathered the younger woman into her arms. "There, there, my dear! Everything is all right. You've done wrong, though I suspect that this deception was not entirely to your liking. Indeed, Belle has staunchly maintained that it was all her doing and that you wanted no part of it in the beginning."

"I am so sorry, Biddy! Pray forgive me," sobbed Cassandra.

"Dear Cassandra, you mustn't go on so. You'll make yourself ill again. And I don't think that your family could endure much more upset just now," said Miss Bidwell. "Your aunt and uncle are below-stairs at this moment, and they are very anxious to have some word of you."

Cassandra drew back, amazed. "Uncle Phineas and Aunt Margaret are here—in this house?"

"Yes, you cannot be any more astonished than I am," said Miss Bidwell. "Sir Marcus had little choice but to consent to their coming, however, when Mr. Weatherstone demanded that he and his wife be allowed access to their daughter." She suddenly chuckled. "Such a to-do as you cannot imagine, Cassandra. And Belle in the middle of it, giving Sir Marcus a royal rakedown. You and your sister accomplished between you what was previously impossible. All of the family is now under one roof."

"Oh, my goodness." Cassandra could scarcely believe what she was hearing. "And . . . and no one has murdered anyone yet?"

Miss Bidwell laughed. "The atmosphere is a trifle uncomfortable, but the civilities predominate."

Cassandra said tentatively, "I have always wondered why my grandfather and my uncle and aunt had such enmity built between them. Can you not relieve my curiosity, Biddy, for I suspect that there is little that you do not know about this family."

Miss Bidwell nodded. "That is very true. Very well! I shall tell you only what is most important. It is my understanding that Sir Marcus arranged a very advantageous marriage for his son. What he did not know was that Phineas had already betrothed himself to your aunt. When Sir Marcus learned of it, he demanded that Phineas renounce your aunt and wed the lady whom he had chosen. Phineas refused, and so Sir Marcus cast him out of the house. They did not speak for years, and only then when you and Belle had to be taken in."

Cassandra shook her head disbelievingly. "What an idiotic turn of affairs! And my grandfather tried to set up the same scheme with Belle and Mr. Raven."

"Yes, one would think that such a harsh lesson would prove a cure for tyranny," remarked Miss Bidwell.

The maid returned, carrying a large brass urn of water. Two footmen followed her, both carrying larger urns filled with hot water. The servants poured the water into the hipbath that was situated in front of the fireplace. Steam rose as the water splashed against the cool metal. A screen had been set behind the hipbath so that the warmth from the fire was reflected back onto the hipbath.

The footmen left the bedroom, but the maid approached the bed. " 'Tis ready, Miss Bidwell."

Miss Bidwell rose. "Now, Cassandra, Meg and I will help you become presentable. There are several individuals who will wish to visit with you once it becomes known that you are awake at last."

"I should like a bath. Have I been ill long?" asked Cassandra, levering herself up against the pillows. She was astonished at her lack of strength.

Miss Bidwell helped her to get up out of the bed and supported her as she replied, "For several days. When Sir Thomas examined you, he gave it as his opinion that you had contracted an inflammation of the lungs. We were all quite concerned."

Cassandra was helped into the brass hipbath, and after she had bathed and the maid had washed her hair, she was given a clean nightgown and her robe. Miss Bidwell directed Cassandra to sit down on a stool in front of the fire and toweled and brushed out her hair until it was dry. While they were thus occupied, the maid changed the clammy bed linens and ran a warming pan over the sheets.

Miss Bidwell put Cassandra back to bed. The clean linens felt wonderful, but Cassandra felt that she should not languish in bed in the middle of the day, especially when everyone wanted to see her. "I really wish to get up, Biddy," she said.

"No, my dear. We must first see that you regain your former strength," said Miss Bidwell firmly. "Meg will bring up a nice bowl of broth. You may begin with that. No, Cassandra, I will have no more nonsense out of you. I will go downstairs now and send up Mr. and Mrs. Weatherstone."

Cassandra subsided, a wry smile on her lips. She wondered if her sister had been so easy for Miss Bidwell to cow as she had been. She thought about all that had happened during her masquerade and in some ways felt regret that it had come to an end. It had been stimulating to act her sister's part, to say the least. However, her strongest feeling was one of relief. Cassandra would be very glad to step back into her own shoes.

Her reflections were cut short when the bedroom door opened and her aunt and uncle entered. "Uncle Phineas! Aunt Margaret!" Cassandra held out her arms and with a glad cry Mrs. Weatherstone ran straight over to her. They embraced, both beginning to cry.

"I am so, so very happy to be with you again," exclaimed Cassandra tearfully.

"We are just as glad to have you back," said Mrs. Weatherstone, settling down beside Cassandra on the bed.

Mr. Weatherstone had been waiting for his turn, and he bent to hug Cassandra. "My very dear girl. What a turn you've given us. I am thankful to see you looking so much better. When we were last in this room, I—" He stopped, clearing his throat.

"I am sorry, Uncle Phineas," said Cassandra softly.

Mr. Weatherstone straightened, and he looked down at Cassandra with a stern expression. "We shall talk about this disgraceful start of yours and Belle's when you are feeling more the thing."

"Yes, sir."

"It was you at the soiree, pretending to be Belle?" asked Mrs. Weatherstone, clasping Cassandra's hand.

"Yes, and it was the most exceedingly uncomfortable night of my life," said Cassandra candidly.

"I can well imagine that it was," said Mr. Weatherstone, and laughed.

The door opened and the maid entered, bearing a dinner tray. "Begging your pardon, but I've brought Miss Cassandra's broth."

Mr. Weatherstone nodded. "Very well. We shall leave you for now, Cassandra. We don't wish to tire you." Mrs. Weatherstone reluctantly rose to her feet.

"No! Please stay. I . . . I have missed you so," said Cassandra, holding out a hand to each of them.

Mrs. Weatherstone glanced at her husband, who smiled. She sat down again. "Well, only if you promise to drink your broth, Cassandra. Here, I shall hold the bowl for you."

Mr. Weatherstone sat down in the chair beside the bed.

While Cassandra was consuming the broth, Sir Marcus entered the bedroom on the arm of his valet. He stopped upon seeing his son and daughter-in-law. "I shall come back," he growled.

"Here is a chair, sir," said Mr. Weatherstone, at once getting up to pull another chair close to the bed.

Sir Marcus grunted and nodded his thanks. He allowed the valet to settle him into the wing chair before he turned to Cassandra and demanded, "What do you mean by impersonating my granddaughter?"

"I only wished to know you, sir," said Cassandra simply.

Sir Marcus tried to hide his pleasure at her answer. He scowled, drawing his brows low over his winter-blue eyes. "Humph. Well, I suppose I must forgive you. And Belle, too. I've already given her a thundering scold, and she declares that she is repentant."

"As I am, sir," said Cassandra. She had finished the

broth, and her aunt took away the bowl, to set it aside on the night table. Cassandra was surprised at how tired she felt and how filling the broth had been.

"We shall see," said Sir Marcus. He gave a grim smile. "There is one other that deserves your apologies, granddaughter. With Phineas's permission, I shall send him in."

Cassandra at once knew of whom her grandfather was speaking. She was dismayed. It had been difficult to face everyone else, but she feared it would be much more difficult to own up to her sins to Mr. Philip Raven. "Pray—"

"I spoke with Mr. Raven at some length during our mutual vigil for you, Cassandra. I am impressed with the young gentleman's character and good sense. I believe that you do owe the gentleman the courtesy of a few words," said Mr. Weatherstone.

Sir Marcus nodded to the valet, and Weems went to the bedroom door. Opening it, the valet spoke quietly, and then he stepped back to allow Mr. Raven to come into the bedroom.

"Good afternoon, Miss Weatherstone," said Mr. Raven politely. His keen gaze was fixed upon her face.

"Mr. Raven," faltered Cassandra.

Mr. Weatherstone looked from one to the other and smiled slightly. "Come Margaret. I believe that we should return below-stairs."

"Yes, Miss Bidwell mentioned that she wished to discuss a certain matter with me when we had finished visiting with Cassandra," said Mrs. Weatherstone, rising. She looked at Sir Marcus and remarked, "I believe that it has something to do with our bringing Belle out this Season."

Sir Marcus at once snapped, "What? Why wasn't I consulted? I have something to say to the purpose, Mrs. Weatherstone!"

Mr. and Mrs. Weatherstone were already at the door. Mrs. Weatherstone paused to glance over her shoulder at her father-in-law. "Then do, pray, come downstairs and join our discussion, Sir Marcus," she said cordially.

"We will be most happy to take into consideration whatever suggestions you might have, sir."

"Am I to be mocked in my own house? Weems! Get me downstairs at once, sirruh! I'll not have Belle run roughshod over Mrs. Weatherstone, as she is likely to do if I am not there to apply the bit," said Sir Marcus.

"Yes, Sir Marcus," said the valet, the slightest smile easing his countenance.

Mr. Raven was still standing beside the door and in fact was holding it open for those exiting the room. Sir Marcus paused momentarily before moving past the door, recommending that he give Cassandra a thumping scold. "For I have not been given time to do it!" he exclaimed. "Weems! Let us be off!"

Mr. Raven shut the door and turned to advance on the canopied bed. Cassandra, who had said not a word while she watched in dismay while her various relations deserted her, shrank back against the pillows. She was feeling very vulnerable and alone of a sudden. She searched Mr. Raven's face, trying to discern some sign of his thoughts. She did not find his bland expression encouraging.

Cassandra was astonished and startled when he chose not to sit in any of the chairs beside the bed, but rather, boldly sat down on the bed itself. His weight caused the mattress to shift, and she felt her face flame. "Sir!"

"Yes, Miss Weatherstone!" He looked at her steadily, his brows raised.

Cassandra could not withstand what she interpreted as his condemnation. "I am sorry that I deceived you," she blurted. "You must think me reprehensible."

"While it is true that you deceived me, it was not for long. And I do not think that you are reprehensible. Outrageous, perhaps," said Mr. Raven. He lifted one of her hands and brought it to his lips.

Much encouraged, Cassandra said shyly, "I suppose that Belle's note confessing to our masquerade came as a great shock to you."

"I knew that you were not Belle before ever her note arrived. Her hastily scribbled confession served merely to convince Sir Marcus of the truth of what I had already told him," said Mr. Raven coolly.

Cassandra regarded him with astonishment. "But how did you know I was not Belle if you hadn't already received my sister's note?"

Mr. Raven smiled tenderly at her. He reached out to tuck a curl of hair behind her ear. "I didn't know at first. But as time went on, I began to suspect that either my memory was completely at fault or there were indeed two different Belle Weatherstones. The latter did not seem possible, and so I had to question myself. You cannot imagine my relief to be confronted with the reality of your twin sister."

"Then you realized the truth at the soiree," said Cassandra.

"Let us say that I strongly suspected it. However, there were so many things that simply did not fit," said Mr. Raven. "And of course, once I began listening to Miss Bidwell and Sir Marcus, I became more convinced than ever that I had not met my old playmate. They, too, had noticed little oddities about 'Belle.' "

"Such as?" Cassandra snuggled closer against the pillows. She found that she was beginning to enjoy her *tête-à-tête* with Mr. Raven. There was something profoundly delightful in having the gentleman one loved sitting on the bed beside one, feeling his weight depressing the mattress.

"First of all, you did not know my childhood nickname. Of course, later at the soiree when Belle addressed me by that detested moniker, I had to consider the possibility of a switch in roles," said Mr. Raven. "Sir Marcus and Miss Bidwell both mentioned their puzzlement at 'Belle's' sudden interest in housewifery and stitching and reading of family histories. And then there was the instance when we stood together in the gallery and watched that magnificent thunderstorm."

Cassandra frowned. "I don't understand why that should have proven to be a clue to my true identity."

"Belle has been terrified of thunder all of her life," said Mr. Raven simply.

"I had no notion," said Cassandra, shaking her head.

Her lips twitched, and she glanced at Mr. Raven through her lashes. "If I had, I might have thrown myself upon your bosom for comfort. That might have been more in character."

"Yes," agreed Mr. Raven reflectively, gazing back at her with a more intent look in his eyes. "Perhaps it is a pity that you did not know that particular idiosyncrasy of your sister's." He slowly leaned toward her.

Cassandra hastily put out her hand, intending to warn him away. Somehow, her hand became cradled in his as he gathered her up in the circle of his arms. Cassandra looked up at him, feeling a little breathless, and asked, "Philip, is this quite conventional?"

"Oh, no. Not at all." He looked down with a smile. "I am going to kiss you, Cassandra."

She felt a flutter in her breast. "Are you?" she breathed.

Without replying, he released her hand and tilted up her chin. His lips caught hers. Cassandra's senses whirled, and she slipped her free hand around his neck.

When Mr. Raven had thoroughly kissed her, he said, "I know now, quite unmistakably, which Miss Weatherstone I've fallen in love with. Will you marry me, Cassandra?"

Cassandra came back to earth with a bump. For a few very pleasant moments she had forgotten. What a stupid little fool she was, she thought unhappily. She drew back against the band of his arms. "You're already married, Philip."

"I have the annulment papers in my pocket at this moment," he whispered. "They came while you were ill." He reached up with one hand to smooth her silky hair. Looking deep into her eyes, he said, "Cassandra, I've never asked this before of any woman. Will you marry me?"

Cassandra threw her arms around his neck and burst into happy tears. "Oh, yes, yes, yes!"

Mr. Raven caught her up tight and kissed her again, which did not shock her in the least.

The bedroom door was thrust open. "Cassandra! You will never guess what Grandfather has just said!"

Cassandra and Mr. Raven broke apart, turning as one toward the doorway. Cassandra felt herself blushing.

Upon sight of the couple, Belle stopped her rush into the bedroom. Her mouth rounded in amazement. "Oh, my goodness."

Cassandra put her hands to her flaming cheeks. "We . . . we are to be wed, Belle!"

"So I should hope!" exclaimed Belle. Her astonished expression altered. Putting her hands on her hips, she glared at Mr. Raven. "This is the outside of enough, Stubby! I have at last extracted Grandfather's promise for a London Season, and now all Cassandra will think about is her wedding to you!"

"Has he really!" exclaimed Cassandra. "Oh, I am so happy for you, Belle!"

"I humbly apologize, Belle," said Mr. Raven gravely, a tremor in his voice. He turned his head and smiled at Cassandra. He held out his hand, taking hers in his clasp. "Shall we go to Rome for our honeymoon?"

"Yes, let's," said Cassandra promptly. "I have read about the magnificence of Rome, and I have longed to see the classical ruins."

"So have I," said Mr. Raven, and lifted her hand to his lips. There was laughter in his eyes as he looked at her. "We shall take Sir Marcus's history with us as a handy reference."

"We would never have suited," declared Belle. She sailed out of the bedroom, shutting the door firmly behind her.